THE ARRANGEMENT

BONNIE POIRIER

To all the women who put their dreams, goals or bucket lists on the back burner for whatever reason.
Dust them off and see what happens!

CHAPTER 1

"You have got to be kidding! Why on earth would you think I would agree to something this insane?"

"I have no choice. I've got too much debt and borrowed from the wrong person. He's demanding payment." My father stood before me with hunched shoulders. His usual commanding voice was shaky, hesitant, and quiet.

"And the only decision you could think of was for me to marry one of his sons?" I shouted. Tears threatened to fall, but I willed them not to. I looked toward my mother, who hid behind my father; she sighed quietly and flitted her gaze to the ground whenever I looked at her. I had expected her to be arguing with me, or at least to appear angry, but she just stood there, holding on to my father's arm, patting it when he needed moral support.

The sun beat down on the parched earth stretching between us. I have welcomed shade, except there was not a cloud in the Texas sky. This conversation was only making me hotter; my temperature had risen at least five degrees since my dad opened his traitorous mouth. They'd both lost their damn minds. This couldn't be happening. My head was pounding and my brain felt like it was going to explode. There was no way I was going to agree to do something like this. Debt or no debt, I wasn't doing it.

"Brian Morton extended the option as a way out of my situation and to save our ranch. I don't have the money to pay him back."

"So you're going to sacrifice me? Use me as a pawn in your little game just so you can save this place? When did this ranch become more important than your daughter?" My voice was just above a whisper as I narrowed my eyes, staring a hole through my father.

He looked toward the ground and scuffed his boot along the gravel. "It's not more important," he disagrees, shaking his head, "but it's our family legacy. It's all I have to leave you one day." Tears filled his eyes, and he turned away from me so I wouldn't see. I could count on one hand how many times I'd seen my father cry. He was the picture of a rancher: tan, weathered face from years of being out in the elements, bowed legs from living on the back of a horse, and his black Stetson only came off for a meal, church service, or bed. Dad was always the level-headed one, the only man in a house full of women, so he learned early on how to solve arguments, heartache, and dodge hormones. He kept his feelings close to his vest. More often than not, you would have thought he didn't care, but that was just his way.

While I'd like to dismiss this crazy idea, I knew how much the ranch meant to him. He was a cowboy through and through. He even wrestled steers in his youth, which is how he met my mom, a rodeo queen in her own right. I worried that if he didn't have the ranch, he would lose part of himself. It was all he knew. Come to think of it, this was all I knew, and the thought of it not being here scared me. I turned away from my parents and wrapped my arms around my waist, closed my eyes, and allowed a few tears to fall. It hurt seeing him like this. It perplexed me how things had gotten this bad. When I came home to help, I thought things had turned around. Wiping my nose on my sleeve, I turned back around to face them.

"So if I do this, it takes care of all your debt?" The words came out far more confident than I felt. I knew if I agreed to this, I would be saving my father and losing myself.

My father nodded, closing his eyes in what I hoped was a silent prayer for my future.

My heart raced, and I began to pace in front of my parents. I fidgeted with my untucked shirt. I felt a wave of nausea hit me. Closing my eyes, I took a deep breath and waited for it to pass. I heard myself say, "Fine." I let out a loud sigh. "So when am I supposed to get married?"

"A week and a half," Mom whispered as she stepped out from behind my father and took a few steps towards me. She tucked her blond hair behind her ear and clasped her hands in front of her, clearly bracing for my outburst like she had for years.

My mouth fell open, and it felt like my eyes would pop right out of my head. I stared at my mother and furrowed my brow, "Wow, you're sure not wasting any time getting rid of me."

A week and a half? They were as nuts as I thought. I looked at them both, waiting for something. Anything. Gratefulness? Praise, thanks or elation—but saw nothing. I turned on my heel and stomped away from them.

"Katherine Jean," my mom called after me, but I didn't stop. I didn't need to hear any more of this twisted bargain. There was nothing they could say that would make me feel better.

CHAPTER 2

I stomped off to the bunkhouse which was across the yard from my parents' house. Years ago I'd converted it to a little apartment, because I was the one who stayed. A whole lotta good that did me.

I paced around my kitchen. It wasn't very big, and the island took up the majority of the floor space. I got dizzy making laps around it. Slamming my hands down on the counter, I let the bottled up tears fall. I wanted to yell. I needed to hit something, or better yet, some*one*, but there was nobody. No one followed me, and that hurt almost as much as this convoluted arrangement. I snatched up a coffee mug that was beside the sink and threw it across the kitchen. It hit the doorjamb, shattered, and fell to the floor. Grumbling to myself, I grabbed the broom and bent down to sweep the china into the dustpan.

"Hey, Kate, it's nice to see you again." My eyes followed his legs up to his head and I saw Tyler Morton standing at the threshold of my home, too good to knock. Or maybe he thought that because we were an unofficial family, what was mine was his. Or I hadn't closed the door when I came home and it was an open invitation for him to come in. With him, who knew?

I had to admit; he was handsome. He was muscular; his eyes rivaled the clearest blue water, brown hair with highlights of gold from being in the sun, and the perfect amount of scruff on his unshaven face. It was just enough without encroaching on beard territory. And most importantly, he had the best Wrangler butt I'd ever seen.

"Hey, Tyler, come on in." I stepped out of the way and most definitely did not look at his butt as he walked by. Removing his ball cap, he sat down at the table. "Would you like a cup of coffee?"

"Sure, as long as the delivery is a little softer than what you used on that last cup." He smiled, and his eyes danced with laughter that he was smart enough to know not to let out.

"You saw that?" I cringed as I walked to the garbage can and dumped the broken cup. It clattered loudly as it hit the bottom of the can. The sound reverberated through my tiny house.

Tyler nodded. "Good throw."

"Do you know what's going on?" he asked, a little apprehensive.

"Kinda… wait. It's you?" I turned away from the counter, full pot of coffee in hand, barely avoiding splashing it, and looked at him. "You're the Morton brother I'm supposed to marry?"

He nodded his head, took a deep breath, and let it out slowly. What? Seriously? I'd had a secret crush on Tyler Morton since they moved here from Montana. Carefully, I turned back to the counter to fill both cups. I looked out the window and fidgeted with the coffee pot, avoiding eye contact. My heart raced and palms suddenly sweaty. I thought back to the times I had seen him around. I had been too afraid to talk to him, and now here he was, in my kitchen, telling me we're going to be married. How was I supposed to pull myself back together to form sentences? I turned to face him again, took the cups back to the table, and went back for the milk and sugar.

"None for me, thanks. Black is good." Tyler shifted in the chair.

I smiled and walked back over to the table and took a seat across from him. "Did you just find out about this, too? It's a bit of a shock."

"No, our fathers wanted to keep this quiet. I told them there'd be no more hiding this from you and I was coming to see you today." Tyler took a sip of his coffee and waited for my response. "What's wrong?" The confused look on my face must have been more prominent than I thought.

"How long have you known about this?" I looked into my cup of coffee, refusing to meet his gaze.

"A week and a half."

My head shot up and my mouth fell open. I had so many words and questions, but not a sound came out. My eyes darted from my cup to Tyler as I searched my brain for the words. I felt like someone had slapped me across the face. This wasn't something that had just happened. Everyone around me knew the plan for weeks, and apparently, I wasn't good enough to be included. They had decided my life for me, and here I'd been wandering around, living what I thought was my best life, only to find out I'd been fooled. The world around me was out of control.

"Look, we've known each other for ten years now, it's not like we're complete strangers. It's not like we're going in blind."

"Tyler, you know who I am, but you don't know me." I pointed to myself.

He nodded his head and took another sip of his coffee.

"May I ask your expectations for this marriage?" All of the sudden, I wasn't sure I wanted to hear his answer. It frankly terrified me to actually know what he was going to say. My hands were folded in my lap. I needed to start thinking of this as what it was - a business deal. I straightened in my chair and took a deep breath, locking my stare on Tyler. I was ready to argue with anything he had to say.

Tyler peered over his mug and smiled. "I want to get to know you. Learn who you are, but ultimately, I want us to have a real marriage. You know, a true husband and wife."

"Well, I'll tell you that's not going to happen for a very long time. And I'm not hopping into bed with someone I've only really known for a week and a half. I'm not that kind of girl." My brow arched, waiting for his response.

"And for some reason, you think I'm that kind of guy?"

The town playboy, the eternal bachelor. He preferred busty blondes who wouldn't last on a working ranch. Yet he sat here, trying to convince me he was an angel.

I rolled my eyes before I glanced back over at him. "You kinda have a reputation. I may not know you all that well, but I've heard stories. Girl's talk."

"My reputation isn't something I can deny. There was a time in my life when I didn't give much thought as to who I was seeing, or how long we were together."

"Days, Tyler. Most of them were days."

"You seem to have kept tabs on me, Kate." A sly grin stretched across his face.

He made my blood boil. He had the nerve to think that I had followed his every move? "That, I assure you, is not the case. It's a small town, Tyler, and gossip spreads faster than flies on a horse's ass."

"Well, I'm happy to be an open book; what would you like to know?"

I stared at him blankly, then shook my head. I dropped my face into my hands. This was not how I imagined my life would end up.

"This is too much, Tyler. I don't know if I can do this."

"You don't have to, but my father will not back down. I'm willing to marry you if you want to save your ranch, but ultimately it's your choice. Saying I'm totally thrilled about this would be a lie. I don't enjoy having choices made for me."

Really, I shouldn't have been surprised by his answer. That was the story of my life. I can't deny that it stung a little to know I wasn't who he wanted to be stuck with. "Well, I'm glad we both can agree this isn't the choice we would've made. I'm not sure I'll ever like it, Tyler. I've had about all I can take today. Thanks for coming over; I'll see you at the wedding."

He stood, walked to the door, and quietly left.

CHAPTER 3

After leaving Kate's house, I balked at the things I had said. I wondered what I would do as an encore performance. Slamming my cap back on my head, I knew I hadn't accomplished a damned thing except making an ass out of myself and making Kate retreat into herself. I said things that sounded like my father's words and not my own. I said things I hadn't intended and weren't completely true.

She had one thing right; this is a small town and word gets around. It won't be long before everyone sticks their nose in our business, and when they do, I don't want them finding out the truth, which is why I hoped to get her on the same page. Dammit.

I shoved my hands in my pockets, my right hand brushed up against the ring I bought for her last week. I should've told her about this sooner. Maybe I should've been the one to tell her. She had every right to be upset about this situation. I know I was, but I'd had a week and a half to cool off and think about things. I'm not sure she'd had five minutes.

Plus, Kate was right. I didn't know her that well, but I had every intention of changing that.

I climbed into my truck and headed back to the ranch.

"Call Dad," I growled to the truck's Bluetooth. The phone rang too long, which made me even more irritated. He was never out of arm's reach of his phone. Finally, the call connected.

"Tyler, what do you need?" my father's gruff voice sounded on the other side.

"Hello to you, too. I just left the Patterson place."

"Ah, and how was your stunning bride?"

"Frankly, she's pissed. I don't know how you came up with this hare-brained scheme, but she ain't pleased."

"What's wrong with her? She's marrying one of the wealthiest bachelors in the state. Does she realize that?"

"Not everything is about money, Dad." I felt my blood start to boil.

"Son, trust me, once she realizes how wealthy we are, she won't give it another thought. This is happening, so whatever you thought you would accomplish with this call, didn't work."

The line went dead, and I slammed my palm on the dashboard in front of me.

Kate was a mystery, always had been. We'd been neighbors for ten years, and I'd only seen her a handful of times at local spring cattle branding days. I had always enjoyed getting together with ranchers from the area and helping them get their calves branded and off to summer grazing. For the life of me, I couldn't remember if I had ever actually spoken to her. We worked side by side at a branding one time... but did I talk to her?

I couldn't remember, but I should have. She was different from other girls, especially the ones I dated. She was strong, confident, could work as hard as any man... and gorgeous.

With her olive skin tone, her brown hair that looked like it had been kissed by the sun, dark brown eyes that flashed almost black when she was mad... just stunning.

I couldn't wait to see what else made them darken.

I'd always wanted an unencumbered life with nobody to answer to, no one to hold me down, or hold me back; a different woman when the mood struck, so they knew nothing would last. But the last few years had not been all it was cracked up to be. I longed for someone to be there when I got home, the comfort and familiarity of the same woman in my bed. Someone who cared about me, not my last name or the fortune that goes with it.

Today I was glad I'd built my home away from the main house where people couldn't see me coming and going. I didn't have to answer to anyone, and I definitely didn't need to be quizzed about having seen Kate today. I lay down on the couch and closed my eyes, hoping the next almost a week and a half would be over soon. Then I could figure out how to start my life as a husband.

CHAPTER 4

I sat in my office surrounded by my grandfather's books on the shelves. Rodeo buckles scattered around the room were passed down from him, although some were my own from my team roping days in Montana. The original ranch deed hung on the wall behind me. I turned in my chair and stared at it. This is the entire reason I agreed to this. I couldn't help thinking back to the meeting I had with Ben and my father.

They both came in to my office together that day…

"TYLER, YOU KNOW BEN PATTERSON." My father introduced him as they walked in.

I stood and held my hand out to Ben. "Of course, how are you? I haven't seen you around for a while."

"Hello Tyler, I have been busy over at my place." Both men took seats, and I returned to my chair behind the desk. "So, to what do I owe this visit?"

"Well, son, I have entered into an arrangement with Ben, and it involves you."

My father looked from me to Ben and continued, "Ben needed a loan from us and can't raise the funds needed to repay it. I don't need the money back but there is something else I need, and Ben has agreed to the terms."

He smiled, and my father rarely smiled. The smirk on his face was slimy, and I felt like I was going to get the short end of the stick over whatever was going on here.

"I'm not sure I really want to know what this is all about." I was hoping it wouldn't be illegal.

"Tyler, I really thought our luck would improve before this loan came due, but it's been a bad few years." Ben looked worn out, and he fidgeted. The crease between his eyes had deepened, and sweat broke out on his forehead.

"Son, we have arranged for you and Ben's daughter, Kate, to be married. It was the only agreeable option we could see." My father looked at me with a straight face, and I figured this must be a joke.

"You are kidding, right? This is absolutely insane. This is not some business move; it's dealing with people's lives!" I looked between the two men.

My father clenched his fists, and his face reddened. I waited for his outburst. I looked over at Ben, who had closed his eyes, dropped his head to his hand, and rubbed his forehead.

Ben shook his head no. "I'm sorry, Tyler, but it's not. I don't like the idea of pawning my daughter off, but I need to keep my ranch. That's all I have left to give."

"So tell me, when is this all supposed to take place?" I spat out at them.

"A month from yesterday. Best to get it over with in a timely manner," Dad said with a chuckle.

"I won't do it," I replied as calmly as I could, while I shook my head. "There is no way I'm going to do this," I yelled and turned away from them, letting out a breath through pursed lips.

"You don't have a choice son; it's done. As long as you hope to have a future on this ranch, you'll go along with it. If not, I will make sure you never work anywhere again."

He was eerily calm; his words were calculated and authoritative. I turned back around to face him, and he smiled smugly. It was a look I had seen many times when he knew he held all the power. My entire life would depend on a marriage I had no control over.

"Well, now that we have discussed it, I think that's all there is to say." The two men stood and began to leave my office.

"Just a moment. I will be meeting with Kate; I won't be going into this blind. We will spend time together. Ben, you have a week and a half to tell her. After that, I do. Am I clear?" Ben nodded, and the two men left the room. I sat there in shock. What on earth just happened?

My father sauntered back into my office. "Well, son, your life is going to change. I think that was the best deal I have ever done." He sat down with a vile smirk across his face, and I could hardly look at the man. The bile rose into my throat. I was disgusted with him.

"The best deal you have ever done? Arranging a marriage between two unwilling people? For what reason?" I tried to remain calm. One of the few things I had learned about my father over the years was not to fly off the handle, because he was volatile when pushed into a corner.

"Son, you are 39 years old. Your reputation in this community is embarrassing to us as a family. You can't fool around for your entire life. I'm doing this to save your future, the future of the ranch, and if we get access through marriage to the Patterson ranch, that's icing on the cake."

He sat back in the chair, folded his hands behind his head and continued, "You won't be keeping company with that tramp of a woman anymore either, so you'd better break it off. What's her name? Lona? Did you really think I would let her in this family? That trash of a woman? Think about it Tyler, she is just looking for the next rung on her way to a bigger fortune."

I looked at him and stammered words, but nothing made sense. I finally gave up and threw my hands in the air.

"The Patterson's are good people. Ben is respected, and Julie is a lovely woman. Kate is a smart businesswoman, a hard worker, and her father should have listened to her. But this worked out well for me," he said as he nodded, looking very pleased with himself.

"What if Kate won't agree to this?" I asked, hoping she wouldn't have any part of it.

"Well, that's up to Ben to deal with. It's not my problem." Shaking his head and holding up his hands, my father stood and began to leave.

"You expect me to take this news and not question it? Dad, come on. This makes no sense."

"Son, it's done. Get used to it or get out. If you choose out, you will never come back, ever." I knew there was no more room for discussion, and with that, he left.

THE PHONE RANG and shook me back to reality. As I looked at the number, saw who it was, and I accepted the call.

"Hello."

"Hey Tyler, it's Kate. I'm sorry for acting all pissy this afternoon. This is all a shock for me. Anyway, I have been doing some looking into what we need for our marriage, and we have to get a marriage license, but we have to be there together. I was wondering about going to Hammond to get it, that way we don't have to explain anything to anyone here."

"Sure, that would work. How about tomorrow? Let's say 10:30? I will pick you up. That gives me time to check a few things at the office and allows you time for morning chores." I suggested that way we would have to talk and we would need to have lunch somewhere.

"Ok, see you tomorrow."

That was it. The line went dead. Our conversation was over. It was going to be harder to win Kate over than I thought.

CHAPTER 5

The sun dipped below the horizon, and all that was left of the day was a fiery red sky. The temperature had cooled, and I couldn't stay cooped up in my house for one more minute. I changed into my running gear, laced up my shoes, pushed play on my running playlist, and headed out. I needed to clear my head and give myself time to grieve the life I built, and the life I thought I would have.

It was just me, the road, and Queen. When I reached the highway at the edge of our property, I stepped onto the pavement and quickly found my pace. My spirits lifted with every foot-strike on the asphalt. The smell of honeysuckle wafted from the bushes along the road. For the first time today, I was in control of myself. The anger towards my parents wasn't going to disappear on this run. I still felt justified in my resentment, but I regretted the way I treated Tyler. I'd been downright rude.

Who was *I* to judge his past life?

Every time I heard Tyler had hooked up with a friend or an acquaintance of mine, I couldn't help wondering, why not me? What's wrong with me? Granted, I had tried to avoid him at every turn. I have no idea what I would have ever said to him, but it might have been nice to have a shot.

Kate, get your head in the game.

I wasn't going to be a notch on his bedpost; I was going to be the last one who saw that bed. A crush was turning into marriage. What I needed to worry about now was how to have a cordial life together.

My crush. How long had he been that?

The first time I saw Tyler, his family had come over to help us brand. He'd just come here from Montana, and was the most handsome man I had ever seen. There was something about him that wasn't like the rest of the guys around here. He had worked and then was gone as soon as the day was over. I looked around for him at dinner, but he was nowhere in sight. We worked side by side most of the day, but I hadn't talked to him beyond the job we were doing. I was certain he hadn't even noticed me.

Eight years was a long time to have a crush on a man you'd only seen a handful of times. I'm sure if anyone drove by, they would have thought I had lost my mind, seeing me talking to myself out loud.

I wasn't sure how many miles I ran, but when I stopped, there was no light left in the sky. I slowed my pace, made a wide turn, and went to the edge of the road. The smell in the air had changed. It became earthy, musky, and fresh. The thunder rumbled in the distance, and raindrops began to fall. I was miles from home and standing here wasn't going to get me there any faster. I took a deep breath and started running.

Out of nowhere, I saw the glow of headlights coming towards me. I slowed my pace to take my pepper spray from the back pocket of my running shorts. I never ran without it.

The truck pulled to a stop. Whoever was inside rolled the passenger side window down.

"Kate, what are you doing out here so far from your place? Come on, get in. I'll drive you home."

"Tyler?" I opened the door and climbed into the truck.

"Are you okay?" Tyler sounded a little perturbed.

"Yes, I'm good, thanks for stopping." He smelled nice; woodsy with a hint of clove and citrus. I closed my eyes and smiled.

He made a U-turn, but instead of heading back to my yard, he pulled over. There was an awkward silence, and I didn't know how to break the ice.

He gripped the steering wheel. "What do you think you are doing running at night with a storm rolling in?" His voice was low and angry, mirroring the distant rumble of thunder through the night.

I didn't really care what he thought.

"What are you doing out driving around in a storm?" I asked in response, even though it was lame.

"Really? That's how we are going to play this? Well, for your information, I had been out with some friends. I needed to blow off a little steam. I had a frustrating afternoon." He turned his head to look at me. I could feel his piercing eyes on me, and saw anger flash across his face in the glow of the dash lights.

I rolled my eyes at his dig towards me.

"Why do you think I was out running? See, I had some random guy walk into my home and inform me that he was going to be my husband, so my afternoon wasn't the best one I have ever had." I stared back at his silhouette.

"Hey, I just took advantage of an open door," he replied. "What if it hadn't been me that stopped? Did anyone know you were out here?" He was angry, maybe a little scared, but that didn't change the fact that he had no right to scold me.

"You think I don't know the risks for a female runner?" I shifted in the seat so I was almost facing him. "Not that you need to know, but I carry pepper spray and a knife when I run, regardless of the time of day. As far as anyone knowing I was out, no, nobody knew. I didn't want anyone to talk me out of it. Running is my stress reliever, my therapy time. It's just me and the road." I folded my arms across my chest in a huff, clenched my jaw, and started tapping my foot in frustration.

"Kate, I just want to know that you're safe." His voice had become quiet and calm, the frustration seemingly melted away.

I could tell he had turned to look at me again. For the second time today, I felt like I was inches tall. He looked back to the road in front of us, shifted the truck into drive, and stepped on the gas. I had an overwhelming urge to reach for his hand. This man would be my husband in a week and a half. He hardly knew me, but he was already very protective. It was sweet and comforting to know he was worried. Needlessly worried, but nonetheless, he was. I needed to reassure him and apologize, yet again, for being snippy at him. Extending my hand, I reached for his, which was resting on his leg. It was warm, calloused from ranch work, and it fit comfortably into mine. I smiled at the feeling, and he gave my hand a light squeeze. Somehow, it felt like we had been holding hands forever. I took a breath but didn't dare look at him for fear tears would fall, afraid it would make him think I was weak. I needed to be strong, put up the shield that had worked so well up to this point in my life.

～

ELECTRICITY SHOT from her hand to mine like the lightning flashing across the sky. Her skin was cold, her fingers long and slender, rough from her work on the ranch. I couldn't help but envelop her hand in mine. I wanted to warm it up; I wanted to warm *her* up.

"I'm careful, Tyler. I pay attention, but you are right. I shouldn't have gone out so late. Someone should have known I was going. Thank you again for stopping."

The glow from the yard light illuminated the cab of the truck, giving me a view of Kate, who looked a little like a drowned rat. My rage decreased. I'd loosened the grip I had on her hand and grabbed the gearshift to park in front of Kate's house. We sat in silence for a few moments.

"You can let me know when you go out if you want. I promise I won't follow you."

"I might just take you up on the offer. Would you like to come in?" Kate looked down at her hands, now back in her lap, then turned her gaze to me. The only thing I wanted to do right now was to follow her into her house and make sure she was okay. But she needed her space, and I needed to not be in such close proximity to her. I wasn't sure I could be so near to her and not hold her.

"It's been a long day, so I think I'll just head home. You've been shivering since you got in the truck. Go have a warm bath and I will see you in the morning." I saw her nod, and she reached for my hand again.

"Tyler, thank you. I truly appreciate it." Her face looked exhausted, her voice quiet.

"Have a good night."

"Night," I replied, trying to sound a little more chipper.

She gave me half a smile, got out of the truck, and walked to her house. At the last second, she turned back, waved, and then disappeared, closing the door behind her. I could still feel the coolness from her hand on mine. I took a deep breath, trying to steady my thoughts.

Why had I scolded her? I wished I could have just held her. She needed a friend, and I was acting like a controlling spouse. Driving home, my body was exhausted from the entire day, but my mind racing a million miles an hour.

CHAPTER 6

Morning arrived too early. I had gotten no sleep with all the tossing and turning because of last night's events, and what we had to do today. With my chores done and two coffees in hand, I paced as I waited on my porch for Tyler to show up. I'd successfully avoided my parents this morning, so I hoped I could keep that up for a little longer.

"Kate!" I heard Delaney call from across the yard. I closed my eyes and prepared for an inquisition from my sister.

"Morning, Delaney." I waved. She was home on a break from school. Her work as an assistant professor in Austin didn't leave her much time to be home helping on the ranch, but of course, she was here now to see the most embarrassing moment of my life: a 37-year-old 'spinster' with no life who needed to be pawned off in an arranged marriage because nobody wanted her. Did Mom and Dad tell Delaney about the upcoming marriage? Or had they just told her she needed to come home for the break?

"What happened last night?" Delaney asked, as she

bounded up my stairs, her curly hair flying wildly about. She was gorgeous, and everyone I met commented on it: blue eyes to go with the perfect blonde locks, dainty, and an airy voice that drew the attention of anyone who heard it.

"I don't know what you are talking about." I lied, blowing her off.

"You know exactly what I'm talking about. I saw you leave for your run and you came home in a black one ton Ford. Now, granted, it didn't stay long, but who was it? Was it a certain Morton brother?" She wiggled her eyebrows and practically vibrated with excitement. Delaney was always gossiping, always the center of attention. Normally she knew everything going on, so I was enjoying stringing her along.

Before I could even start to tell her the story, Tyler drove up in the mysterious black Ford F-350.

Delaney watched his truck before slowly turning her head towards me. Her eyes were as big as saucers, and her mouth fell open like she wanted to say something, but no words would come out.

I waved at her, smirked, and climbed into the truck. "Good morning," Tyler said with a smile. Damn, why did he have to smile?

I smiled back.

"Are you ready for this?" he asked.

"Yep, I think so." I handed him the second travel mug of coffee. "Peace offering?"

"It will do." He arched his brow and smirked at me. "I was busy this morning and didn't have time for a coffee." He put the cup to his lips and took a long sip. "You remembered I take it black. Thank you, Kate." He smiled. We pulled out of the yard and headed for Hammond.

"Should we get to know each other? We have the time."

Good job, Kate, I berated myself. Where did that come from? I had expected to sit here in silence.

"Sure, that sounds good. I'm aware of what you have been doing since we moved here, but what about before? What did you go to college for?"

"I took Animal Science at Texas A&M, then carried on for a Master's degree. Afterwards, I worked for an animal nutrition company in Austin for five years."

"You have a Master's degree and work as a ranch hand for your father?" Tyler asked in disbelief.

"Well, I'm not just a ranch hand. I manage the herd and the grazing schedules. I oversee the nutrition of our animals and the artificial insemination. He needs me."

"Hmm," was all Tyler said, and he looked like he was thinking.

"What about you? Any college?"

"I didn't go right to college. Started working on the ranch in Montana and learned I had a head for numbers, so I decided that a degree would always be an asset, so I took business, specializing in marketing. I started at the University of Montana, and then transferred to the University of Texas when my parents moved. I manage all the ranch's business dealings."

We chatted about different things, but as we got closer to Hammond, we both got quieter. The reality about what we were going to do hitting us both.

I PARKED in front of the county office. I took a deep breath, got out of the truck, and walked around to Kate's side to open the door. I held my hand out to help her down.

"Thank you," she said with a faint smile. We let our hands

linger together for a moment as we looked at each other. She seemed hesitant, and a little pale. I felt her tremble slightly, but then Kate pulled her hand away and started walking. I ran to catch up to her.

The entire process was painless, and ten minutes later, we walked out with a marriage license.

"That seems like it should have been harder," Kate said in a hushed tone as she stared at the paper in her hands.

I could see her reading it over and over. She bit the corner of her lip and furrowed her brow. Were her eyes glistening with unshed tears? She put the license back in the envelope, took a deep breath, and stared straight ahead as if looking at me would release the floodgates. I reached over and took her hand in mine. She didn't pull away; she squeezed it and turned to look out the passenger window but not quickly enough, as I saw one tear fall.

"I'm sorry," she whispered. "I had no idea it would hit me like this. Please don't think it's you. It's just the situation." She looked back at me and forced a smile.

I smiled at her. I didn't want to pull my hand from hers, but I needed to start the truck and shift into drive. Afterwards, I quickly grabbed her hand again. The drive to the restaurant was silent. I wasn't sure what to say, and I was afraid that if I started talking, Kate would start to cry. I didn't want to be the cause of her tears.

We were seated quickly and ordered our meals. "We should probably discuss living arrangements," I said, looking up at Kate, and she nodded.

"I don't know how much room you have at your place, but my house is pretty much what you saw last night. One bedroom, one bathroom."

"My home is two stories, has three bathrooms, five bedrooms, and a large kitchen." I was being a little vague, but I wanted her to see it for herself.

"Well, I think that pretty much settles it," Kate said between bites of her meal.

"Would you like to go back to my place to see where you'll be living? I also want to show you where I plan to build up a road; that way you won't have to take the long way to get back to your Dad's. The pasture east of my place butts up against your property. I thought I could put a cattle gate in and then you can just zip back and forth whenever you need to."

"That would be nice, thank you." She didn't even hesitate in her response. Once our meal was done and I purchased a few things I needed for the ranch, we headed home.

We drove onto the sprawling ranch. I looked over at Kate, and her jaw dropped when she saw the main house.

"This is where you live?"

I shook my head and took a right turn. We carried on down a long tree lined road.

"I don't live too close to the main house. When I came home, I was used to independence, and I didn't want prying eyes knowing my every move, so I built out of the way. Rob, my middle brother, lives about 75 yards to the north of the main house. The bunk house is just south of him, and it would drive me crazy knowing that they all were going to be able to see me come and go. So before I decided to build, I looked around and found this spot. Unless someone happens to see me drive in, nobody really knows what I'm up to."

We drove down a road flanked on both sides by lilacs. My window was down and their deep floral scent wafted into the truck. I closed my eyes and drank in their smell. Since I was a little girl, lilacs have always lifted my spirits. They're a special flower to me. I was taught to love them by my grandmother, and I felt like this was a good sign. Rounding the corner, all I could see before me was the most beautiful two-story log home with a wonderful porch.

"Tyler, this place is stunning," I exclaimed, peering through the windshield.

"Wait until you see inside!" Tyler was almost giddy. He parked the truck, and we went in. It really was breathtaking. "Think you could be comfortable here?"

"Comfortable? How about spoiled?" The entryway was spacious, with a wall of closets to keep outside clothes tucked away. I wandered into the open living room and looked up at the giant stone fireplace that stood as the focal point of the room. I kept walking around and found the kitchen, which was state-of-the art. It would be easy to cook together in here.

"Follow me." Tyler took my hand and led me upstairs. The feel of his skin on mine sent a flurry of goosebumps up my arm. I liked how happy he seemed to be, showing me around his home.

We headed for the second floor. "This will be our room," he said, as he turned towards me. "You are very confident, Mr. Morton," I replied, arching my eyebrow and smirking. He grinned and opened the door. The double doors swung open to the master bedroom. It had the most amazing view of the hills, pastures, and cattle. The room took up the entire width of the house. An enormous stone fireplace stretched up the wall at the end of the bed. It was a man's room; there was no doubt about that. There was what looked to be a hand-hewn log king size bed with matching nightstands on both sides of it, and a large rusted metal globe pendant chandelier hung above the bed. *I could be comfortable in that bed,* I thought to myself, but then stopped and wondered how comfortable I could possibly be with Tyler right next to me.

The master bathroom was at one end of the room, and there was a large nook filled with bookshelves, and two very comfy looking overstuffed brown chairs in the other.

"You have a beautiful home, Tyler."

He looked into my eyes. My brain and my heart were at war. I wanted to open up and let Tyler in, but I had been hurt too many times. My heart couldn't take another beating.

"*We* have a beautiful home, Kate. I want you to be completely at ease here. Change anything you want, nothing is off limits." We went back downstairs and walked out to the porch. Sitting on the swing, I let out a contented sigh. Yesterday, I thought I'd never feel content again, but damn, Tyler was just so easy to be around.

I let my head fall back onto the oversized swing and turned my head to look at the handsome man sitting beside me.

"What are we going to tell people, Tyler? This is all so strange. If we tell people the real reason, it makes my father look like a horrible man. I can't come up with a decent story."

"Well, what if we say we have been seeing each other quietly? We feel like we are soulmates, so we're getting married." He had moved his hand to rest on my thigh, and I didn't swat it away. It felt nice to be the one attracting attention, instead of always stroking the ego of the men I'd dated.

"Not the best explanation, but not the worst." I smiled at him.

I shifted on the swing and dug around in my pocket.

"I wanted to give you this yesterday, but our visit was cut a little shorter than I had planned." She let out a little chuckle. I pulled the ring out and held it in front of me.

"It seems redundant since the decision has been made for us, but Kate, will you marry me?"

She smiled, "Yes, Tyler, I will marry you."

I'd picked a two carat solitaire surrounded by a halo of smaller diamonds, with more of the sparkling gems running down the sides, all set in a platinum band. Kate stared at the ring.

"Tyler, this is the most beautiful ring I have ever seen." She held out her hand, and I slid the ring on to her finger. It looked beautiful on her hand. If we were in different circumstances, I would have kissed her. I wanted to kiss her now, but I was worried I would end up with a fat lip.

We sat in silence side by side. I didn't realize how much I liked just being with someone. I looked over at Kate. She looked at her hand and twisted the ring around. I couldn't help but smile.

It would have been very easy to sit beside her all day, but I had things that needed to get done.

"I have to go feed the horses, and check on a heifer that should calve soon. Want to come with me?" I stood and held my hand out to help Kate off the swing. She jumped up and took my hand.

We wandered to the barn. I opened the door and let Kate walk in first. She walked over to the hay bin, grabbed it, and pulled it over to the stall. I opened the first stall, reached for the water bucket, and filled it. Kate stayed one stall ahead of me and circled back to put out their grain. My phone rang, and I stepped outside to answer it. When I came back in, Kate had started mucking stalls.

"Kate, you don't need to do that. I can do it later."

She stopped and turned to look at me.

"Well, it has to get done, right? We might as well do it together; it gets done twice as fast."

I stared at her for a moment, watching her effortlessly clean the stalls with a smile on her face. Was this what I had been missing all these years? Someone who didn't look at this life as a headache or a life sentence? Someone who genuinely loved it. Someone who was mine.

I smiled, "I'm not going to argue with you."

"For once," she mumbled. I laughed and heard her chuckle from the other side of the stall I was in.

We talked about our separate lives and our work, and discussed when to bring Kate's stuff over. The shrill ring of my cell phone brought us back to the real world, and I excused myself to answer it. Several minutes later, I hit end and walked back into the barn.

"Kate, my mother would like to know if you want to go to their home for supper. A kind of a welcome to the family. I told her I would call her back."

She looked like she was about to run away when she paused and took a deep breath, "Sure, that would be nice." Her face didn't match the words coming from her mouth. She looked in the direction of the main house, biting the corner of her lip, brows creased with uncertainty. I felt like I had watched my bride-to-be morph from a strong independent woman into a shy teenage girl in a matter of seconds.

eeting his parents for supper was not in my plans for today. We finished in the barn and walked back to the house.

"Tyler, would you mind if I freshened up here? I don't know what will help, but maybe I can salvage a decent look."

"Absolutely. The bathroom is just through there. We can head over in half an hour or so."

I nodded and was off to 'fix my face' as my grandma used to say. I came out of the bathroom and Tyler smiled.

"You look beautiful."

My face turned crimson, and I felt flustered. "I guess it's finally paid off to carry a purse the size of a carry-on bag. Tell me about your family," I said.

"Well, my mom was from here, but you know that. She and Dad met when she went to Montana for school." I looked up at Tyler, who seemed to be in another world as he told his story. "Dad grew up in Bozeman, the son of a ranch hand, always wanting more out of life. They got married, had kids, and then moved here after us boys were gone from home. My grandfather left the ranch to my parents." We walked out to the porch and Tyler leaned up against one of the large posts. "Rob was married, and he has Addison. She's seven and the light of this family. We all try to get along because of her. We want her to have the best childhood she possibly can." Tyler pushed himself away from the post he had been leaning on, and we started walking towards his parent's house. "Gavin is three years younger than Rob. and he lives in Dallas. He's an architect and wants nothing to do with this place. He drew the plans for my house, actually; it was one of the first things he did after school. He's single, and I would think he'll stay that way for quite a while. He enjoys single life."

"So why did you all move to Texas if Montana was home?"

"We are a close family. Rob and I wanted to work on this place and take over one day. Gavin didn't like the prospects of Montana for his career, so Dallas seemed like a good fit for him."

"I like that you are close. My sister and I haven't ever been close, so it's hard to understand," I said.

I was glad that we could walk over. It gave me a few extra minutes to talk myself out of running away. I bit the corner of my lip and stared at the ground. One chunk of my hair kept falling out of place, and I relentlessly tucked it behind my ear. Walking close to the lilac hedge, I ran my hand along the deep purple blooms as we passed by. That scent once more calmed my fears and settled my nerves. We rounded the corner of massive hedges, and ahead of us stood the largest home I had ever seen. It was three stories with a peaked roofline. A wall of windows covered the second and third floors. The stone and wood columns stood on either side of the door like guards. The second story had a beautiful wrap-around terrace. There were wings off the second and third floors, with peaks that faced north and south.

We arrived at the grand wooden door that seemed like it should belong in a castle. Tyler opened the door and motioned for me to walk in first. Huge log beams crisscrossed above me. A staircase led off of either side of the great room we had just walked into. A giant stone fireplace stood on the south wall, climbing up through the three stories of open space. I knew I was out of my depth. Standing in the foyer of this grand home, I felt like an imposter. I had grown up in an old two-story farmhouse that was drafty all year.

"Mom, Dad?"

"In the den, Tyler." I heard a voice call from our left.

Tyler grabbed my hand, and I followed him into the front room. It was as grand as the room I had just left. There were pictures of the ranch throughout the years, and a wall of family pictures that looked like they dated back generations. Beautiful paintings of western life adorned the other walls, and furniture that looked far too expensive to be sitting on filled the floor space.

"Hello son, I am so glad you were able to change your plans and be here." Sandra Morton walked over to Tyler and hugged him.

"Kate, it's so nice to see you again. It has been far too long." Sandra held out her hand for me to shake. I had to release the death grip I had on Tyler's hand to take hers. Sandra was very put together; her blonde hair immaculately cut and colored, and there wasn't a visible wrinkle on her flawless face. She was always dressed well and in the height of fashion. Today she wore a long leather fringe skirt and a fitted button-down navy blouse. I wore jeans, looking like I had rolled in from the pasture. This was a far fancier dinner than Tyler had led me to believe.

"It is nice to see you again, Mrs. Morton. Your home is absolutely breathtaking. Thank you for the invitation."

"Please, dear, it's Sandra. No need to be formal here."

I smiled, took a step back, and grabbed for Tyler's hand again. He gave my hand a little squeeze.

"Tyler, glad you could make it." His father had walked in behind him and gave him a slap on the back, nudging his body forward. "Moving pretty fast I see." Looking at our hands, he mumbled into Tyler's ear just, loud enough for me to hear. Tyler closed his eyes for the briefest of seconds. I let go of Tyler and folded my arms in front of me. Heat crept up from my neck into my cheeks. I hoped they weren't the color they felt like they were. I bit the inside edge of my lip, trying to relax.

"Kate, pleasure." Brian Morton said as he stuck out his hand for me to shake. I took it and was happy when he released it.

"Mr. Morton, nice to see you."

There was no offer for a more familiar greeting, which I imagined was a tactic to keep me intimidated. If that was the case, it was working well.

For about twenty minutes, it was just the four of us. Tyler and his parents carried on a casual conversation and included me often enough that I didn't feel left out.

"Hi, are you Kate? I'm Addison, but you can call me Addie." She dropped into a whisper, "But don't let my dad hear or he will correct you. He says my name is Addison; he didn't name me Addie." She mimicked his voice and rolled her eyes. I couldn't help but smile. I could tell she must have run over to the main house because her dark brown hair was all over the place. It was as if someone had released oxygen into the room.

"Well, hello Miss *Addison*." I stressed Addison and winked at her, and she winked back.

"I am happy to meet you. Your Uncle Tyler has told me a lot about you."

Addie beamed and jumped into Tyler's arms and sat on his lap.

"I like her, Uncle Ty." Her blue eyes were as big as saucers and she had a smile to match.

Rob walked over to the chair beside me and sat down. He was tall like Tyler, but not quite as broad.

"Kate, so good to see you. It's been a long time. Your dad must keep you busy over there."

"Things have been a little crazy. I'm thankful we are done calving and have awhile before branding starts."

"I wish we were done here. I'm getting a little tired of the night checks," Rob said, rubbing his face.

"Give me a week and a half, and then I can take a shift if you need a break," I replied.

"Really?"

"Yeah, I don't mind a bit. I don't usually sleep much, anyway."

"Thanks, I just might take you up on that."

I TURNED to look around and saw Gavin walk into the room.

"Well Kate, let me be the first apparently to welcome you into the family." His arms opened for a hug.

I stood from the couch and Gavin gave me a hug and whispered into my ear.

"They aren't going to bite."

"Thanks, Gavin." I smiled at him and took my place next to Tyler.

Gavin was seven years younger than Tyler, and a few

inches shorter, but they could have almost been identical. I knew Gavin better than his brothers. He was around more after the family moved here and had helped with branding and fence fixing along our shared fence line. He went to Montana for school and decided ranching wasn't for him.

Sandra got up and excused herself.

"I need to put the finishing touches on supper. We will be ready to eat in about five minutes."

"May I give you a hand?" I asked, standing from the couch.

"That would be wonderful." Sandra smiled, and we left the front room.

Sandra handed me dishes, and I took them out to the dining room, which is yet another gorgeous spot in this massive house.

"Well, I think we are ready. Thank you so much for your help. It's been a long time since I had anyone help me get the table ready for family supper. With a house full of men, they don't always think of these things, especially when they get talking business. I assure you, I did raise Tyler better than that."

I couldn't help but smile. "Tyler has been the epitome of a gentleman. In my opinion, you did a wonderful job."

She beamed from ear to ear.

"Before I call those men to the table, I would just like to welcome you. I want you to feel comfortable here. I know things aren't easy right now, and I'm sure you have your own feelings and resentments, but you are welcome here anytime."

"Thank you," I said quietly, as once again I felt the heat rising from my neck.

Sandra walked over to the kitchen door.

"Boys, it's supper."

The chatter grew closer, and closer as the mob descended into the dining room.

The brothers bantered back and forth. Like most families in business together, the talk turned to the latest things happening and what needed to be done.

"So Kate, have you thought of where you will have the wedding?" Brian asked between bites.

Any hopes that dinner wouldn't be awkward were dashed. The table went silent, and all eyes turned toward me.

"I um, well, I haven't given it too much thought since I only knew there was to be a wedding yesterday." Frowning at Brian, I hoped the jab would let him know I wasn't a pushover and that I could and would stand up for myself.

Rob let out a quick laugh, and Gavin gave me a coy smile of approval. From the looks of things, not too many people spoke their mind in front of Brian, unless it pertained to business.

"Kate, can I be your flower girl?" Addie asked with a mouth full of salad.

"Addison Morton, you don't blurt out a question like that," Rob said, slightly perturbed.

"Rob, it's okay. Addison, I would love it if you would be my flower girl." The little girl beamed and looked at Tyler, who nodded yes as well.

She shot off her chair and ran around the table and wrapped her arms around my waist.

"Thank you, Auntie Kate."

I wrapped my arms around her and whispered, "You are so welcome. You better go back to your seat and finish supper."

She smiled and went back to eating.

The remainder of supper was eaten in silence. It wasn't until dessert was brought out that anyone dared to talk again.

"Kate, not to make things uncomfortable again, but if you would like to have the wedding here, I am more than happy to host it. It's the least we can do," Sandra said flatly, looking at her husband.

"Thank you Sandra, we would like that very much." I was surprised at the generous offer. It took a lot of the headaches off my plate. I looked over at Tyler, who smiled at his mother.

"Thank you, Mom, this means a lot."

CHAPTER 8

She was basically being forced into marrying me by my father, so meeting my family officially was daunting, I'm sure. I felt her take slow, deep breaths, as if she needed to calm her nerves. I reached for her hand under the table and entwined my fingers through hers, giving it a squeeze. She looked over at me with wide eyes and half a smile. Nobody outright said *arranged marriage,* but it was in the back of everyone's mind. My father looked rather pleased with himself the entire evening for making the deal.

"I'm going to take Kate on a tour of the house." I stood from my chair and held out my hand for her to go with me.

Kate slowly smiled, and I saw she let out the breath she had been holding. She took it and stood. We left the dining room while the others went to the den.

"I figured you needed a break from all of that." I frowned as I motioned with my head toward the dining room.

We wandered around the house together, holding hands.

"Before you built your house, where was your room?" She smiled at me, so I walked toward the room I had used. I opened the door. Kate walked in, and I closed the door behind me.

"It looks just like I imagined."

"You imagined my room?"

"Well, ah—I, ah—no. It's just a figure of speech. What I mean is it looks like something you would, ah, be, umm, comfortable in." Kate played with that piece of hair that kept falling out of place. I enjoyed getting to know what I could tease her about.

Not wanting to leave her fumbling for words or feeling shy, I broke the silence. "You pulled that out of the air, didn't you? You have thought of my room. What other thoughts about me have you had?" Smirking and moving closer to her, I backed her up until she was trapped between the door and me.

"We should probably get back to the den. I'm sure your family is wondering where we are." Kate's voice was barely above a whisper.

"They won't even miss us. I really want to know, Kate. How often do you think of me?" Leaning in close to her, I felt her warm breath against my face. Her eyes darted around. I could tell she was searching for something to say, but the words wouldn't form.

"Over the last two days it seems constant." Her eyes changed from searching to confident.

My laugh was huskier than I thought it would be.

"Well, that's not what I was looking for, but it will have to do." Reaching behind her, I grabbed the doorknob and turned it. She slipped out of the way and let me open it, but our closeness made it difficult to maneuver without contact. Her breasts grazed my chest, sending a shock through me. I immediately felt her nipples stand at attention. Arching my eyebrow, I grinned at her. I got a half smile back. With the door open, Kate bolted out of the room and down the hallway.

"Sorry, I just need a second," she said, turning to look out the window behind her. I walked up to her and put my hand on her lower back, quietly standing beside her.

"Everything okay?" I asked quietly. She didn't talk, only nodded her head and took a deep breath.

"It just got very real in there," Kate whispered. "I haven't felt feelings like that for a long time."

"Feelings like what?" I pushed her to talk.

Kate looked up to my eyes, "Wanting, longing, hoping to be touched. Needing someone else." She was open and vulnerable. I took her in my arms, and we stood in each other's embrace for a moment. I felt her take another deep breath, and she moved away from me.

"We should get back."

Her smile returned, and she took my hand. With the tour finished, we went back to the den to visit for a few minutes.

REGARDLESS OF THE SITUATION, I had a decent evening.

We said our goodnights and left the house to walk back to Tyler's. In this moment, I understood why he had wanted his privacy away from the main house - and away from his family.

"That house is incredible. I've never seen anything like it."

Tyler stopped walking and looked at me quizzically.

"You've never been here?"

I shook my head no.

"Not for one of mom's events? Branding parties? Just to be neighborly?"

Again, I shook my head. "Nope, never."

It had been a nice evening. We had shared an intimate moment, and I felt like flirting, which was out of my comfort zone. Before I gave it a second thought, I heard myself say, "I was too afraid I might run into the Morton brother I had a crush on." I looked up at Tyler, arched my eyebrow and turned to face him.

Tyler pointed his index finger at himself. "Would that have been me?" He moved closer to me, grinning from ear to ear.

"We may never know." Shrugging my shoulders, I looked away and wandered off ahead of him. I could hear him chuckle behind me.

"It was me, wasn't it?" he whispered in my ear when he caught up to me. I stopped walking and turned to look at him and nodded.

He took a step closer to me. "That's why you said it wasn't marrying me that was causing your tears. You *have* thought about me more than just the last few days." His eyes widened, and there was that smile. I nodded again, and he puffed up like a peacock.

"I'm not sad it's you I'm marrying, Tyler. I'm sad we didn't get to meet properly, fall in love with each other, and get married like a normal couple. As for thinking about you... well, you aren't exactly the easiest person to forget." I bit my lip and looked him over from head to toe and back up. Tyler chuckled. If he only knew what that did to me, I was sure he would do it all the time. Tyler grabbed my hand, and we continued our walk.

WE GOT BACK to Tyler's house and went in to relax.

"Would you like a glass of sun tea?" he asked.

"That would be great." I smiled at him. Tyler walked into the kitchen and I followed. He grabbed the glasses, and I opened the fridge. I poured, and he handed me my glass.

"Thank you." My smile wasn't hidden, and his smile back at me was all I needed. He was easy to be around. I could see us making a life together. These moments when it was just the two of us together doing mundane things, it was easy to forget why we had been thrown together.

As we walked back to the living room, I sat on the couch across from him and folded up my legs under me.

"So, dinner wasn't terrible," I said straight faced, looking directly at him.

I could tell he tried to hold back his laugh, but it didn't work.

"What did you think was going to happen?"

Bringing the glass up to my lips, I took a sip. "Well, I wasn't sure. I haven't ever been taken home to meet parents, so you can imagine what was going through my mind."

"What do you mean, you have never met parents? Surely you've dated."

"Oh, I have dated a lot. But when it came time to meet family, I broke it off or, they did. Or I had known them my entire life. I guess I just figured nobody really wanted to take me home."

"Who have you been dating all these years?" he blurted out. "Kate, I didn't mean…"

"The men I have dated are really none of your business, but since you think it is, I will tell you. They were guys that I couldn't imagine sharing a life with. Or they saw our ranch and thought it would be a payday. So I'm sorry if all these years I have been a little pickier about who I let into my life, and my bed, unlike you." I hadn't meant to say the last part, and I winced as I said it. Looking up at Tyler, I could see he didn't look angry. To be honest, he looked slightly amused.

"I'm glad you were." He took a sip of the sun tea. I tried to avoid eye contact.

I looked at my watch; it was late. "Oh man, I better get going. My mom, Delaney, and I are heading to Dallas for the weekend to find a wedding dress. I should probably be awake for that."

Tyler nodded and looked a little disappointed. The drive back to my place was quiet, neither of us sure what to say, or how familiar to be, but there was so much left to talk about.

"Your mom gave me the number of the event planner she is using, so I will call her tomorrow while I'm on the road. Is there anything you want or really don't want to have at the wedding?" I asked as we drove into my yard. Tyler sat quietly for a moment and turned to look at me.

"Doves. I hate doves." I turned to look at him in the dark, only illuminated by the yard light behind us. The surrounding glow made him seem bigger, more protective. I burst out laughing.

"We are being thrown into an arranged marriage, and all you could come up with was doves?"

"I don't like birds." Tyler threw his hands in the air. "Okay, but being serious for a second, I really am not worried about our wedding, Kate. I already know you're practical, and I can't imagine that will change, but really no birds."

The words *you're practical* stung. I was only that way because I had to be. There was no room for frivolous living here. We barely scraped by, and obviously weren't succeeding at that either. I shook it off and tried to accept it as a compliment, but just once in my life, I wanted to not worry about how one decision affected the foreseeable future.

"OK, no birds." I tried to pout, but my smile gave me away.

We sat in the truck for a while, just talking.

"Night, Tyler, I will call you when I get home from Dallas."

"OK, sounds good. Have a good night."

"You, too." I hopped out of the truck and went inside.

Tyler only drove away once he saw a light go on in the house. I crawled into bed, exhausted but excited from the day, knowing that tomorrow wouldn't be any easier.

SHE WAS VERY easy to talk to. When I took her home and came back to the house, it felt empty. I don't know how someone I just met could make me feel like this. My phone rang, surprising me. "Hello?"

"Hi, it's Kate. I couldn't sleep and I thought maybe you would still be up."

"Well, I'm not going to turn down your call, so what's keeping you awake?"

"Why did you agree to this? I didn't have much of a choice or my family would have been forced to leave the only home they have known for the last 150 years. But why do you feel you have to do this?"

I was silent for a minute.

"Kate, my dad told me if I didn't do this, he would ruin me. I don't know if he has the power to do it, but I don't want to find out. He said he would also make it so none of this place is left to me. Like you, this place is my heritage, and I don't know if I'm ready to give up the dream of owning it." I ran my hands through my hair and closed my eyes. "I have business dealings in Montana. The ranch I grew up on came up for sale a few years ago, so I'm a partner in the old place. Actually, Rob and Gavin are the other partners, so I always have something to fall back on." Lying back down on the couch, I tucked my arm under my head. "But it's not just that. I said yes, Kate, mostly because I'm tired of living my life the way I have been. A new girl every few days who only sees money and doesn't see me, doesn't understand when I'm up all night, or offer to help before I even know I need it myself. I have brought girls home that won't even go into a barn because it smells, or they realize that I actually work and they don't want the life their parents had." I let out a sigh, not knowing if I should continue, but I pushed ahead with my thoughts. "You are the first person who has ever taken control in that barn and got things done. I want a life that I can be proud of. One that when I'm old, I can look back on and say I lived a good life. I had the greatest of loves. We grew together and made a life that generations can look back on and be proud of. Like your family."

Kate was silent on the other end of the line.

"Kate, did you fall asleep?"

"No." Came quietly.

"Tyler, what if I don't live up to your expectations? What if I'm not the great love of your life? We have been forced into this, and I don't know if I can be that person."

I knew I should have censored myself a little, but I wanted her to know my feelings.

"Tyler, I need to go. Tomorrow is going to be a long day. Good night."

"Night, Kate."

Her line went dead, and I was more awake than I had been before she called. I couldn't understand how a woman as great as Kate could think so little of herself. Suddenly I had an idea, and I had to work fast because it had to be done by morning.

$\mathcal{I}$ didn't want to get out of bed; this trip to Dallas was just making things even more real. Being alone in a vehicle with my mom and sister for three hours wasn't really my idea of a good time. Add in trying on dresses... it would be a torturous weekend. Swinging my legs out of bed, I quickly showered and got dressed. Knowing there was no hope for my hair, I threw it up in a messy bun and went to the kitchen. Checking my watch, I saw I had just enough time to make coffee. I had barely sat down to enjoy my lifeline when a horn sounded outside my house. Delaney was getting anxious to get on the road. I grabbed my suitcase and the mug of coffee and headed out the door. I stopped when I saw Tyler talking to Delaney and Mom. My heart skipped a beat, and I started fidgeting with the strap on my suitcase. Tyler smiled when he saw me walk out of the house, and once again, I thought about the fact that his smile was going to get me in trouble.

"Good morning, everyone. What's this meeting all about?" Looking around at the three of them, I could see they all looked guilty. Mom and Delaney were looking everywhere but at me, and Tyler was grinning from ear to ear.

"I just wanted to talk to you real quick, if that's okay?" Tyler looked at Mom and Delaney, and they both nodded yes.

"I don't get a say?"

Tyler laughed and took my suitcase from me, put it in the trunk of the car, and motioned to the barn. I followed until I caught up, and we walked side by side.

The barn was empty when we walked in.

"I'm sorry if I caught you off guard this morning; it wasn't my intention. I just wanted to tell you to have a good time in Dallas." He held out his hand with a very official-looking paper in it. Could this be the pre-nup I had been waiting for? I looked down at the paper he handed me and my eyes shot directly back up to his.

"I hope you don't mind, but I made reservations at these restaurants, and booked you into this hotel."

"You booked us into the Rosemont, as well as supper, at The Steak House tonight? Tyler, this is too much, we can't—"

He cut me off before I could finish.

"It's not too much. I want to do this for you. Your supper tomorrow night will be at the Rosewood. I have hired a driver to take you anywhere you want to go. Let me do this for you, please."

I could tell he was genuine; he truly wanted me to take advantage of the luxury that he was able to give.

"Thank you, Tyler. I don't know how I will ever repay you." I looked down at the confirmation papers in my hands. He put his finger under my chin and lifted my head to look at him.

"You deserve to be spoiled, Kate. You work hard; you have kept this place afloat for the last few years with little to no help from what I can see." He frowned.

I knew I should have argued, but he wasn't wrong. I worked very hard on my own most days.

"Go have a good time. The only request I have is that you call me tonight and tomorrow. Not because I want to control you. That's what's running through your head, I can tell. I only ask because I want to hear about your day. I want to know you, and the only way to do that is to talk to you." He took my hands in his. "I'm making a rule right now that we talk at minimum once a day until our wedding. After that, we really have no choice but to talk to each other."

I let out a laugh, hoping to lighten the mood that had gotten quite heavy.

"Deal. I can do that. It will be the bright spot in my day, I'm sure. I better get going before Delaney starts honking again." I smiled up at him.

"Please enjoy yourself. I'm only ever a call or text away if you need someone to talk to."

"I know, and you better keep your phone close." I walked closer to him and wrapped my arms around him. Closing my eyes, I took a deep breath and drank in his cologne. Strong arms wrapped around my waist and pulled me closer to him. We were closer than we had been before, and I rested my head on his chest. I could hear his heartbeat, steady and rhythmic. At this moment, I didn't want to move.

"I have to go," I whispered, and my heart soared when he groaned.

"Okay, have fun," he whispered in my ear.

We pulled away from each other and walked back to the barn door, hand in hand.

"We can't go out there holding hands. I will never hear the end of it this weekend." The squeeze he gave my hand before he let me go was the last encouragement I needed to begin the dress search.

"It's about time; let's get going," Delaney said from the driver's seat. She had pulled her car to the barn and was waiting for me.

"Have a wonderful time ladies. I better get back to work. Bye, you." Tyler leaned in and said huskily.

"Bye," I said, smiling back at him. He opened the door, and I climbed into the back seat as he closed my door. I looked at him and thought maybe this wasn't going to be terrible. Rummaging around I, got my book out, and I'd just started reading when my phone vibrated. I picked it up and looked at the text.

Tyler: Smile, this is supposed to be fun ;)

I smiled and shook my head. I pushed the camera button and took a selfie of my forced smile and sent it back.

Me: I am! See!

Tyler: Beautiful.

Me: Oh, please.

Tyler: I'm going to tell you until you believe it.

Me: Well, it's probably good we will have a lifetime together, because it will take at least that long.

A few minutes passed before his reply.

Tyler: I won't let it take that long. I have to work now. My fiancée is supposed to call me later.

Me: LOL Bye.

"We aren't even out of the county, and he's already texting you? Turn your phone off and enjoy this drive," Delaney said, looking back at me in the rear-view mirror.

I'm happy she didn't notice me taking a selfie, because she would never have let me live that down. I just smiled.

"We're flirting; isn't that what everyone wanted us to do? I mean, let's face it. We are getting married in eleven days, and we need to build some kind of foundation for this relationship we have been forced into."

Delaney scoffed, "Come on. If you hadn't been so terrified, you might have run into him, then this would have happened a long time ago, and you wouldn't have been forced into this situation. Kate, tell me honestly, would you be this easy-going about it if it was Rob or Gavin?"

If I could have stared holes into the back of her head, it would be smoldering. My very own sister, one of the few people who actually knew about my secret crush on Tyler, just called me out.

"I can't say how I would have reacted. There is nothing wrong with Rob or Gavin. They are both nice guys, and any woman would be happy to have them interested."

"Yes, but they aren't Tyler."

I had no rebuttal to her statement. Once again, I suddenly felt vulnerable and used, which led me back to feeling resentment towards my parents. I looked over at my mom, who had been staring out the window, disengaged from the conversation.

"Mom, you must have an opinion," I said accusingly.

She turned away from the window to look at me and took a deep breath. "Katie, when this option was brought up, I was against it. Your father and Brian had been going around in circles." She took a deep breath before she continued. "Your father did everything he could to find any other agreeable alternative. When we finally saw that there was only one decision, I made the risky declaration that the only person it could be was Tyler. As much as you think your crush was a secret, I'm your mom. I know more than you have ever told me, and your sister has a big mouth."

Mom and I looked at Delaney and laughed when she decided to pout.

Mom took a deep breath. "I knew both Rob and Gavin would make good husbands. They are good men, but it would have been a disruption to Rob's life when he had just finalized his divorce and the custody of Addison. Gavin is so much younger and just trying to establish himself in Dallas, and I didn't want you that far away. So that left Tyler. I knew you would make an easy transition to being his wife. Well, maybe not an easy one, but the cards weren't as stacked against this pairing as they were with the others." She turned back to look out the windshield, and the rest of the drive was quiet.

CHAPTER 10

My phone buzzed, so I picked it up and smiled when I saw the text was from Kate.

Kate: Supper was amazing. The restaurant was beautiful, and we were treated like VIPs. Then there is the hotel. Tyler, it's breathtaking. There is no way we will ever be able to repay you for this weekend.

Me: I'm so very glad everything has been perfect for you. You are repaying me; you are becoming my wife. That's all the payment I need.

Kate: Well, I will think of something someday.

Just when I was going to answer back, Rob and Gavin came barreling through the door to my office.

"Are you ready for your bachelor party?" Rob asked, coming around to the back of my chair and slapping me on the shoulder.

"What are you two talking about?"

"We are headed out to commemorate the end of your single years."

"Thanks guys, but I don't want anything. This isn't exactly how I thought I would get married. So thanks for the offer, but

I'm just going to head home." Standing from my chair, I started to pack up when both Rob and Gavin started laughing.

"Nice try, brother. You stayed late here for a reason. We knew you would be responsible and try to get out of this, so the party's happening at your place."

"Let's get this over with," I said as I headed for the door.

I WALKED INTO MY HOUSE, and the party had already started. Six of the best friends a guy could have in his corner sat on my sofas, beers in hand, eating what looked to be nachos, wings and mini bacon burgers.

"Tyler!" they all shouted at the same time. Rob had gone to the kitchen and come back with drinks for the three of us. I cracked my beer and walked over to the sofas.

"Well, old man, you are finally settling down. How does it feel?" Tony, my oldest friend from college, asked.

"It's good. I think it will be good. You guys all make it seem like a cake-walk." The guys laughed.

"Ty, it's a little quick, don't yeah think?" another one asked.

Our story was flimsy, and I felt like all the people in this room could see through it. I chugged the beer in my hand, "When yeah know, yeah know." I grabbed a mini burger and popped it in my mouth, hoping that would stop the questions.

We watched an old Cowboys vs Eagles game and got rather loud yelling at the TV. Drinks flowed, and the food kept coming. I had no idea how it got here, and I didn't care. One by one, the guys called a ride share until it was just my brothers and I left.

I sat on the sofa, staring up at the ceiling. I hadn't had a night like this in a very long time.

"Well, how was your bachelor party?" Rob asked, slapping me on the leg.

"It was great. Thanks for arranging it." I looked at my brothers and realized we had become friends somewhere between the fights, the disagreements, and growing up.

"OK, tell us what you are really thinking. I have known you long enough to know there is something happening under that calm exterior," Gavin said as he tossed back another drink.

"I just don't understand it. What's the purpose of this? Dad has never pressured any of us to get married. I'm 39 years old. Doesn't he think I am smart enough to figure out what I want or don't want?" I was fully aware that at this moment I sounded like a whiny child, but I didn't care.

"So I found out that we all have to be married by forty for the ranch to fully transfer from Grandpa John's estate to dad. If we don't, everything transfers to Uncle Adam." Rob and I whipped our heads up to look at Gavin. "I would think that Rob has met the qualifications, but the issue is you. You just turned thirty-nine and had no prospects close enough to ensure our future on this ranch. I have a feeling that this arrangement wasn't a coincidence as far as the timing goes. If he had waited any longer, it would have come across as very suspicious to Uncle Adam, but you will have been married almost a year before the deadline, so it looks plausible."

"So keeping the ranch in our name is more important than my future. Maybe I shouldn't have come back here. How long can a grown man work under his patronizing, bad-tempered father? I wonder some days what would have happened if I had stayed in Montana." I opened another beer and didn't really care how I was going to feel in the morning.

"OK, hear me out; you don't have to do this. You can walk away. So what if Uncle Adam takes over? It's not like we can't find other places to work." Rob chimed in, "You shouldn't have to marry Kate because of this. I mean, she's not a terrible choice. She's pretty; she can out work most people." Rob was loudly pleading his case, but I wasn't able to follow what side he was making it for.

"I know she's pretty. I know she's a hard worker, but one woman for the rest of my life?" I stood up from the couch. Staggering a bit, I steadied myself on the fireplace mantle. "She's kind and thoughtful. The more time I spend with her, I wonder why I never saw her. I know I was chasing blond's and boobs, but she's still hard to miss."

Both my brothers held up their drinks and cheered. "I have been so stupid. I can't get married. What do I know about being a husband?" My words were jumbled, and I went from pro-marriage to against marriage faster than even I could keep up.

"Listen, you have decided to do this, and we are behind you. But right now, I think you need to hit the sack," Rob said as he swayed side to side. "I also think I'm crashing here for the night." He plopped onto the sofa as Gavin and I laughed. I staggered up to my room and noticed my phone on the bed. I picked it up and saw a few missed calls from Kate.

MY PHONE RANG. I rolled over thinking I was dreaming, but the shrill ring went off again. I fumbled around in the dark for the phone before it woke up the entire suite. I saw it was Tyler and got worried. It was four in the morning. I quickly pressed the green answer button and sat up in bed.

"Hello?"

"Hellooo Kates, you called and I missss. Missss, I didn't hear it. I'm very, very sorry."

Frowning, I rubbed my face, trying to wake myself up.

"Tyler, have you been drinking?"

"No. Well, yes, yes, I have been."

"Quite a bit from the sounds of it."

"That may be a yes, too. See, Rob and Gavin threw me a bachelor party at our house. Oh don't worry, it will get cleaned up before you get home. But things got a little drinky. No strippers or things like that, just a few friends of mine."

"Tyler, I'm not concerned about it. It's four in the morning. I would be happy to talk, just not right now." From the sounds of him, he was going to be hurting in the morning. "OK, listen to me. Where are you in the house?"

"I'm in the… our bedroom."

"You sure about that?" I couldn't help but tease him.

"Yessss."

"Go to the bathroom and get a couple of Advil and a glass of water." I could hear him opening cupboards and picking up the bottle.

"Ha, got it." He shook it into the speaker of the phone. "See!" Hearing the faucet turn on and off, I figured he had accomplished getting water into a cup.

"Great. Now put them beside your bed. You will need them in the morning. Get into bed."

"Done. Now what should we do?" He sounded like a five-year-old trying to avoid bedtime.

"Good night, Tyler."

"OK, nighty night, wifey." I was taken off guard. The familiarity made me smile before the line went dead. I shook my head, turned my phone off, and went back to sleep.

• • •

THE ALARM WENT off at 8:00am, and as I lay in the luxurious bed, I was quickly dreading what was to come today. The sooner I started, the sooner it would be done, I hoped.

"Kat, did your phone ring at four this morning?" Delaney called from the other room.

"Yes, it did. It was Tyler."

Delaney flew into my room and landed on my bed like a sack of potatoes.

"Why was he calling at that time of the night?"

I rolled over to face her, "Well apparently there was a surprise bachelor party, and I had a very drunk fiancé worried that he had missed my call last night."

"Well, that was sweet, he called." Delaney rolled on to her back.

"Sweet if it hadn't been four in the morning but, the last thing he said was 'nighty night wifey'."

She shot straight up in bed, her eyes huge and she looked like she was ready to burst. "He said that?"

I started laughing with Delaney.

"How did it feel to be called that?" Delaney asked through giggles. I immediately looked at her and stopped laughing.

"I don't know. It seemed like just a funny thing at that moment." Flopping back down on my pillow, I covered my face with my hands. "Delaney, I'm terrified… and a little excited. Sometimes I feel so silly imagining a life with him, but that's exactly what's going to happen." I looked over at her and gave a crooked smile. I fidgeted with the sheet and we lay there quietly, lost in our own thoughts.

We had a full day of dress shops lined up, but before we got to the first one, I called Tyler.

∼

A PHONE RANG RIGHT in my ear; I must have fallen asleep on it. Well, maybe more like passed out on it. I peeled it off my face and answered it.

"Hello." My tongue felt like it was glued to the roof of my mouth, so I'm not sure an actual hello came out.

"Well, hey there, cowboy. How are you feeling this morning?" On the other end of the line, the very perky and loud voice of Kate made me snap awake.

"Kate, do you always talk so loud? Is it morning?"

"Yes, it is. How does it feel being woken up from a dead sleep?" She was laughing, but I couldn't remember why. "You called me after your bachelor party."

"I called you?"

"Yes, you did."

"What time did I call you?"

"Four this morning."

Groaning, I put my hand to my head, "Kate, I'm so sorry. Did I say anything…?"

"Well, you called me Kates and then there was the wifey comment." She was enjoying this a little too much.

I sat up in bed and the room spun, so I lay back down. "I'm sorry, I assure you that's not the normal me."

"It's fine Tyler, I was just calling to tell you to take the Advil that's beside your bed." She managed to get out through a few giggles. I looked over to the table beside my bed and there they were; two Advil and a glass of water.

"How did those get there?" I asked.

"I walked you through, getting them from the bathroom. I was happy you didn't have childproof caps." Her laughter on the other end of the line hurt my head, but it made me smile.

"Thanks. I appreciate it."

"I will call later tonight to see how you are. Bye-bye, hubby."

I groaned again, "Bye, Kate, thank you." Hanging up the phone, I grabbed the Advil, downed the glass of water and fell back to sleep.

I HUNG up the phone and turned to look at Delaney, who had her hands clamped over her mouth and burst out laughing.

"I can't believe you just flirted like that. My big sister had a moment of not being so serious. Maybe this situation will break you out of being the responsible one. You deserve to have a break. Let someone else play that role for a while."

"Like who? You?" I said, slightly accusingly.

"Well, ya. I was approached by the high school; they need a principal, and I have the credentials to be one. I had been putting feelers out, knowing Mr. Keeting was looking to retire. The assistant prof job isn't going anywhere for a few more years, and I want to come home."

"Delaney, I am a little surprised, but I'm so glad you are going to be around. When do you start?"

"Next week, after the wedding. My stuff is in storage, and I will stay with mom and dad until I find a place I want to call home."

I grabbed a throw pillow, swung it at her, and hit her square in the face. It was an all-out pillow fight when mom walked in.

"You two, this is a nice hotel. Stop it and get ready to go or we'll be late."

CHAPTER 11

We ate breakfast in the hotel restaurant and walked out to the sidewalk, where we climbed into the limousine Tyler had arranged to take us to the bridal shops.

We arrived at the first one and walked in.

The shop was exquisite, cream-colored couches and carpet, chandeliers hanging all over, and mirrors everywhere. Beautifully dressed mannequins were spot-lit in every direction, employees who all had porcelain skin, perfectly manicured nails and not a hair out of place on anyone's head stood around the perimeter, waiting for clients. The smell of perfume wafted from every corner of the shop. All the girls looked like they could walk the runways of Paris or Milan. Feeling slightly intimidated, I walked up to the front desk.

"Hello, I have an appointment booked under Kate Patterson."

The receptionist smiled and typed on her computer.

"Ah yes, Miss Patterson, your consultant, will be Stella. I will just run and get her."

A lady in her late thirties walked over to us. She was tall, with black hair and red lips you would never be able to miss or forget.

"Hi Kate, it's a pleasure to meet you."

She stuck out her hand toward me, and I shook it.

"Let's get you ladies settled in, and Kate, I will take you to your fitting room."

My mom and Delaney sat on the sofa in front of a mirror and I was whisked away to the fitting area. I had no idea what type of dress I wanted. I always thought brides that were indecisive were just playing to the cameras on all the bridal shows, but here I was, trying to answer Stella's questions, and I had no clue what to tell her. She showed me pictures of all the dress styles and I managed to narrow it down to a few different options, so she ran off and found dresses for me to try on.

"Ready?"

I nodded and exited the dressing room for the first time in a huge diamond-white ball gown. It had sparkles and bling all over it. It was off the shoulder and had long tulle sleeves. I knew it wasn't the one, but I had a feeling mom and Delaney needed to see it, or I wouldn't have a moment of peace.

They both gasped when I walked out.

"Kate, you are beautiful." Delaney said just above a whisper.

"Kate, it's gorgeous. What do you think?"

I looked at my mom, and then looked at myself in the mirror and shook my head.

"It's a beautiful dress, but not exactly me. It's just too much." I grabbed handfuls of material in the skirt.

"Next one it is," Stella cheerfully answered.

Dress on, dress off was the game we played for the next

hour. Nothing seemed to be me, and I didn't think Stella really had any idea about what to pull from the rack.

The last dress was the complete opposite from the first one. It was a satin sheath dress with tiny spaghetti straps. The front had a draped neckline that exposed most of my chest and a slit up the middle that ended at my upper thigh. I was completely uncomfortable, but decided they needed to see it. If I had to show this dress, I decided to strut out of the dressing room like I owned the shop. I stood on the pedestal and waited for the reaction.

SILENCE. That's what the reaction was.

"Stella, could you please give us a few moments of privacy?" Most would think this was a question, but my mother had made it a statement. Stella looked from her to me and walked away with a huff.

"Katie, that is an entirely inappropriate dress," my mom whispered. "Well, I guess if you need a very expensive nightgown it would work." I looked into the mirror at my mom and then to Delaney, who was doing her best to keep her giggles under control.

"Kate, now given that you have known Tyler only a few days, and that this is an arranged marriage, is this the look you are going for because this says… " Delaney whispered.

"Delaney shh, don't you dare."

"If you are wanting to be intimate at the altar, I suppose,"

"Laney, stop." I started giggling.

My mother placed her hand on her head. I couldn't tell if she was embarrassed by us, the dress, or trying to maintain her Southern lady manners.

"Don't laugh, you are going to pop out." Delaney was

almost falling off the sofa, laughing so hard. She had put her hands up to her breasts and flung her hands open.

I started to bend over to pick the dress up and she and mom both yelled, "NO!"

I stood straight again and picked up the draping neckline and tucked it under my chin, bent down and picked up the dress, and stepped off the pedestal.

"You two are terrible people."

I strutted off to the dressing room with the neckline still tucked under my chin.

"Stella, I don't think this will work."

My time was up at that salon. I was tired of trying things on, but we had fun. I put my clothes back on, thanked Stella for her time, and went to the next appointment I had booked.

Arriving in front of the second shop, I sighed. I knew this wouldn't be easy, and we had the crazy time table to contend with, which meant I needed to find a dress that could be taken home today.

I pushed the door open, the bell above us chimed to signal our entrance. We walked into a sea of white tulle, satin and lace. It looked like minimal organization, and couldn't have been more opposite than the last shop. This shop advertised 'buy and go' as their specialty, which is why I thought we should try here.

A woman in her mid-fifties came flying out of the back room, her hair disheveled, but smiling like we were the first people she had seen today.

"You must be Kate. I'm so happy you made it. I'm Nancy. Now come with me, ladies." We followed Nancy to the back of the shop.

"Mom, sister, please take a seat. I'm going to steal Kate and you will see her again in a few moments.

"Is it just me, or does this place seem like it needs an update?" Delaney whispered to Mom.

"Delaney Anne, shhh. But, yes."

Delaney laughed and settled into her chair.

In the fitting room, Nancy and I had quickly chatted.

"Kate, I have been dressing brides for 25 years. Trust me, and I know we will find your gown."

I smiled at Nancy; she seemed to have all the confidence in the world which I was glad of, because mine, at this point, was in the negative.

She zipped out of the fitting room, and in less than three minutes, she came back into the room with two dresses. Neither of them were amazing, but I tried the first one on. I walked out to no reaction.

"I suppose if you had the theme of Southern Débutante, that would work," Delaney said, eyeing me from head to toe.

"You would know about being a débutante." I stuck my tongue out at her, and she stuck hers out at me.

"Girls, behave."

Nancy laughed at us and ushered me back to change dresses.

With the second one on, I stepped out to show it off. There weren't even words, just turned-up noses and a shake of heads.

Nancy flew out of the fitting room and came back with one dress.

"This one just recently became unavailable from the designer. It's your size, and I'm not sure you would need many alterations."

I looked at the dress and nodded. Nancy helped me into it, and I knew I was done looking. A delicate V neck top of lace and iridescent crystals led to a plain brushed satin skirt. Turning to look in the mirror, I saw a plunging back with a few buttons starting at my lower back and went all the way down to the end of the train, which was edged with lace and sequins like the bodice. It was very fitted to mid-thigh, then flared out gradually.

"This is it, isn't it?" Nancy put her hands on my shoulders and whispered in my ear. And it wasn't a question. She knew it was. Looking at myself in the mirror, I was stunned. I never thought this moment would be one I would have, but here I am. A strange wash of contentment flowed through me. As crazy as life had become in this moment, in this dress, life slowed, and I could breathe. I nodded yes.

"Let's show them."

I turned in the fitting room, and Nancy pulled open the curtain. I looked from my mom to Delaney who had both just let out a gasp. Stepping out of the fitting room and up onto the pedestal, I waited for their critique.

"You have to get this dress. You are going to drive that man crazy," Delaney said, looking me up and down.

I looked over at my mom, who was digging through her purse, desperately trying to find a tissue to wipe the tears that were rolling down her cheeks. Nancy grabbed a box and handed it to Mom. Finally dabbing at her eyes, she looked up.

"Kate, you are stunning. It's like it was made for you. What do you think?"

I looked at myself in the mirror and smiled.

"Wait, let me add a few things." Nancy rushed off and came back with a light veil that was edged with the same lace as the dress, a pair of large sparkly teardrop earrings and a bracelet. She put the accessories on, and I looked at myself once again. Whoever the woman looking back at me was, I didn't recognize her. I had never been in anything so beautiful in all my life. I smiled and nodded.

"This is it."

The three women cheered.

"Now Nancy, what can you do about the maid of honor dress?" Delaney's turn was up.

Back in the fitting room, I took my dress off and began to change back into my clothes. My phone buzzed in my purse, so I grabbed it.

Tyler: Well, how's your shopping?

Me: Great! I have found my dress at Nancy's Bridal.

Tyler: Do I get a picture?

Me: No. And besides, I literally just took it off.

Tyler: Hmmm, do I get a picture of that?

Me: Tyler Morton! No, you do not.

Tyler: Can't blame a guy for trying.

Me: No, I suppose I can't.

Tyler: Good thing I have a good imagination.

Me: Goodbye, Tyler. I have to get dressed.

Tyler: A very good imagination.

I laughed to myself and shook my head and tossed my phone back in my purse.

I walked out of the fitting room and took my place in the chair.

Nancy had gone in and out of the fitting room four times before Delaney came out. I didn't have any preference when it came to her dress, so I left it up to her.

Once she finally came out, she was in a strapless royal blue lace dress. I knew it would complement mine, and she looked stunning.

"Delaney, that's gorgeous. I love it."

We stood at the counter waiting to pay. Nancy was on the phone and writing frantically. Finally, the call ended, and she turned around and gave Delaney her dress bag and then handed me the bag with my dress, veil, earrings, and bracelet. I looked at her, confused, as she came around to the front of the counter.

"All I ask is a picture of you both in the dresses to post on social media, if you will allow me to."

"Nancy, there is the small matter of payment," I said, confused.

"Darling, it's taken care of. Go have a wonderful remainder of your day, and a happy life. If I had a fiancé like yours, I would still be married."

I should have known he would do this. The man was good, but I expected there was a spy amongst my party.

"Thank you Nancy; you made this painless." She beamed and walked us out of the shop.

Sitting in the limo, I grabbed my phone.

Me: You are too much.

Tyler must have had his phone in his hand because he replied back within seconds.

Tyler: Is that a thank you?

Me: Tyler, thank you. You didn't need to pay for my dress; I had enough tucked away.

Tyler: Keep that tucked away and buy something you have been wanting.

Me: Thank you from the bottom of my heart.

Tyler: You are so very welcome.

I TUCKED my phone back into my purse and smiled.

CHAPTER 12

With our dresses in hand, we headed back to the hotel for our supper reservations. We all changed and walked down to the restaurant. "Miss Patterson, this way, please." I looked at my mom and Delaney and shrugged, but followed the Maitre'd. He led us to a table in a private dining room. It was already set up with refreshments and appetizers.

"Umm, I don't think this is for..."

"Please have a seat. This will explain everything." The Maitre'd handed me a note and pulled out the chair for me. He walked to the other side of the table and seated Mom and Delaney.

I opened the note. It read:

Kate, better known as Wifey,

Sorry about last night, or more like this morning.

I hope you all enjoy your meal. Don't worry about anything. I have also covered your evening for anything you want to do."

Tyler aka, hubby

I couldn't suppress my laughter. I shook my head and handed the note to Mom. She read it and looked up at me.

"Katie, he is very thoughtful, when he's not calling at four in the morning that is." Shaking her head, chuckling a little, she continued "This entire weekend has been lovely with you both, thanks to Tyler." Mom smiled and placed her hands on ours.

"Thank you for forcing me into this weekend. I would have put very little effort in if it wasn't for you."

"We know you pretty well, Kate, and knew exactly what you would do." Delaney picked up her glass of wine. "To Kate, making the best of an unconventional situation, and managing to fall into marrying one of the hottest men in the county."

"Delaney, please. You're not wrong, but really. What a thing to say during a toast." Mom raised her glass to me, as well as Delaney. We both laughed.

Full from dinner and a few glasses of wine, we retired to the suite where Delaney and I said our good nights to mom. We crawled into my bed like we had when we were girls.

"What a day." Delaney sighed.

"You got that right. I was so worried we wouldn't find a dress." I flopped my arm over my eyes, exhausted and emotionally drained from the last few days. the bed shifted and I moved my arm to see Delaney propped up on her elbow, looking like she was going to burst. "What?" I whined.

"What else is worrying you?"

"I don't want to talk about this, Laney." I stared at the ceiling and gave her the silent treatment. The seconds passed and all I could hear was Delaney breathing and calculating how she would make me talk. The silent treatment never worked on her. She could wear a person down just staring at them.

"Nope, it's not going to work. Talk to me Kat."

Groaning, I tried to think of something witty, but I had nothing. "I'm worried about dad, Brian Morton, and uprooting my life." I hoped that was enough to satisfy her, but my inquisitive sister would not be blown off.

"You have been thrown into this situation against your will, basically, so tell me how you really feel. I know you are worried about more than dad and Mr. Morton."

Rolling over to face her, I took a deep breath. "I can't do this, Laney." Shaking my head, I saw the terror I felt was mirrored in her eyes. "But there isn't anything I can do about it." I felt a tear roll down my cheek.

"Go back and tell dad you changed your mind. We can come up with a way to fix this." Delaney grabbed my hand and held it tight.

"There's no other way, Laney. He borrowed half a million dollars, and it's gone." I slammed my fists on the bed. "On what I don't know, but there's no way to repay that, and I can't be the one that kills him because that's what will happen." Both of us were crying at this point. I took a deep breath and slowly let it out. "I will hold my head high, paste on a smile, and marry Tyler Morton," I said, sounding far more confident than I felt. But I wasn't sure she bought it.

"You are a better person than I am." she said through a yawn. "I'm going to bed. Night Kat."

Watching her leave my room, I felt more alone than I had since this entire thing started.

Picking up my phone, I dialed Tyler's number.

"Well, how was your dinner?" Not even a hello, just right into conversation. Somehow, after only a few days, he got me.

"It was wonderful. This entire weekend has been, and that's because of you." Flopping back down on the pillow, I suddenly felt like a teen talking to him. The only thing I was missing was a phone cord to twirl around my finger.

"No, it's because of you. I just provided a few perks. I know this isn't easy, but I thought if I could spoil you a little bit, maybe you would be more at ease with a decision that should have been yours to begin with." His voice trailed off, and I wondered what he was thinking.

"I can't lie and say I'm over the moon about this now, but I can say each day that passes and the closer to our wedding we get, I'm more accepting of our future life together. That sounds so ungrateful, I'm sorry."

"No, it doesn't. I will freely admit that when the party was over last night, and it was just my brothers and I, I expressed the same feelings." Tyler hesitated, but continued talking. "In fact, until that point, I was very much in control of myself. When it was just us, that's when I drank too much."

I was silent. So he was having to drink himself into oblivion to accept the fact we were getting married. I had hoped we were on the same page, both not overly thrilled about this arrangement, but willing to accept it and start to build a relationship. I was hurt, but not surprised.

"I see," was all I could think of.

"No, Kate, I know exactly what you are thinking, and that's not what I'm saying at all. I want a life with you. These past few days have been some of the best in my life. You challenge me, make me want to do better, be better. I have only just gotten to know you, and I feel like you have been beside me my entire life. I can't wait to watch us grow together. Gavin kept pouring, and I kept drinking, that's all. Kate, are you still there?" He was silent for a second. "Kate, I can hear you breathing. I know you didn't hang up."

"I'm here." A sniffle gave away that I was crying.

"Oh Kate, please don't cry. I never meant to hurt you."

"I'm not hurt, and it does make me feel better that you are feeling the same way. I'm a few glasses of wine in and sometimes I get sensitive."

His chuckle on the other end of the line sent a thrill through me. "For future reference, what do you normally do when you feel this way?

His attention toward me was endearing. The longer we talked, the lighter my heart became. "I have to sleep it off, and wine hits me like a ton of bricks, so sleep comes easy." My voice trailed off, and I stifled a yawn.

"Well then, get some sleep. I hope your head doesn't hurt too badly in the morning. I will talk to you tomorrow."

I giggled a little, "Good night, Tyler."

CHAPTER 13

Our drive home was uneventful. We left Dallas around ten thirty, so we were home in good time. I took my dress and hung it in my closet. My phone rang, and I dashed into the kitchen to grab it.

"Hey you, are you home yet?" That voice on the other end of the line was the one I needed to hear. I had become more anxious the closer to home we had gotten. I'm not sure if it was nerves or because I was hungover and just needed a nap.

"Hi, yep, got in about fifteen minutes ago."

"Great, I'm on my way over. Your mom invited me for supper. See you in a few." The phone went dead, and I looked around at the mess that was my living room. I only had a few minutes to get things tidied up. My dress was safely tucked away, but I grabbed the bag with the accessories and set it in my room. I had also picked up a gift for Tyler with some of the money I hadn't spent on a dress, and I put it in my dresser. There was a soft rap on the front door as I walked back towards the living room. I quickly checked myself in the mirror, took a deep breath, and turned the doorknob.

I couldn't help but grin when I opened the door. Tyler had been so wonderful to us this weekend, it was hard to believe we hadn't been together for years.

"Come in." I motioned him in. As he walked in, I took his hand. I could tell by his wide eyes looking down and the smile spread across his face that I had surprised him, but he was happy about it.

"Well, can I start the search for your gown?"

He took me a little off guard, but then he started to laugh.

"Kate, I'm kidding. I don't want to see it until Saturday."

I breathed a sigh of relief and rolled my eyes.

"So we have a job to get done today, that's why I'm here so early. We need a guest list. Jessica, the wedding planner, is making Mom crazy because we don't have one." He sat down on the couch and patted the seat beside him. I walked around and sat down beside him. "Here is my list, so now we just need yours."

I took his list from him and looked it over. Family and a few, I assumed, friends. He had no more than twenty-five people written down. It made my decision easy, knowing he wasn't inviting a lot of people.

Shifting, I crossed my legs under me, which made me sit closer to Tyler. I grabbed a pen off the coffee table and flipped his list over and began making mine. His hand rested against my leg. It felt warm, comforting, and that small, more intimate touch made my heart flutter.

With that done, we were left with a few hours alone before supper. I grabbed the remote and turned on the TV. Tyler slipped his arm around me, and I slid over closer to him and rested my head on his shoulder. It felt comfortable. Nothing was expected. We just watched TV.

Six o'clock rolled around, and we walked over to my parent's house.

"Tyler, come on in," Mom said, meeting us at the door. She pulled Tyler in for a hug.

"Thank you for making this weekend one I will never forget."

"It was my pleasure, Mrs. Patterson," he replied.

"Oh, you are just too much, and it's just Julie to you, dear." Fanning at her eyes and blinking a mile a minute to keep tears from falling, she smiled at him.

"Take your boots and coat off, and come in."

I took his coat and hung it in the closet. Mom had laced her arm through his and was chattering away as they walked to the sun-room at the back of the house.

My dad came in behind us. I turned to look at him and saw that he seemed to have aged before my eyes. This was taking a toll on him. "Your mom said you had a nice weekend."

"It was wonderful, Dad. How are things here?" I took his coat and hung it up as he sat to take his boots off. He rattled on about what he had gotten done while we were gone, and it sounded like he had kept busy.

When he stood and started to move down the hall, I stopped him. "Dad, we're OK." I hugged him tight and his arms wrapped around my shoulders. We stood there together for a moment, nothing more was said. It didn't need to be. We walked into the sun-room and joined Mom and Tyler.

"Mom, where's Delaney?"

"Oh, she will be down in a few minutes. She's just finishing her resignation letter to the university." Tyler looked from Mom to me and I explained what she had told me in Dallas.

"That will be nice having both girls close again," he replied.

My mother beamed, "Yes, it will, and a new son-in-law too."

She knew how to make people feel at ease. Everyone always knew what she thought because she couldn't hide her feelings.

"Alright, let's eat." Delaney said as she ran down the stairs. The five of us moved into the kitchen and sat around the table.

"Did Kate tell you she did her first semester in senior year of high school in Scotland?" Julie said, making small talk.

"No, she hasn't mentioned that. I would like to hear more about it though." I looked over at Kate, who was obviously not enjoying this supper as much as I was. She had lowered her head into her hands and shook it back and forth.

"She came home and asked if we could change the herd from Red Angus to Highlands. She argued for weeks, even came up with pro and con lists. Obviously, the cons won out. She did manage to have a few of them for quite a few years though."

I could just see her coming home from her semester and trying to argue with her father about making the change.

"Hey Kat, did you tell Tyler about the time you drove through the barn door?"

All eyes turned towards Kate.

"Do you really think I would have told him that?"

"Come on Kat, tell me."

Kate pointed her finger at me. "Oh no, cowboy, Kat is not going to stick. She—" her finger switched directions to point at Delaney. "Only says that to tick me off. As for the barn… Delaney and I were pretending to be on a trip and were playing in the car. Well, the keys were in it because, why not, and I turned it on. Delaney thought we should try to drive. It didn't look that hard, so I pulled on the gearshift and it went into reverse. Delaney pressed the gas pedal with her hands and we were launched backwards. Before I knew it, we were in the barn. Thankfully, there was just enough incline that we stopped before we went through the other side. We climbed out of the car and walked out of the barn… and there was Dad, standing there and scratching his head, trying to figure out what he had just witnessed." Kate stabbed her fork into the cheesecake and shoved it into her mouth before I had a chance to ask her more questions.

"See, when the car started to move, Kate dove to the floor, and we couldn't figure out how a car could be moving by itself." Julie finished the story.

I choked back a laugh, but I was about to burst.

"You can laugh. It's taken us a long time, but it's quite funny. Seeing these two come out of the very large hole in the barn, looking a little dazed and trying to figure out a good story was quite the thing." Ben put his hand on my shoulder and I saw his shoulders start shaking. His lips pursed, trying not to grin, but he couldn't hold it in.

I laughed with Ben, Julie and Delaney.

"Oh, you all laugh. I'm the one that had to help put the door back together. Delaney was too little." Kate scrunched up her face and made talking motions with her hands. "It was all her fault." Now pouting a little.

The room was filled with laughter, and Kate couldn't help but smile.

We visited through supper and into the early evening, moving from the table to the living room. Kate and I sat on the love seat. Her father was in what I would assume was 'his chair', and Julie and Delaney on the couch opposite us.

"4-H didn't go so well for our girl here either," Ben said, pointing at the one and only picture of Kate with her 4-H uniform on. Looking over at her, I saw her shake her head.

"What is this, a Kate tell-all night?" Folding her arms over her chest, she sat there trying to look angry. I put my arm around her and drew her close to me. It felt good to feel her melt into my side.

Ben laughed and continued, "You see, my girl here is a wonder with cattle, and her project steer was no different. She won Grand Champion that year, so when it came time to put Fred through the sale ring and she realized what was next for him, she was devastated. Cried all the way home from the fairgrounds.

She marched up the stairs and came back down, changed and carrying her uniform. I will never forget the look she gave Julie when she handed her the clothes. 'Mama, do what you want with these. I'm never wearing them again.' Then she turned and walked outside to the barn. I found her there at supper, crying in Fred's stall."

Looking over at Kate, I felt a heaviness in my chest for her. Even though this was many years ago, I could feel her sadness. Tightening my arm around her, she looked up at me and smiled, with tears glistening in her eyes.

"He was the perfect steer," she said quietly. I couldn't help the smile that grew across my face. Seeing her now, I could envision her sitting in that stall, crying for this poor animal she loved so much. Suddenly, I thought about having kids, and what our little girl would look like. I couldn't help but stare over at Kate.

Julie hopped up from her seat and got a picture off of the piano to hand to me. "This is Kate's senior year of basketball. She played all through her school years and was very good."

I looked down at the picture in my hands. She looked

exactly the same, but there was a confidence about her in this photo that I didn't see now, and I wondered why.

Looking over at Kate, I could see the blush creeping from her neck up to her cheeks. It sent an arrow straight into my heart. I needed to protect this woman. She needed to know she was more than just these old pictures and stories, the first daughter, the responsible one who hadn't gotten to do the easy things growing up. She was groomed from day one to work hard and take over.

I could see Delaney's sense of adventure and drop of a hat decision making. She only cared how the outcome would benefit her. But Kate took her time, weighed every decision, to see how it would affect those around her before herself. The love Ben and Julie had for their girls was beyond measure, and showed in every story, every glance at them and between each other.

I was having a hard time swallowing the lump that had formed in my throat. It wasn't every day that you saw two people so compatible or so comfortable in each other's presence. My stomach curdled thinking how parents were rarely in the same room for anything other than a meal. To sit down and talk didn't happen often. I doubted that Kate could tell me one thing about my childhood after her supper the other night at my parent's place. I didn't want us to be like my parents.

CHAPTER 14

Kate and I said goodnight to her family, thanked them for supper and the nice evening. We walked back to her place, hand in hand.

"I can see why our supper was intimidating. That's how a family meal should be. Relaxed, laughing, and genuinely loving each other." Looking off through the darkness, I realized how dysfunctional my family really was. I wanted our kids to come home with their partners and feel welcome, at ease, and know they are loved. This is the life Kate and I would strive for.

Arriving at her door, she opened it, turned towards me, and leaned against the door frame.

"Come in for tea?" Her arched brow intrigued me. I looked at my watch. It was still early. I nodded my head and smiled.

Sitting at the kitchen table, Kate handed me a cup of tea and sat down across from me. Maybe now that a few of her walls appeared to be cracking, I could break down one or two and get some answers about why she didn't run *from* this, but *to* this arrangement.

"I have to admit, I was a little surprised when you said yes to this arrangement. I want to know why you haven't fought it more. I get that you want to protect the family legacy on this ranch, but you are smart. You probably could have figured out another way to clear the debt."

Kate looked up from her tea, which she had just removed the bag from. Her eyes shone brightly in the kitchen lights, but she looked exhausted. I wished I could gather her in my arms and hold her as she drifted off to sleep.

"Maybe I'm tired of being overlooked. This arrangement takes all the chemistry out of it. I don't have to pretend I'm someone I'm not." She didn't look up from her cup. "I'm able to see the real you immediately and not have to wait until date five or six. Look, we can sit here and put our best foot forward for the next week, but after that, we will be together in close proximity. I don't feel a person can hide who they really are for very long in that environment."

I looked back down at the cup in my hand and nodded. My heart sank. There was no way this woman should have been overlooked. It made me sad to think that she felt over-looked, not good enough, when in actuality, she was too good, especially for me. All the years I wasted not noticing her, and she was right down the road. I was kicking myself.

"So… are we going to talk about our revelations over the last few days?"

Kate looked up at me.

"We aren't going to talk about fluff tonight, are we?" Kate smiled over her cup of tea.

"I just want our feelings to be out in the open. We know each other a little better than the first day I walked through the door."

"That wasn't my finest moment, but I don't feel much has changed, Tyler. We need to get to know each other better before intimacy happens. I'm sure that's not what you want to hear, but it's what I need to do. I hope you can understand that."

"Kate, I'm fine with that. Like you said earlier, someone else has decided we would be a good fit. While I feel the chemistry between us, I won't push anything. I do want to make some ground rules though."

"You like to make rules, don't you?" Kate arched her eyebrow and smirked.

"Well, I have always found it takes the questions out of things so we both know where we stand." Kate nodded in agreement.

"I didn't say they were bad." Kate sat back in her chair, letting me lead the discussion.

"Alright, so no intimacy until we are both in agreement and comfortable about it. I want us to eat breakfast and supper together. If your work here makes you stay late, I'll come here. If I have office stuff that is making me late, you come to the office and we'll have a picnic on the floor."

Kate nodded. "I can agree to that rule. I like picnics." She had the most beautiful, genuine smile. It's what I noticed every time we were together. No matter how anxious she was or how relaxed she was, the one constant was her smile. It never changed.

"OK, second one, we sleep in the same bed." I could almost feel her getting her back up, and I knew I needed to talk fast. "Hear me out. We can't only get to know each other halfway. If we are hoping to have a forever marriage, we need to be open and vulnerable. I want to see you first thing in the morning, and you need to know how bad I snore."

Kate burst out laughing.

"I hate to disappoint you, but mornings don't look much different than I am right now. I'm not one to completely change her face with makeup."

I smiled, silently grateful that at least the woman I go to bed next to will look like the same person when she wakes up.

"Any more rules?"

"Not that I can think of, but we are both free to reevaluate, add or delete as needed, with good reason and discussion."

Kate stuck out her hand, and we shook on it.

It suddenly struck me that I had no idea about Kate's personal details.

"When is your birthday?"

"August twelfth. When's yours?"

"April fourth."

"Happy very belated birthday."

I couldn't help but smile. It had been almost a month since my birthday, but it felt like it could have been yesterday when she wished me a happy birthday. Kate was thoughtful. From what I had seen, she put others' needs far above her own. She wasn't one to ask anything of anyone, and it was something I was going to have to pay attention to. I wanted to take care of her, and that meant it was time to go and let her get some rest. The thought of leaving here tonight was disappointing.

"Well, I better head out." We both stood from the table, and Kate walked me to the door.

"Night, Kate. Talk to you tomorrow."

Standing at the door, her hand in mine, I pulled her close to me. I wrapped my arms around her and she did the same. I felt her sigh, and melt into me, her head rested on my chest. She felt relaxed, and I would have been comfortable standing like this all night.

Whispering, "I should go, before I make our rules null and void."

Kate looked up at me and smiled shyly. Her lips were beautiful. She didn't wear lipstick, and she didn't have to. They were a rosy pink. They looked soft and extremely kissable. Would she kiss me back? Would it make her mad if I tried? I found her extremely sexy when she was angry.

"Night, Tyler." Kate backed out of my arms. Turning, she opened the door, and I left. I heard it close softly behind me and I hoped it would open again, but I wasn't surprised when it didn't.

I climbed into my truck and made the quick trip to my lonely, quiet house. How had I overlooked Kate all these years?

I climbed into bed but found that sleep was not going to come easily while I was stuck thinking about her. Kate had me bewitched. She had a genuine, caring personality. I smiled thinking, about her fiery temper. I wanted to grab a hold of her perky rear end and never let go. Her breasts bounced gently as she walked, and I couldn't wait to see them free. Her lips looked so kissable, and I was in agony, not having them on me. My hand snaked down my abs to my already standing cock. Wrapping my hand gently around it, I pictured Kate beside me, her hair tickling my chest as she ran her hand up and down my shaft. Letting out a moan, I sped up my pumping. My erection was harder than I had ever experienced. If this is what Kate did to me without even being here, I smiled thinking about what would happen with her next to me. I didn't last long; a few more motions and I let out a groan and exploded. My breathing returned to normal, and I laid there for a moment, and smiled. I reached over and grabbed a handful of tissues, and cleaned up. Sleeping naked had its advantages.

CHAPTER 15

I felt uncomfortable driving on to the Morton's ranch and not going to Tyler's, but I needed to get some things figured out with his mom. I parked my truck, walked up the sidewalk and knocked on the door.

"Kate, how nice to see you. Come on in," Brian said, smiling.

"Hello, sir. I'm supposed to meet Sandra to go over a few of the plans."

He nodded. "She will be right down."

"Thank you." I smiled, but really wished I didn't have to be alone in the same room as him. I wasn't afraid of him, but I didn't trust him. I saw Sandra coming down the stairs and breathed a quiet sigh of relief.

"Kate, I'm so glad you could come today." She walked over to where l stood, extended her arms and wrapped me in a hug. I hesitantly returned her embrace, and she let me go. "Why don't I walk you around the areas we have picked out?" She showed me where the wedding would take place, the spot for the cocktail hour, and then we went to the barn where the reception and dance would be held.

"It's all so perfect, Sandra, thank you."

"Do you have time for a cup of coffee?"

"Yes, that would be nice." I looked around, hoping to catch a glimpse of Tyler, but I didn't see him anywhere. We sat down on the porch and there was coffee waiting for us.

"Kate, I know your entrance into this family isn't exactly the way you or any of us would have hoped, but I want you to know that this is your home now, and you are welcome here. I'm thrilled you're marrying Tyler." I genuinely felt welcome by Sandra; Brian on the other hand, was a different story.

As if she could read my mind, "Don't worry about him. All bark, no bite." I smiled at her.

As I saw Tyler walking up the sidewalk, I started to fidget. I hadn't seen him in his work attire. He was casually professional in Wranglers, but he also wore a white button-up shirt and a suit coat. The top two buttons of the shirt were open, and I could just see a hint of chest hair peeking out. I hadn't seen him in a cowboy hat before, but he was going to have to wear one more often. Handsome wasn't enough to describe him. He was confident, strong, and just plain sexy. I bit the corner of my lip and took a deep breath.

"Dear, he's just a man, and I think he's crazy about you." I looked over at Sandra and she was smiling.

I opened my mouth to say something but was interrupted by Tyler's commanding, low voice.

"Well, isn't this a pleasant surprise," he remarked, smiling at me. His eyes never left me. I could feel a blush creeping up my face, my heart skipped a beat, and I felt like it was just him and me on that porch.

"Hi, I was just having a meeting with your mom about the wedding."

"Did you get all the planning done?" he asked.

"Yes, I think so." A smile crossed my face, and I let go of the button I had been playing with on my shirt. Slowly, I rubbed my sweaty palms on the legs of my jeans.

Sandra set her mug back on the table and smiled. "Well, I have a list of calls to make, so I'm going to leave you two alone. Kate, please call me if you have anything you want to talk about."

"Thank you for the afternoon. I had a wonderful time." Sandra turned and went into the house, and Tyler sat down across from me.

"Were you going to sneak out without coming to say hi?"

I looked down at my coffee and bit the corner of my lip. I nodded.

"Can I ask you why? I thought things had been going well between us. We have been spending quite a bit of every day together, then all of the sudden, you want to avoid me?"

Everything in me was screaming to let him in, to go to him willingly, maybe even go eagerly into this marriage, but I was stubborn. This marriage wasn't because we were madly in love, and I knew that. I felt like a pawn in a game that I had no control over. My future was decided for me, and I couldn't lose myself in the process. What made me even more frustrated was everyone else's forgetfulness of why this marriage was happening. To pay a debt. I was a bill my father couldn't pay, the simple way to get rid of a daughter who was destined to be alone. The woman nobody wanted, and no matter how I tried to forget, I couldn't. I could flirt and I could imagine all the things Tyler and I could do together, but it didn't change the fact that I wasn't his choice and he wasn't mine.

"Tyler, I wasn't trying to avoid you. This is over-whelming and the closer to the wedding we get, the more I feel like I'm being swept away. I'm sorry." I didn't know what else to say, but from the look on his face, I hadn't made things better.

"Well, I'm glad Dad told me you were here."

I looked at him and gave him a half smile.

"OK, I know I said I was good with anything for the wedding, but what have you gotten me into?" Tyler said, grabbing a cup of coffee.

"Picture it," I said as I swept my arm out in front of me "flowers everywhere, archways covered in pink tulle, a walkway of dark pink rose petals leading to white rose petals down the aisle; carriage lanterns in all the trees, and flower sprays on the back of every chair." I looked at Tyler, waiting for a response. He forced a smile and looked a little, no, a lot, apprehensive.

"That sounds... lovely," he said, but it sounded more like a question. I decided not to tease him anymore.

"Tyler, I'm kidding." I burst out laughing and laughed harder when I saw relief flood his face. "I'm sorry; we needed a laugh." By then, he was laughing with me.

"You had me going for a minute. I kept thinking I was sure we were on the same page with something simple. I know I don't know you that well, but that didn't seem like you."

"I wish you could have seen your face. It was priceless."

"This was good. It feels good to laugh about all this." Tyler grabbed my hand and didn't let go. "Are you going to actually tell me anything?"

I nodded. "A white carpet will mark the aisle. Your mom has picked a pretty spot where the trees meet, and that's where the officiant will stand and where we will meet. After all the I do's, we will have a few photos done around the property, and then our moms have planned the reception and it sounds like a simple supper in the event barn."

"Simple and my mom doesn't mix, so I'm sure it will be a little more elaborate," Tyler said as he stood from the table.

"I guess I should be going," I said as I followed him and stood as well. Tyler walked me to my truck and opened my door.

"Drive safe," he huskily told me as I put the truck in gear. I had a feeling that's not what he wanted to say, but he changed his mind.

As I was backing out, he ran and jumped on the running board.

"Come over for supper. I don't know what's in the fridge, but I don't want you to go."

Looking into his eyes and being drawn in by his smile, I melted. I nodded.

"Get in."

He ran to the passenger side and hopped in. He was grinning from ear to ear, and I couldn't help but smile. My arm rested on the console, and Tyler reached over absentmindedly and gently traced his fingers in small circles over the back of my hand. A trail of tingles left in his wake sent sparks deep inside, awakening a need I had pushed away for too long.

Standing in the kitchen, watching him rummage through the fridge, grabbing things, smelling them, setting them on the counter or launching them into the garbage made me giggle. The view from behind him wasn't one I was going to complain about any time soon. I walked over to the fridge and placed my hand on his lower back. The electricity from the truck returned.

"I think we can work with this," I said. He stood up and was only inches from me, my arm wrapped around him, hand resting just at his belt, made me weak in the knees. He smelled just as good as the night he picked me up on the side of the road, and it made me just as turned on.

"What are we going to make?" he asked quietly next to my ear.

My breath quickened, and my heart had apparently turned into a butterfly fluttering away. I needed to move. There needed to be space between us. I grabbed the hamburger and moved toward the stove. "Spaghetti and meat sauce, I think. I saw a French baguette over there; we can toast it for garlic bread. Why don't you cut it while I get the beef frying?" I grabbed the bread and tossed it in Tyler's direction. He caught it easily with his large hands.

I flung cupboard doors open looking for pots and pans. Nothing was handy for cooking. "How do you cook here? Everything I need is across the kitchen and all your useless things are right here." I motioned toward the stove.

Tyler looked at me and shrugged, "Move things then." He turned back to the bread.

I stirred the beef and poured tomato sauce into the pot. "OK, bread's ready for the oven," Tyler said as he came up behind me and placed his hands on my hips. I turned around and faced him.

"It's warm and I'm ready for it to go in." The words came out of my mouth before I had time to stop them. Tyler arched his eyebrow and smiled.

"Are you now?"

I glanced down at his lips. He ran his tongue slowly across his bottom lip. My breathing quickened, and I had to move. He was too close. Sliding over so he could get to the oven, I caught his sly smile before he bent down and slid the bread in.

I turned back to the bubbling sauce. It splattered and sputtered until I poured it on the ground beef. "Can you drain the pasta please?" I faced him for the first time since the oven incident.

His eyes danced as he reached up and brushed his thumb

along my cheek. My heart raced, and I saw him glance down at the quick rising and falling of my chest. "You had sauce on your cheek." My hand went to my cheek. "Don't worry, I got it all," he said, as he brought his thumb to his mouth and licked it. I was relieved when he turned and grabbed the pasta so he wouldn't see the red hue creeping across my cheeks.

Supper was over, and it was delicious. "Kate, that was wonderful. Thank you for cooking. Why don't we move to the living room? I will clean up later."

"Thanks for inviting me over. I would probably have had toast and called it a night." I sat down beside him and grabbed my glass of sun tea and settled in for an evening of TV and small talk.

"I can't believe that in four days, this will all be over." I flopped my head back onto the couch and rolled my head to look over at Tyler.

"Well, it won't be over, but I know what you mean." I thought I saw disappointment flash in his eyes.

"What's wrong?" I quizzed, resting my hand on his leg.

"Nothing's wrong. I'm just disappointed that this time in our relationship is drawing to a close. I have really enjoyed spending time together on this level. In four days, we will legally be husband and wife, and I'm afraid we will fall into the married couple's routine and I won't get to know you like I am now." He turned and looked at me. He looked like a little boy who had just told his deepest secret to his best friend, hoping not to get laughed at.

"There is still a lot we don't know about each other, and when we get married, I won't be leaving at the end of the night, so we will have way more time to spend together." I scooted closer to him and rested my head on his shoulder. Hoping I eased his concerns, I wrapped an arm around him and sighed contently.

CHAPTER 16

The four days flew by, between work, wedding planning, and spending all my free moments with Tyler. There was barely time to breathe. Although we had only invited family and close friends, it seemed a lot still needed to be done. I left it mostly to Sandra and my mom, but I worried I gave up too much control.

But I shouldn't have been concerned; they had made it perfect. Everything was beautiful, from the well-landscaped, manicured lawns to the flowers everywhere. It was the bright spot in this entire nightmare. I loved flowers, and I hoped I would get the opportunity to have my own garden and flowerbeds here.

My hair was in what felt like a giant up-do and I'd had makeup plastered on my face, so I only had my dress to get into and I would be ready to walk down the aisle. I wandered around the ranch, trying to calm my nerves before the ceremony. Everything on the Morton ranch was top of the line. If you could think of something, it was here. A cattle producer's dream.

Tyler's father approached me.

"Kate, how are you holding up?"

"I'm doing OK, sir. Thank you for asking." He made me nervous, and today I really didn't need anything extra to set me off.

"Good, good. The ranch looks wonderful. I'm so glad all the hard work and deal making has come to fruition." I stared at him blankly.

"What do you mean deal making? What other deal besides me did you do?" My voice shook. I was on the verge of tears. I didn't need this today.

"Just so we are clear, this gets your father back square with me, but I win in the end. I know that the ranch passes to you when he dies, which then will be incorporated with Lone Star Cattle. That's the only reason he's getting out of this, because one day it's going to be mine, anyway. Don't worry that pretty little head about anything, though. It will be a long time before that happens. See you in a few hours." My stomach dropped and I could feel my anxiety rising as I watched the man walk away. He was shorter than Tyler. Brian was a heavyset man, who I was sure hadn't actually worked cattle in the last five years. I never thought of what would happen when my father passed, and it never occurred to me his debt would now become mine. I thought this wedding would take care of things, and it would, but now the loss of my father's ranch would be held over my head.

My thoughts shifted to Tyler. Did he know all of this? Is this the reason he has been so accepting of an arranged marriage? I wanted to be a runaway bride, but that wouldn't help my father at all. I needed to throw up. Frantically, I searched for the closest bathroom. There was no way to make it back to the house, so I found the tallest hedge and went behind it. I needed to speak to our lawyer as soon as possible. Monday. There had to be ways to protect what was ours.

∼

I SAW my father talking to Kate. At first, their exchange looked cordial, but something changed in her face. She turned as white as a sheet. What was that old man up to?

I should have approached him, but I didn't have the time to get into it with him before the wedding. I put my black suit jacket on over a crisp white shirt. Kate had asked for a relaxed wedding, so black wranglers and a new pair of boots it was. To be honest, I was glad. It was what I was comfortable in. I looked at the clock, took a deep breath, and walked out to the backyard. The wedding planner had done an amazing job of getting Kate's vision out of her head and set up for the day. I was glad that this part could be normal, even if the arrangement wasn't.

We had spent the last week and a half in limbo, waiting for this moment. In some ways, it would have been easier to only give us a few days, but this right here was at least part of what I had always thought about. The guests had arrived. I stood at the front of the aisle with the minister and my younger brother Rob, waiting for Kate to appear. The music changed, and I watched Delaney walk down the aisle and take her place. Addison followed next, her smile lighting up her entire face. She looked wonderful in her light pink tulle ball gown. I bent down and kissed her cheek, and she giggled. The music changed again, and I looked back to the end of the aisle. There stood Kate. *My* Kate.

"Please rise," the minister said, startling me with his deep voice. Kate walked in on her father's arm. My breath caught in my chest. She was radiant. Rob nudged me and I took a breath. Her gown fit her perfectly. It hugged her curvaceous hips, and the neckline provided just the right amount of cleavage to turn me on. But I also wanted to cover her up so nobody else would see. She had the most stunning figure, and it was going to prove difficult to live day-in and day-out with her and not touch her. She was gorgeous, but I wasn't about to make her feel uncomfortable or like I was pushing her for more. I respected her wishes to hold off on being intimate, but that didn't mean I didn't long for the day that she'd be ready. In the meantime, my imagination would have to do the work, but I can't wait for the day I can slip her out of her clothes.

THE SUN BEAMED down through the trees. The shadow over Tyler made me able to see his facial expressions. His smile was sincere, and he looked like he wanted to run up and take my hand. My heart jumped as I looked him up and down. He was dashing in his wedding attire. I was glad I chose a little more than casual wear. I felt like I was the only person in the world when he looked at me. I felt beautiful in my dress, but still insecure about everything.

"Who gives this woman to this man?"

Interesting choice of words, I thought to myself.

"I do." My father replied. He kissed my cheek and whispered, "I'm sorry I got you into this." He turned and sat with my mother. I handed my flowers to Delaney and turned to look at Tyler. He gave me a smile, and I returned it.

"Dearly beloved, we are gathered here today to join Katherine and Tyler in holy matrimony. If any of you can show just cause why these two shouldn't be lawfully married, speak now or forever hold your peace." The minister waited, and I secretly prayed for someone to stand up, but nobody did.

We exchanged our vows, Tyler and I gave each other our rings, papers were signed and we stood back in front of our family.

"What God has brought and joined together, let no person separate. Tyler, you may now kiss your bride." How did I forget that a bride and groom kiss? In picturing this day, I never once thought of having to kiss him. Tyler and I were holding hands as he stepped toward me. He let go, put his arm around me, leaned down and kissed me. I had full intentions of standing there like a statue, but the moment his warm, soft lips met mine, my breath was momentarily taken away. The butterflies in my stomach increased, if that was even possible. I wrapped my arm around his shoulders and leaned into him. The kiss seemed like it lasted forever. I hadn't kissed anyone or been kissed for a very long time. It was full of passion and promise. It was amazing. He broke the kiss, and there was a round of applause which brought me back to the here and now. My heart felt like it was going to beat right out of my chest. Standing there for a moment to let people take pictures, I hoped I was smiling. The world seemed to be spinning. Tyler offered his arm and took a step, and I instinctively followed as we walked back up the aisle.

After our pictures were done, we retreated to Tyler's office for a few moments alone. He pulled the blinds, and I let out a sigh of relief.

"Katherine? How did I not know that?"

"I only get called Katherine when I'm in trouble."

"I will have to remember that." He arched his brow and smirked.

"Guess we forgot a few topics." Leaning against the desk, I felt more relaxed than I had in the last week and a half.

"How are you holding up?" he asks, walking over to stand in front of me.

"Better than I thought. How about you?"

"Good. You're stunning." Reaching out to me, he placed his hands on my arms.

"I am pleasantly surprised at how simple that was." My words trail off as Tyler placed his palm gently on my cheek. He bent his head and brought his lips to mine. My heart stopped beating for a moment and my breath quickened. The kiss was gentle at first, but it became more passionate as I fully gave in to his lips. He closed the already tiny space between us, wrapped his arms around my waist and pulled us together. Our hips met, and I felt the pressure from Tyler's arousal.

My hands seemed to have a mind of their own. They trailed down his arms, brushing his hands, which were holding onto me. I slid them under his suit jacket to the small of his firm, muscular back. Before I gave myself time to think, I moved my hands down to the pockets of his jeans.

Lingering there, I grasped his ass, pulling him closer to me as he explored my neck and collarbone. I was putty in this man's hands. My heart pounded as he lightly ran his work-worn fingers up my neck and entangled his massive hand in my hair. Slowly, he pulled the bobby pins out and my hair tumbled down to my shoulders. I heard him take a deep breath as he buried his nose in my locks.

"I prefer your hair down," Tyler whispered in my ear before nibbling on my earlobe.

I had never felt passion like this. My mind was racing a million miles a minute. After a week and a half of being with him every day, I was finally in his arms. The falling asleep, dreaming of what it felt like to be held by him, imagining what he would feel like in my arms, was over.

He slid his hands down my sides and brushed the edge of my breasts. My breath caught in my throat, and I heard him let out a husky moan before his large hand engulfed my breast.

The thin lace fabric let the warmth from his palm radiate to my skin. Between the pressure of his arousal, the intoxicating kisses, and him fondling my breast, I let out a moan that built from deep inside me. I had never made that sound before.

Suddenly, there was a knock at the door. Tyler let out a guttural growl as he realized our secretive moment was over.

"Are you two going to attend your reception?" Rob called out.

We both laughed, and I rested my head on Tyler's chest as he held me.

Returning to my level-headed self, I whispered, "Tyler, this doesn't change the way I feel about being intimate. I'm just not there yet."

His shoulders slumped and a look of disappointment replaced the lustful gaze. I was worried he would be angry. He tightened his arms around me, kissed my head then quietly said, "Kate, I'm not going to push you into anything. It will happen when it's supposed to." My heart jumped at his response. Even after what just happened, he understood I needed time.

Pulling away from me, he smiled and said, "Guess we should go." I nodded in reply.

I grabbed the bobby pins off his desk and tried to quickly fix my hair. Tyler took gentle hold of my arm, "Leave it." Two regular words said full of passion… It never crossed my mind that they'd sound as sexy as they did coming from his puffy, red and perfect lips. We walked out of his office hand in hand.

Our reception was simple. We chose to forgo the speeches and just have a good time. Tyler and I danced our first dance, 'To Make You Feel My Love'.

Tyler leaned down and whispered, "This is nice, but I preferred our time in the office."

I could feel heat creep up from my core, and I was sure I

had just turned lobster red. Letting out a nervous giggle, he smiled down at me. We lingered when the song was over and kissed again, gave the guests what they were hoping for. I couldn't deny that I hoped for the kisses also. It felt like a natural progression.

We danced until my feet hurt. I thought back to the barn dances of my youth, the good times with family and friends, and I knew that tonight it had been just that. I hadn't often pictured what a wedding day for me would look like, but this small, only slightly over the top day was perfect. With the reception over and guests heading back to their homes, Tyler extended his arm for me to take.

"Are you ready to go home, Mrs. Morton?" he asked, his voice still husky from our shared kisses.

"I am very ready, Mr. Morton. Lead the way." Wrapping my arm around his, we walked back to our home. I was glad it was tucked away from the main house and any prying eyes. This would be hard enough to get used to without everyone and their dog trying to be involved.

*H*er anxiety was palpable as she stood beside me, clutching her hands together outside the closed front door of our home.

"Do you want me to carry you over the threshold, wifey?" I flirted as I turned the doorknob and opened the door. Kate turned to look at me, face lifted, the corner of her eyes crinkled as she started to giggle. The giggle turned into a full-blown laugh.

"No, I will walk in, but thank you for the offer, hubby." She reached out and placed her hand on my arm.

Her laugh was light-hearted, musical, and it made my soul soar. I wanted to hear that laugh every day for the rest of my life. It would be my mission to make her laugh as much as I possibly could. I walked into the house, following close behind Kate. I wasn't sure how the remainder of our wedding night would play out, but I knew holding her would not be part of it. She had made that quite clear the day I went to her house, then during the evening we had spent together, and again in my office after the wedding ceremony. Our relationship had changed over the past week, but that wall was still up. I longed to have her soft skin against me, her long slender fingers reaching out for me, her full, very kissable lips against mine.

Kate turned and looked at me, "I am going to get ready for bed," she said so faintly I almost missed it.

Intently, my eyes followed her as she climbed the stairs. When I could no longer see her, I took in a deep breath, trying to relax my overactive imagination. It had been a long day, and I was ready for crisp sheets and an overstuffed pillow.

"Tyler, I need your help." I turned to see her gracefully gliding back down the stairs, her white gown still on. I sensed something was wrong, a look of failure clear to see on her face.

"Umm, so I can't get myself out of this thing." Her hands went to her hips, her lips pursed, staring at me like she could see into my thoughts. Holding out my hand, I motioned for her to turn, and I ever so slowly walked closer to her and reached for the small satin-covered buttons.

Button after button popped open, slowly exposing her toned and tan lower back. The last buttons barely above her round butt sent a thrill through me as I neared the end. This alluring, strong, impressive woman before me had no idea how sexy I thought she was. Ever so slightly, my hand brushed over her ass as I unbuttoned the last button. Pushing the lace off her shoulders and down her arms. I saw her breathing quicken, and her back stiffen straight as a board. I heard a throaty "Thank you," as she rushed back up the stairs and out of my proximity.

After turning the lights off on the main floor, I climbed the steps to our room. The master bathroom was set up his-and-hers style, so it was easy to quickly get ready for bed on my side while Kate was at hers. Climbing into bed, I propped my pillow up against the headboard and relaxed for a moment.

The stress of the last a week and a half was over. Kate and I had made it to our so-called destination, a moment neither of us really wanted but one that had come and gone smoothly and without a scene being caused.

The bathroom door opened, and Kate walked into the bedroom. She looked a little taken off guard when she saw me in bed. Bare chested, with the sheet forming a tent big enough to camp under. I followed her gaze, and smirked at where her eyes stopped. I'm not sure what she thought I would sleep in, but I wasn't changing my habits. Kate had changed into a white satin tank top and shorts. She looked sensational. Her long legs were strong and chiseled from years of hard work, and her arms were lean and muscular. Her round, perky rear end was going to get me into trouble. I just wanted to spank and pinch her teasingly when she walked by. Her breasts were free and bounced gently as she walked to the bed. I was grateful for the sheet covering me right at this moment as I shifted so my arousal wasn't as obvious.

Kate climbed into bed beside me but stayed as close to the edge as she could. It was comical, but I didn't dare say anything.

"I know it probably wasn't what you were expecting, but did you have a nice day?" I didn't look up from my book when I asked. Kate put down the book she had grabbed and looked over at me.

"I did. Did you?"

I looked over at Kate and smiled, "Yes, I did too."

Leaning over to the drawer in her bedside table, she said, "I um, I got you something. It was hard to decide, but I hope you like it. I think it will work well for business meetings and everyday wear." She handed me a box, and I smiled as I opened it. It was a sleek, matte black watch with gold accents. The second hand swept effortlessly around the watch face. I looked at it and noticed the back had been engraved. 'Tyler, to our lifetime together.'

"Kate, it's wonderful, thank you." I wished things between us were different, because I wanted to kiss her again. I reached over to my bedside table and handed her the gift I had waiting. She took it and pulled the bow loose and carefully unwrapped the box, and put her hand to her mouth.

"Tyler, it's beautiful." She pulled the necklace out. It was a solitaire diamond on a white gold chain. "Help me put it on?" she asked as she handed me the necklace and moved closer. I reached over and fastened the clasp. I rested my hand on the back of her neck and she leaned into it.

"Thank you, it's the most beautiful thing I have ever had. Well, it's a close second to my engagement ring." She smiled as she looked down at her hand. She turned and was only inches from my face. Our lips met when she leaned in to me. Slowly she melted into me, and the kiss intensified as she hungrily explored my lips.

I wanted this woman more than I had ever wanted a woman before. I wrapped my arms around her and pulled her close to me. I couldn't control what was happening between us, and I didn't want to. Our hands roamed over each other's bodies, and Kate let out a soft moan.

He was so tender. I heard myself moan, and I began over thinking again. Before I could second guess myself, I pulled away from Tyler. He let out a small groan of disappointment. I looked into his eyes; I could see he wanted more, and I was so close to letting my guard down, but I couldn't. I didn't really know him yet. There was too much I needed to figure out. Did he know his father planned to take over my home?

"Tyler, I…"

"It's okay, Kate."

I doubted his words, but looked into his eyes again and knew it was. I placed my hand on his cheek, smiled, and softly kissed him again. We both moved back to our respective sides of the bed and picked up our books. I don't even know what I read after our kiss; I couldn't think straight. He was hypnotizing, from his smile, to his laugh, to his kiss.

It was no use; the words in my book weren't making sense. Closing the book, I put it on my nightstand and looked over at Tyler. Somehow, in all the craziness of the last a week and a half, I never imagined this part of our life together. I hadn't thought much past getting married. We were husband and wife. Meant to lean on each other, be there for one another. Fall asleep and wake up together. I would get to do mundane life with this man. A slight smile crept across my face, and Tyler noticed.

"What's all that about?" he asked, pointing at my mouth.

I shook my head, "Nothing. Just thinking."

"Thinking about what?" I was quickly learning that Tyler was inquisitive. He didn't let things be blown off. If he asked a question, he wanted to know the answer. There was no use fighting it. I opened up and told him what had been on my mind.

"I was just thinking about life after today. Beyond this past a week and a half, it wasn't something I thought of. I thought of our wedding because that took up most of my focus, but after today, that's not a worry anymore." I looked down at my hands, hoping I wasn't sounding like a total fool. Even if I did, I kept talking.

"We have the rest of our lives to spend together. You are now my primary contact, next of kin, the person who has to put up with me. It sounds silly now that I say it out loud. I'm sure you are wondering how I couldn't have thought of it." I shrugged my shoulders and looked at Tyler.

He rolled over onto his side and propped his head up on his hand. "It doesn't sound silly at all. We didn't have time to think past today." He reached for my hand and held it between his. "I'm glad I get to be the one to put up with you." His smile beamed from his face and I laughed.

THE SUN SHONE through the windows, which woke me up much earlier than I had wanted. I could feel her looking at me and wondered what she was thinking in the light of day.

"How long have you been staring at me?" I startled her, and she began stammering.

"I, I just rolled over."

I smiled, "Right. What did your inspection show?"

"You have a scar above your left eye, and a dimple in your right cheek I never noticed before. You had the softest expression while you slept."

Not daring to open my eyes for fear of embarrassing her, I said, "I got hit with a baseball when I was ten." I pointed to my eye. "I was born with the dimple, but you just don't see it unless I'm clean shaved and the expression must mean I'm content." Opening my eyes, I turned my head slightly to look at my wife, who was propped up on her pillow leaning on her arm. I watched her smile creep over her face.

"How did you sleep?" she asked as I stretched.

"Pretty good. I was a little chilly, could have used someone to hold," I said and looked over at her again.

She grabbed the throw pillow and hit me in the head with it, swung her long, lean legs out of bed and headed for the bathroom. I watched her walk away with what seemed like added sway this morning.

"How did you sleep?" I called from the bedroom.

"Like a rock, but maybe a little too warm." She peaked out around the bathroom door, smiling. I laughed at her response. She was quick, and I knew she'd keep me on my toes.

"What do you have planned today?" she called out as I dressed.

"Well, I took everything off my schedule for the next week. I was wondering if you wanted to go on a little getaway. There really isn't any place better to get to know someone, than on a trip."

She was doing up the last of the buttons on her blouse when she came back into the room.

"What did you have in mind?" Kate asked, sitting on the edge of the bed in front of me. I was nervous she would think I was putting too much pressure on her, but I barreled ahead with my plans.

"New Orleans. We leave at 3:00 this afternoon. Private plane."

Looking at me in disbelief, she whispered, "Are you serious?"

"Yes."

She was speechless.

"We will be staying at the Soniat House, in one of the grand suites. I have booked it until next Monday."

"Do you have everything planned?" she asked quietly.

"No, just day one, and then we will figure things out as we go."

"I have always dreamed of going there one day, but couldn't find the time to leave the ranch, or the money to go."

I got out of bed and walked around to sit beside her.

"You won't ever have to worry about money again. I know things haven't been easy around your dad's place these last few years. We wouldn't be here otherwise, but please know I truly want you to be happy. I want a marriage in the truest sense of the word." Taking her hands in mine, I continued, "I don't mean now. We need to get to know each other, but I have high hopes for our life together. That's why I think we need to get away, away from prying eyes and work that never seems to end for both of us." I saw the wheels turning in her head. She was figuring out excuses not to go. "I have already arranged to have one of our hired men help out at your dad's, so he won't be alone. You don't need to worry about that. I want uninterrupted time for you and me this week."

"Me, too," Kate replied and smiled. "But how did you know I wanted to go to New Orleans? It's not exactly like it's the honeymoon capital of the world."

"I asked Delaney. That's what we were talking about the day you left for Dallas. I asked her what's the one place you've always wanted to visit. I had expected Paris or London, but she said you had been talking about seeing New Orleans for years." Looking into Kate's eyes, I could tell she was touched that I had taken the time to find out what she wanted.

"I will go get the suitcases. You and I better get packing." I stood and left the room.

ater that afternoon, we were sitting in a private plane waiting to take off. I was so nervous.

"Are you ready?" Tyler asked. I nodded yes and looked out the window.

"Kate, what's wrong?"

"I don't really like flying," I said, not looking at him but straight ahead instead. He didn't say anything, just put his hand on my leg, palm up, for me to take as the pilot started to taxi down the runway. I took it and held on for dear life. Thankfully, we weren't in the air very long before we were descending into New Orleans. I dozed off at some point in the flight and woke up when the captain was announcing it was time to land. I squeezed Tyler's hand, which I hadn't let go of the entire flight. Nestled into his shoulder, I had fallen asleep. With the plane on the ground, our bags already in the waiting car, we headed to the hotel. I watched intently as we entered the heart of New Orleans and the French Quarter.

"It's even more beautiful than I pictured." We arrived at our hotel, and it was a two-story French Quarter historic landmark, with a wrought iron second-floor balcony, dormers along the roof line, and beautiful arched doors. Tyler and I went to check in and the concierge took our bags.

"Mr. and Mrs. Morton, welcome to Soniat House. You can follow Alcé to your room. Enjoy your stay." The receptionist behind the desk handed Tyler our keys, and we turned to catch up to the gentleman she had pointed out to us. I grabbed for Tyler's hand as we went up the grand staircase.

When we arrived at our room, Tyler tipped the gentleman that assisted us, and he closed the door behind him.

"It's magnificent, Tyler," I whispered, as I took in the exquisite furnishings. Beautiful antique chandeliers hung in each room, and the sitting room had a sofa that looked too gorgeous to sit on. I wandered into the bedroom to see an antique four-poster canopy bed with the most delicately embroidered curtains I'd even seen.

"This is too much. I don't deserve this," I said as I turned and looked up at him.

"Kate, this is our honeymoon, a time for us to just be together. We have been thrown into a situation that in this day and age is almost unheard of, and if I want to pamper you a little, that's what I'm going to do." He came and stood in front of me and took my hands. Just that gesture sent shivers up my arms. His touch was electric, and it was quickly becoming my new favorite sensation. "You absolutely deserve it, so let's enjoy our time, this wonderful hotel, and have fun." His eyes were dancing, his smile contagious, and I couldn't help but smile back at him. This place made me feel like we were living in the French Quarter, rather than just visiting.

SHE CAME out from the bathroom in a stunning black dress. It hugged her perfectly in all the right places. The V-neck was just high enough as to not be scandalous. Kate looked gorgeous. Even though we were taking things slow, I was very aware of her body and what it did to me.

"Kate, you are gorgeous."

She scoffed, shook her head, and grabbed her purse. I was sad to think nobody ever told her that, or if they did, it wasn't often enough. Walking up behind her, I wrapped my arms around her waist and whispered low in her ear.

"You are gorgeous, and I am so very glad you are mine."

Stepping back as she shivered deliciously, I offered her my arm, and we walked out of our room, down to the main floor. Our reservations were close, and we decided to walk there. There was soft jazz music being played on the street.

"Listen, isn't it wonderful? I thought this was just something that happened in the movies."

"No darlin', this happens all the time. I think it's one of my favourite things about New Orleans."

When our supper was over, we meandered back toward the hotel. The air had cooled and Kate hadn't brought a jacket, so she walked closer to me. I stopped and let go of her arm, took off my suit coat and put it over her shoulders. I put my arm around her waist, and we continued on to the hotel.

"Thank you for a wonderful evening. I wouldn't have ever dreamed this was possible."

The jazz music from the street below wafted into our room through the open door to our private balcony. Kate was leaning against the door frame, lost in her thoughts. I walked up beside her and leaned back so I was resting against the other side, looking at her.

"What are you thinking?" I asked. A smile crept across her still face as she looked over her shoulder at me.

"I'm thinking that somehow I have fallen into a dream. I know it sounds crazy Tyler, but you have done all this for me."

I saw tears welling up in her eyes, "Nobody has ever gone to these lengths for me." A single tear fell to her cheek, so I reached out and wiped it away with my thumb. I brought her closer to me with a gentle grip on her arm. I didn't say anything, nothing needed to be said. Kate looked up at me and smiled. I took this moment to claim her lips. She wrapped her arms around my neck and leaned into the kiss.

Kate broke the kiss, took my hand and led me to the swing on the balcony. We sat down and she gently placed her hand on my neck and pulled me down to meet her lips. The cool New Orleans night, beautiful music serenading us from somewhere below us, and my wife in my arms; the world in this moment felt perfect. Nothing else mattered.

The next day, we wandered around the French Quarter hand in hand. Kate had taken charge of our honeymoon and quickly planned the other days of our time here. We took it all in. New Orleans was full of life, and so was Kate. I had never thought of having a honeymoon, and if I had, it wouldn't be unfolding like ours was. But it was working, and it was almost everything I had dreamed of. We took in as many sights and touristy things that we could, and the food, the music, and the people everywhere we went were amazing.

The tour of the Saint Louis Number One cemetery was fantastic. Walking around the crypts should have felt ominous, but here in this moment, hand in hand with Kate, it was beautiful.

"You see this place on TV all the time, the history, the tombs and the fact that most are so very old is fascinating."

I laughed, "You sound like Gavin when he sees an old building." Wrapping my arm around her waist, I pull her closer. "Come on, let's go find some coffee and music, or something more cheerful than a cemetery. This is a honeymoon, you know." Kate laughed at me and we wandered to find some snacks.

"Ty, I want to stop and find something I can take home for Addison." It was the first time she hadn't used my entire name. It was sweet, and I hoped it was a sign she was more comfortable around me.

"Sure," I said. "Why don't we find a gift shop after we get back from the cooking class?"

Kate nodded her head and smiled at me. I took her hand, and we rode in silence, but it didn't matter. We were having another great day.

Finding our cooking class proved to be easier than expected. Kate and I walked in and waited for someone to assist us. She had a death grip on my arm.

"What's wrong?" I whispered.

"I'm nervous. You are pushing me out of the comfort zone I have worked so hard to build." Her words struck me. She had put walls up, protecting herself from something that I didn't know about.

"Well, darlin' get used to it. I'm determined to get you out of that comfort zone." I chuckled as the hostess walked out toward us.

We were in a class with six other people. There was a chatty, newlywed couple beside us. They quite often forgot they were in public. I caught Kate glance over at them during one of these times, and her eyes were as big as plates.

"Wanna show them up?" I asked quietly as I took a step closer to her, eyebrows wiggling suggestively.

"Tyler, I, ah, stop teasing me." She finally giggled after she stumbled through her answer. "Hand me the Cajun spice." She swatted me across the chest. Our hands touched as she took the spice, and she looked up at me and smiled.

"What does the recipe say next?" I hadn't ever enjoyed cooking. Take-out menus took up one drawer in my kitchen, but watching Kate move around this strange kitchen was hypnotic. She navigated everything effortlessly. If I hadn't known she ran a ranch, I would swear she was more at home in a commercial kitchen.

"Tyler, I need the shrimp. Earth to Tyler." She was snapping her fingers in front of my eyes. Before I knew what I was doing, I leaned down and kissed her. I took her by surprise, but she wrapped her arms around me; an onion in one hand and a spatula in the other. We stepped away from each other and I turned to grab the shrimp and ended up with a stinging butt cheek thanks to a quick flick of the spatula. I spun around and Kate was stirring the sauce for the shrimp with a sly smile on her face. How was it possible that I had been wanting to slap that round ass of hers since the moment I saw her, and she beat me to it? I felt like it was some cruel joke, but I would get my revenge.

Sharing a table with a couple who had been married for forty years at the end of the class was the highlight of the day. They talked of their family, which included seven grandchildren, how they had met and fallen in love, and so many stories in between. I looked over at Kate and smiled. She took my hand and we continued our casual conversation.

CHAPTER 19

It was our last night in New Orleans. I couldn't have dreamed of a better trip.

"This has been wonderful, Tyler. Thank you."

"I'm glad. That was my plan. I'm not done with the surprises though. I booked this next one before I knew you didn't enjoy flying." Tyler looked apprehensive as he handed me the brochure. I looked down; an evening flight over New Orleans. I gulped and looked up at him.

"Well, let's go." I forced a smile, and we left the hotel room.

The plane was small. My pulse raced and my breathing quickened. My palms were sweaty and my steps slowed. Tyler must have sensed it, because he grabbed my hand as we walked toward the plane. The pilot was young, too young. He had finished all his checks and walked over to introduce himself. We climbed onto the plane and were given headsets. Seatbelts on, Tyler grabbed my hand again, and the pilot began his taxi down the runway. I hated flying in a large plane, so this little plane was pure torture. Tyler let go of my hand and wrapped his arm around my shoulders. The plane leveled off, and I pried open my eyes and looked out the window.

"Kate, how on earth did you fly to and from Scotland in high school?" he asked once I opened her eyes.

"Dramamine, lots of Dramamine. I was out like a light before we took off and barely awake when it was time to land." Looking straight ahead, not daring to look over for fear of turning lobster red. I felt his shoulders move and heard the chuckle he tried to suppress.

The sun was setting over the west side of New Orleans, and the light was beautiful. We toured the bayou, flew around the Superdome and over the French Quarter as the street lights were coming on. It was amazing and romantic. I leaned into the crook of Tyler's arm and he tightened his grip around my shoulders. I looked up at him and smiled. Shifting in my seat, reaching over, I put my hand on the back of his head and pulled him towards me. We kissed tenderly at first and then it became more passionate. Remembering we were in a small public space, we ended our kiss, and I rested my head on his shoulder.

Once back on the ground, I was much happier and relaxed.

"Tyler, let's hit a bar," I said, wide-eyed and grinning at him.

He stopped and looked at me. We had been so busy during the days; we didn't venture too far from the hotel at night.

"Sure, have a place in mind?"

I scanned the street and pointed to Maison Bourbon.

"There?" He was hesitant as he looked across the street.

"Come on, don't be a stick in the mud on our last night." Pleading with him, I grabbed his hands and started to pull him across the street. He sighed and gave in to me.

PICTURES OF JAZZ musicians lined the walls of the bar. We managed to get a table and order drinks. The atmosphere was electric, the live music phenomenal, and Kate visited with almost everyone in the pub. I watched Kate interact with strangers who all became her best friends. Here, she was outgoing, thoroughly enjoying herself, extra flirtatious with me, promised people we would be back, and offered a place to stay if anyone came to Texas. I had no idea how spontaneous Kate was. I was disappointed tonight was our last night here.

Looking at my phone, I saw it was very late. I made a quick call and watched Kate walk over to the table.

"We should probably head to the hotel, Ty. It's three in the morning. Our flight is supposed to leave at nine."

"Already ahead of you, I have a car waiting for us."

She smiled at me, "Always thinking ten steps ahead, and always making sure we're safe." I grabbed her purse and coat, and we walked out of the pub with our arms wrapped around each other.

We got into the car and began our drive back to the hotel.

"Thank you for humoring me tonight. It's been a long time since I have had that much fun." Resting her head on my shoulder, she let out a contented sigh.

Inhaling the scent of her shampoo, I asked quietly, "Why don't you let your hair down more? You work so hard. I want you to be able to have fun with your friends. I want to have evenings like this together when we get home. It's time for someone to take care of you." Kate lifted her head and looked at me. Moving my hand up to her cheek, I leaned in to claim her lips.

I had a wonderful time getting to know my wife and shutting out the outside world. Right now, everyday problems from home didn't matter. Getting ready for bed that night, I felt closer to her than when we arrived. I climbed in and watched Kate walk towards the bed. She was a little tipsy and grinning a lot. I rolled over on my side to look at her, propping myself up on my elbow.

"Thank you so very much for this trip, Ty. I've had such a wonderful time exploring the city, and a great time with you." She scooted over in bed until she was right beside me. We kissed. Kate ran her hands across my chest while I entwined my fingers in her hair and pulled her carefully closer to me. Sliding my other hand down to her hip, I repositioned and pulled her until she was straddling me. Exploring her body, I slid my hands up under Kate's sleep shirt. I grasped her breasts and rolled her perky nipples between my fingers. Kate sat up, knees on either side of me, positioning herself perfectly to grind against me. I sat up and made quick work of removing her shirt. Taking one pointy bud in my mouth, I nipped at it, and Kate threw her head back and let out a sigh. She was perfect. Every fiber of my being wanted me to continue, but I stopped.

"Ty, what's the matter?" she whispered, putting her hands over mine, which were still holding her breasts.

"You've had a little too much to drink, and as much as I want you, baby, I don't want our first time to be like this."

Suddenly, as if a switch was flipped, she was back to her level-headed self. Closing her eyes, she nodded and gently slid off my lap. Finding her shirt, she slid it on and laid down facing away from me.

Wrapping my arms around her, I pulled her close. "Please don't pull away." Kate rolled over to look at me.

"I'm sorry; I don't know what got into me." She closed her eyes, as if she were ashamed of her behavior.

"Don't apologize, baby. I would have liked nothing more

than to take you right here and now, but I don't want you to regret anything in the morning." The look on her face changed. She hadn't said a word, but I knew she was beginning to trust me. Kate cuddled in beside me and fell asleep. I held her close all night. When we woke up, we were still laying together. Our flight home resembled the flight to New Orleans. Kate was quiet, maybe even distant. I hoped it wouldn't last beyond the jitters she had about flying.

When we were back home, real life came flooding in. The Kate that I saw in New Orleans wasn't the same person as who she was here at home. My phone was constantly ringing or chiming. Taking over a week off had left me with hundreds of emails to answer and dozens of calls to return. Apparently, people thought I should have worked on my honeymoon. Over the next few days, Kate became shy, cautious, and always watching how she said things. It made me think back to the first time she had been here. I wanted her to feel like this was her home, but what else could I do?

Me: Kate, are you on your way back home now? If you are, do you want to come to my office in the main house?

A few minutes later my phone chimed, and it read:

Kate: I'm on my way.

There was a soft knock on the door, and then it opened. Kate came into my office and sat down at one of the chairs in front of my desk.

"How has your day been?" I asked, giving her my undivided attention.

"It's been good. Busy, but I like that. How about yours?"

"Long. I'm thinking of calling it quits for the day, but just wanted to see what you were up to. Think you could be done too?"

"I don't see why not. Everything on my end is ready for weaning at Dad's tomorrow. I could probably be persuaded to not go back over there." I put away the things that were on my desk, grabbed my laptop and bag, and we left my office. I reached for Kate's hand. We walked to her truck together, holding hands. She didn't have the same grip she had while we wandered around the French Quarter together.

CHAPTER 20

Finally, I was taking a day for myself. It had felt like forever since I had done something without having to think about Tyler coming with me. It was time for some shopping in the city. I was wandering down the street when I heard, "Are you who I think you are?" I didn't pay much attention, but I heard it again, "So you are her? Yes, I'm talking to you." I turned to see a blond, slender, and very pretty woman walking towards me.

"I'm sorry. Do we know each other?" Furrowing my brow, I looked at this woman in front of me.

"No, I don't suppose we do. I'm Lona, the person they forced Tyler to leave, only to get stuck with you. That's right, me." She held her arms out and did a little shimmy. My mouth fell open and I couldn't find words, not that she gave me any time to respond.

"You see, Tyler's father didn't think I was good enough to be in his family, so they found you." I felt sick to my stomach. I was too far away from the truck to slink away, and part of me wanted to know what else she had to say.

She looked me up and down and obviously didn't approve.

"We still talk every day. I just hate how miserable he is." She stuck her bottom lip out and pouted. "I can't wait until the dust settles and life goes back to normal." Looking at her nails, she arched her brow and appeared to wait for a reaction. I didn't give her the satisfaction of one. "Anyway, I just wanted to let you know he's in love with me, and as soon as he can figure out how to get rid of you, he will."

Tears were filling my eyes, but I forced myself not to cry. I was clasping my hands so tightly my nails were digging half-moons into my palms.

I WATCHED HER WALK AWAY. I unclenched my hands, and they started shaking. Of course, there was someone else. A reputation like Tyler's doesn't just go away overnight. I was the reputable woman he could parade around to events and nobody would take a second glance at. Lona was the typical hot blond who would be the lover on the side who kept his fire alive. Tyler never meant those things he had said about me being beautiful. He was a businessman, and he was used to telling people what they wanted to hear. I took my frustration out on the empty bottle that was on the ground in front of me. I stomped on it and kicked it across the sidewalk. People walking by looked at me like I had a problem. Walking over to it, I picked it up and tossed it into a garbage can.

Wandering back to the truck, I got in and slammed the door behind me. Resting my head on the steering wheel, I let the tears fall. I didn't know what to do. I couldn't go home. Tyler wasn't who I wanted to face right now, and I couldn't go to my mom's. There would be too many questions.

I forgot what I had wanted to get today. I didn't remember driving home, but I ended up there. This had all been a horrific mistake. I was going to do everything I could to make Tyler want out. If he really wanted that woman, I wasn't going to stop him. It didn't matter that I was falling in love with him. It was over before it even got started.

I decided that I wouldn't mention this exchange with Lona, but I wasn't going to be lovey- dovey with him. I had been a fool to think that he really cared about me, found me attractive and wanted me for me. No man would ever feel that way about me. They just used me for their needs and then walked away. I wiped my eyes and got out of my truck. I was happy his office wasn't here; then I wouldn't have to face him until supper.

WHEN I GOT HOME from work, I was happy to see Kate's truck in the driveway. I walked into the kitchen and found her getting supper ready.

"It smells great in here. How was your trip to the city?"

"It was fine. Supper will be ready in five minutes," she replied coolly.

I frowned, "Is everything OK?"

"Fine," was all she said. We ate in silence, and that was how the rest of the night went. I knew something needed to be done, but I wasn't sure what. She had become more and more distant, but today was different. Something was definitely off, and my warning bells were ringing.

As we climbed into bed that night, I saw Kate's puffy eyes and red nose. This was more than nothing.

"Kate, whatever is bothering you is not fine. I want to know what it is." I frowned at my wife. I knew she was hiding something.

"Tyler, it's been a long day. Sometimes I just need a cry.

I'm fine." Rolling over, she turned off her light and left me in the dark, literally and figuratively.

Hearing a few sniffles from her side of the bed, I reached out and pulled her to me. Her quiet tears worried me. Thinking back over the last few days, I tried to figure out what could be bothering her, but came up with nothing. My heart broke because I couldn't help her through this. She didn't resist, but she wasn't relaxed either. Kate's breathing eventually became soft and rhythmic. The sniffling had stopped, and I knew she was asleep, but I stayed awake, laying there and wondering what was going on.

The next day, Kate had plans to do a few things around our house. I took the opportunity to sneak off to see her parents.

"Julie, Ben, thank you for agreeing to meet with me."

Kate's mom had motioned for me to sit at the table while she poured coffee for the three of us.

"I wanted to talk with you and see if you could give me any insight on how to crack that tough exterior Kate puts up. I know we haven't been married that long, which means we don't know each other that well yet. When we went to New Orleans, her guard was down. We had a fantastic trip; we laughed and talked. But as soon as we got back here, she shut down again." I leaned forward and propped my elbows on the table. "I see glimpses every once in a while of the woman I saw on our honeymoon. For lack of a better term, I want to draw that woman out. I know this is far from a normal situation, but I have to say I am falling for your daughter. She is a wonderful person, she's beautiful, and I want to be a good husband to her." I had just admitted I was falling in love with Kate. My hands started sweating, and I rubbed them on my pants to dry them. My breathing increased, and a smile crept across my face. "I'm falling in love with Kate."

Ben grabbed for Julie's hand, and they both smiled. Ben looked relieved, like a weight had lifted. Julie shook her head and said, "Oh Tyler, our Kate has always been a little tough to crack."

Kate's dad let out a little chuckle. "That's an understatement."

Julie swatted at Ben, giggling to herself. "She's cautious, always thinks five steps ahead of where she needs to be. Kate had to build a wall. She wasn't like the other girls in school. She didn't worry about dances, parties or boys; all she wanted to do was work hard and figure out how to make this place successful. She has always struggled with feeling wanted, feeling like she is enough." I smiled, thinking of a young Kate, and I hurt thinking she thought she wasn't enough. Julie picked up her cup of coffee before she continued, "Past relationships were just fleeting because she wanted to feel like someone needed her. When that fell through, she would shut down. She has had no control over what happened here, with you, and getting married. I really think she has no idea how to get things back under her thumb."

"She would have been relaxed in New Orleans, and that's when my girl truly shines." Ben interjected.

"When you asked where you should take her, we knew you would see the true Kate while you were there. She's in there Tyler, you just need to need her, make her feel useful." Julie took a sip of her coffee and looked at me.

"Give her time, make her comfortable, let her know you need her and not just for a ranch hand. Kate has always longed for a man to make her feel like a woman, not just one of the guys. I promise you that is the way to her heart. Don't let her shut down. If that happens, there'll be a long road ahead."

I picked my coffee cup up as I nodded. I spent the better

part of the afternoon with Ben and Julie, getting to know Kate through family stories and photo albums. My wife had been selling herself short almost all of her life. I knew I needed to make her see her worth.

"Thank you both for sharing your stories and pictures. It has really helped me to know what I need to be doing."

"Tyler, all I can tell you is you need to court your wife, not just now, but always. Right now, you need to get to know her, go out on dates, make plans with friends, saddle two horses and just ride. Spend time together away from the ranch, get her away from here. Find out from her what she likes, what she wants from life. It's also not just all about her; tell her about you, tell her about growing up, your dreams for the future, what you want from your life together. If you do that, you'll have a strong marriage," Ben said.

"Please don't tell her I was here. I don't want her feeling like I was tattling to you both." They were in agreement, and I headed home, formulating a plan that would bring not only my wife closer to me, but me closer to herself.

I knew I could not let what was bothering her go on another day. We needed to talk. Kate was on the couch, filling out thank you cards.

"Kate, something is bothering you, and I would like to know what it is."

She turned and looked at me as I walked into the living room and sat down across from her.

"New Orleans seems like a lifetime ago, and I had a wonderful time. Since we got back, something changed, and something even worse has changed in the last few days. I want to know what I can do to make you happy. Is there something I'm missing?"

Kate set the cards and pen down on the coffee table between us and leaned forward.

"Who is Lona?" Kate asked, looking down at her hands, making no eye contact with me. I could feel the blood drain from my face. I closed my eyes and took a deep breath.

"Lona is an ex-girlfriend. I have not seen or talked to her since I broke up with her, months before my father made the arrangement for us to be married."

Kate didn't look too convinced.

"Why do you ask?

"She approached me in the city the other day. She said you talk every day and tell her how miserable you are being married to me." Kate's chin quivered, and I watched her eyes glisten with tears.

I put my palms to my face. I clenched my jaw and felt the anger building inside of me. Of all the people she had to run into, it had to be Lona.

"Kate, I swear I have not spoken to her since we broke up. The reason I broke things off was because she was getting very possessive, demanding, and saying we were soul mates; that we belonged together. She decided she would move in."

"She said you were trying to figure out how to get rid of me."

Looking at the tears falling down her face, I worried about how to make her see that was not even close to the truth. Would she believe me? Then again, why would she believe me? She had no reason to.

Kneeling down in front of her, I took her hands in mine,

. "I don't want to get rid of you. I have never been so happy in a relationship. There is no way I would go back to her. I want you, and I want our lives to grow together." I wasn't sure I alleviated her fears. Her face remained pained and tears were still falling. I hadn't wanted to tell her I went to her parents, but in this moment it was all I had to prove to her I was in this marriage for keeps.

"Does a man who is looking to get out of a marriage spend the day with his in-laws to find out how to get you to open up and be more like you were in New Orleans?"

"You went to see my mom and dad?" she asked quietly.

I nodded.

"What did they say?"

"Nope, you don't get to know that." I smiled. She cracked half a smile.

"So, this person is not someone you think about all the time?"

I sat on the couch beside her and gathered her in my arms.

"Kate, I'm telling you the truth; she means nothing to me. The only woman I want in my life, as my wife, best friend, and one day, hopefully soon, as my lover, is you. You are all I need. You're all I want."

A shy smile crept across her face.

"Are we okay?" I asked, and she nodded.

"We're okay," she whispered, wrapping her arms around me. We stayed wrapped up in each other for a few minutes, heart to heart, locked in each other's arms, with a newfound trust between us.

CHAPTER 21

"Tyler, I'm going out with some friends tonight. I'll probably be late," I called from our room. I was getting ready to go, and I didn't really care if he had any objections. He walked in and his mouth dropped open as he looked at me from head to toes. I had put on my tightest black jeans, a hot pink, low-cut blouse with lace accents down the center and on the cuffs of the sleeves. Large drop rhinestone earrings and black high heels completed my outfit. I had just sprayed on a small mist of my favorite perfume that smelled fruity with hints of lilacs.

Tyler walked over to me and brought me close to him. "You look and smell too good; better not find another cowboy to take you home."

I laughed and gave him a peck on the cheek. I stayed close to him, looked into his eyes, and smiled. As I turned to go I slid my hand down his arm and held onto his hand. Just when I was about to let go of it, I looked over my shoulder.

"I think I will just come home to the cowboy I already

have," I replied, winking at him. He laughed, and I walked out of the room.

"I think some of the guys and I will head to a bar. I will text when I know," he said as I was walking down the hallway.

I grabbed my purse and headed downstairs.

"Where are you going?" he asked.

"Um, I'm not totally sure. It will be somewhere we can dance, I hope." I saw Jane drive up through the window. "Have fun. See you later." I kissed him on the cheek and ran out the door.

We got to the bar and found tables to sit at. Karaoke night was the best night to go out. There were six of us girls who, at one time or another, had been on the rodeo circuit together.

I was up singing the song "José Cuervo" when I saw Tyler walk in. Judging by his shocked expression, he saw me, too. I focused on him as I sang the rest of the song and flirted with him from the stage. When the song was over, he was waiting for me at the bottom of the stairs and helped me down.

"You sing?" he asked quietly in my ear.

"I sing, yep. What are you doing here?" I asked as he walked me back towards my table.

"We started at another place but it wasn't any fun tonight, so someone suggested here. Boy, wasn't I surprised when we walked in and saw my wife putting on quite the concert." Looking up at Tyler, it suddenly struck me at how him being here changed me. I would still have fun with the girls, but I wanted to flirt. I wanted him to watch me.

"Excuse me, you've had her all to yourself since your wedding. She's ours tonight, Tyler." Jane pulled me back to our table. I would catch him looking at me every once in a while, so I arched my brow or gave him those 'come get me' eyes.

The music changed and "If Tomorrow Never Comes"

came on over the speakers. I saw him leave the guy's table and walked over to where we were sitting. He came up behind me, placed his hands on either side of me.

"Care to dance with me, ma'am?"

My pulse raced. He smelled so good. I could feel the heat from him radiating onto my back. I would be lying to myself if I said I wasn't attracted to Tyler.

I looked at his strong hands, up his toned arms, and turned on my stool. I wanted to say something flirtatious, but I just took his hand, smiled and let him lead me to the dance floor. He pulled me close, and we danced as close together as we possibly could.

"Why didn't you tell me you could sing?"

"It's not something I think of blurting out very often." I shrugged.

"How did all you girls become friends?"

"We used to rodeo together."

"You used to rodeo?"

"Yep, barrel racer," I answered.

"What else don't I know about you?" he asked as he spun me around.

I moved my head so I could look at him. "Did you drive here?"

He nodded yes.

"When you are ready to go, take me with you. We can find out more about each other tonight." I arched my brow and smiled at him.

"That sounds wonderful."

The song was ending, and I knew all eyes were on us. Other than the group of friends we each came with, nobody knew us. They didn't know we were married. That was free-ing, so I threw my normally cautious self to the wind, put my hand at the base of his neck and pulled him down for our lips to meet.

He returned my kiss; it started out tender, but he quickly grabbed the back of my head, entangling his fingers in my hair as our tongues danced. Tyler let out a low growl, and if possible, pulled me even closer. The song ended, and so did our kiss. I turned away from him and left him standing on the dance floor alone.

My girlfriends hooted and hollered when I got back to the table. I looked over to Tyler's table where he had returned, and he was getting pats on the back. We caught each other's eye. I smiled at him, and he winked at me. This man was making it very difficult to keep my distance from him, but I still didn't feel like I knew him. There were things I needed to know before I could trust him completely. He was intriguing, caring, and, more importantly, my husband.

I stole glances throughout the night. Once, I turned and Tyler wasn't at his table. Quickly scanning the bar, I saw him being pestered by a large chested bottle blond. Annoyed that I couldn't hear what he was saying, I started to get huffy. He pointed at his ring, and I could clearly see him say, 'I'm married but thanks for the offer.'

The woman kept trying, and finally he held up his hand and pointed to his ring again. Then he pointed at me and I could see him mouth the words "to her." I smiled and waved, turning my hand so she could see my ring. I pointed to it and then I pointed to him and mouthed, "he's mine." The woman scowled at me and flounced away. Picking up my glass, I held it up to him, and he held his up to me. Watching him turn that woman down was not only satisfying, but a turn on as well.

I walked around the table and whispered into Jane's ear, "I'm going to head out."

"Well, ladies, this has been great. We need to do this more often. Since we are both here, and I'm the wrong way for you all to drop off, I will catch a ride home with Tyler. Night, ladies."

I grabbed my purse and Tyler slid his hand from my lower back to rest on my butt. As we left the bar, my friends squealed at the table. We got to the truck and instead of opening the door; he backed me up into it until I couldn't move. He placed his hands on either side of me, bent down, and kissed me. Hungrily, passionately, possessively.

"Two things you need to know. One, I've wanted to do that all night. Two, you care about me, Kate, and I know I'm not wrong if I say you care a lot. You were jealous when that woman wouldn't leave me alone. I could see it. A woman that doesn't care would have turned around. You didn't turn around." He moved me out of the way, opened the door to let me climb into the truck. I was kind of dumbstruck by his observations, but didn't have any rebuttals to his claims. He was right on both counts. Dammit. He climbed into the driver's seat and started the conversation up again, as he if hadn't just left me feeling dumbfounded by his observation skills.

"You sing. You barrel race. What else?"

"You know about basketball and 4-H," Shifting in the seat, I turned and looked at him. "Well, I sang in the choir at school and played the clarinet. I was pretty much a nerd. I didn't have a lot of friends, which, in a small town, is pretty lonely, except when I work with the cows. Barrel racing was the one place I found friends that have lasted."

I TURNED into the yard and parked at the house.

"Just because we're home, doesn't mean you get to skip out

on the childhood talk," she said, surprising me.

We got out of the truck and walked into the house. It was late, but I didn't want our night to end. About twenty minutes later, Kate came out of the bathroom and crawled into bed next to me. "Tell me about you."

"Dad was a ranch boss, so we didn't have free run of the ranch. I played football most of the year in one league or another. Actually I got into the University of Montana on a football scholarship. I started team roping with Rob when he was old enough, but nothing serious."

I looked over at Kate to see she was listening intently. "Our life wasn't exciting, and absolutely nothing like it is now. At that time, I knew the only way to get out of there was school, so that's why I went into business and marketing."

"I bet you were popular," she said as she rested her head on the pillow.

I nodded yes. "I had friends around all the time, and always a girlfriend."

We sat in silence for a few moments and Kate leaned in to me. "Good night, thank you for turning tonight into a fantastic evening."

I kissed her. This kiss was different from the one we'd shared in the parking lot of the bar. It was tender, loving, and sensual. Kate sighed contently, laid her head on my shoulder, and fell asleep.

That night when we went to sleep, I finally felt like I knew my wife. We had shared more intimate moments, more about our lives before each other, things that we should have found out before our marriage. Tonight I felt like I had gone on a date with my wife. It was not just the day to day, but we'd really spent time together. We flirted and had fun. It was the kind of time we had together in New Orleans, but had not had here. I would plan a night out for us in a few days.

CHAPTER 22

My phone chimed just after lunch.

Kate: Hey are you busy? I need some help at dad's if you're available?

Me: I'm always available for you ;)

Kate: Oh brother, insert eye roll.

Tyler: Can't blame a guy for trying. I'll change and be right over.

Kate: Thank you, I'll be in the barn.

I was at the Patterson ranch in ten minutes, and I parked in front of the barn. Opening the barn door, I saw my wife struggling to help a cow deliver its calf. I grabbed the calf puller from the wall by the door and ran over to the maternity pen.

"Kate, move out of the way." I could tell she was exhausted. I knew it for sure when she moved out of the way without arguing.

Blindly, I found the calf's legs and slid the chains on. I placed the puller under the cow's rear end and started to winch the calf. I repositioned and cranked on the handle again.

"Kate, steady the end. I need you to hold it on the ground. I need more leverage."

She immediately did what I asked, and with a few more tugs and another reposition, the calf plopped onto the ground. I dropped the chains and moved to the calf, and pulled the bag away from its mouth and nose. Kate was frantically rubbing it, trying to get it to take a breath. The cow hovered and nosed at the calf. Finally, after what felt like hours, the calf gasped and started to flounder around. I grabbed on to Kate, and we scrambled out of the way so the cow could take over.

Kate leaned up against me as we sat in the corner of the maternity pen, watching the mother and baby bond.

"Thank you. I haven't had that much trouble for a very long time. Dad's gone to town, and this one was supposed to be dry, so I'm not sure how this little one happened."

"I'm glad I was around. You never have to ask if I'm available. If you need me, I will drop everything to help you."

I wrapped my arms around her and we sat there silently, waiting for the calf to start sucking on its mother.

I sat in my office the next day, not working. I was planning how to spend more time on the Patterson ranch with Kate. There was no reason I need to be here every day. There were enough ranch hands around to cover me. My business dealings could be done from anywhere. I didn't really think I needed to be sitting in an office five, or sometimes six, days of the week. She worked herself ragged. I watched her drag herself home at the end of the day, barely able to stay awake for supper.

There was a knock on my office door as it flew open.

"Tyler, are you going to make it a habit of only being here for part of the day, or can I actually count on you? I came to your office to talk to you about Montana and you were gone.

Getting married seems to have made you pay less attention to the ranch business."

I looked at my father and didn't have anything to say to him.

"What did you need so badly that you didn't try to call me?"

"I guess you aren't thinking straight these days. Not getting much sleep, I bet. I know I wouldn't be with an alluring woman in my bed."

I slammed my hands down on my desk and shot out of my chair.

"If I ever hear you utter another word about my wife in that manner, I will not hesitate to hit you."

"Ah, so you haven't sealed the deal then. Son, don't forget who set this up. I haven't so much as heard a thank you. If it wasn't for me, you would still be screwing the trash that you found in bars. I'm the one that made you respectable. I'm the one looking out for this ranch and its future. Don't you ever forget that." He was almost nose to nose with me, leaning across my desk.

"Here's a newsflash Dad, nobody cared who I was sleeping with except you. Why haven't I ever been good enough for you? Even now, after all the sacrifices I made to be here. I'm not enough. I know all about the marriage clause in Grandpa's will. You sure snuck in under the wire with that one. The only reason I went through with this marriage was to protect Kate and her family. I couldn't care less about what was going to happen here, but what you were doing to them was crazy." How I kept from yelling was beyond me, but I was standing toe to toe with my father, and I wasn't backing down.

"Tyler, it's business. He couldn't pay when it was time to collect, so I used it to my advantage. Not to mention that when he dies, the land will transfer to Kate, who is a Morton now. It will be a part of the Lone Star empire anyway, which means we will be the largest cattle ranch in the northern half of Texas. We are respected, Tyler, and this will make us power brokers in this area." He stood and puffed out his chest.

"That's where you're wrong, Dad. We may be one of the largest, but you can rest assured we aren't respected. Rob, Gavin, and I work hard to clean up our name, but as long as your shady dealings keep happening, we won't ever be respected." I sat down in my chair, feeling overwhelmed at the prospect. My father shook his head and walked out of my office.

Rob walked through the doorway, passing our father.

"What was that all about?"

"Father being father. One day, he's going to get what he deserves," I said, still sitting behind my desk, feeling defeated. "I have to get out of here."

"Go. The day is almost done anyway," Rob said.

"Thanks. We'll talk tomorrow." I walked to the barn, saddled two horses, and rode home.

I HEARD someone stomp up the steps, and the door swung open.

"Kate!" Tyler called from the front room. I walked out of the kitchen and saw him pacing the floor.

"Ty, what on earth is wrong?"

"I need to go for a ride. Do you want to come with me? I have a horse saddled for you."

I looked back to the kitchen where I was making supper.

"You're busy; it's fine. I'll go by myself."

I could tell he needed to get something off his chest.

"No, it's alright, I'm just making supper. Just let me turn

the stove off and I'll come with you." I got my boots on, and we were out the door. He'd saddled the most beautiful chestnut horse with a blaze face for me. I swung my leg over the horse and sat in the saddle. Tyler gave his horse a nudge in the side, and he took off. I did the same. He kicked his horse and flew. I caught up to him. When he finally slowed down, we were at the lake on Morton property.

"Tyler, what's wrong?"

He turned in his saddle and looked at me.

"Some days, I wish I could walk away from this place. No, it's what I wish for most days. I hate that you were brought into this insane family without a choice." He got off his horse, and I got off of mine. The horses walked to the water, and I joined Tyler at the water's edge.

"Kate, I feel like I can't fully be me here. I have always known I would be under my father's thumb, but my life has changed so much now. I don't want to be behind a desk for the rest of my life. When I dreamed of taking over this ranch one day, it wasn't from an office. I turned down amazing job offers that would have had me behind a desk, but I knew that's not what was going to make me happy. I want to work, get my hands dirty, know the cattle inside and out because I handle them."

I walked to him and laced my arm through his, standing in silent support with him. I looked out over the still water, smooth as a pane of glass. Occasionally there was a ripple from a bug landing on the water, but at this moment, it was just us, surrounded by nature and seclusion.

"My father has let power go to his head, and I don't know if I can take it much longer."

I was silent.

"I'm sorry; I shouldn't be dumping on you like this."

I walked around Tyler until I was in front of him. I took both his hands in mine and held them.

"Tyler Morton, I'm your wife. I'm your sounding board. Your helpmate. I'm your confidante. I'm who you are supposed to dump your problems on. We didn't get here the traditional way, and that puts us in a different place than most newlyweds, but you can count on me for anything and everything you need."

He looked at me and smiled.

"Do you have any idea how much of a balm for my soul you are? I wish we got together under different circumstances, but I don't think the outcome would have been any different. I still would have made you my wife."

I could feel a blush creeping up my cheeks and butterflies in my stomach.

SHE SMILED AT ME.

"I'm glad we got married, Ty."

I leaned down and kissed her. There was no hesitation; she wrapped her arms around my neck and returned the kiss. While we were standing at the lake, the sky suddenly went black, and I watched a storm building on the horizon. I knew we didn't have time to get back home before it broke, but there was an old trapper's cabin close by. We jumped on the horses and rode as fast as we could. We tied the horses on the sheltered side of the cabin and ran inside, soaked to the skin. The old shack looked like it could be blown down with one gust of wind, but it had been on the property for a hundred years. We were laughing at each other at the state we were in, and I got a fire going.

"Take your clothes off."

Kate's face changed, and she started to stumble over the words she was trying to say.

"We need to hang them up to dry, or we are going to be a little chilly."

"Won't we be just as chilly with no clothes on?" Kate said suspiciously. I looked at her and smiled. She burst out laughing after she gained her composure and got over being stunned. "You just want to get me out of my clothes, Mr. Morton."

"Well, you can't blame a husband for trying, Mrs. Morton," I responded as I closed the distance between us.

I walked closer to Kate until I could feel the heat from her. Slowly, I reached up and started to unbutton her shirt. I slid her shirt off her shoulders and down her arms. My breath caught in my throat and my pulse pounded in my veins. She stood before me, her breasts barely covered by her black lace bra. I longed to have the perky globes in my hands. Reluctantly, I turned to the fireplace and hung the shirt up. "You are on your own for your pants."

Kate did a little shimmy to get out of them. In that time, I had managed to peel my soggy clothes off and hung them up. We stood before each other in wet underwear and I moved to the couch and sat down. There was no denying how much I wanted my wife. The tented front of my boxers was not easy to miss. I leaned back and stretched my arm over the back of the couch. Kate slowly walked over, her hips swaying hypnotized me. There was no way I could hide my frown when she grabbed the blanket and wrapped it around herself before she sat down.

"We'll wait for this to pass and head back home." A clap of thunder echoed outside, and she jumped. I pulled her closer until she tumbled over onto my lap. The pressure of her cheek made me groan in need.

~

"THIS PLACE IS PRETTY WELL STOCKED for an old trapper's cabin," I said, looking around and trying to take my mind off the storm. It was just one room. There was a small kitchen with dark cupboards that looked like they were ready to fall apart, a two person table to my right. No fridge, a propane stove that looked as old as the cabin, and delicate looking lace curtains on the window above the sink. We held each other close on the sofa, as I perused the bookshelf on the far wall, trying to ignore his erection under me.

"Well, you never know what you are going to run into out here, so we check it every month. Rob and his ex-wife honeymooned here."

Tyler looked down at me, and I couldn't resist any longer. I kissed him. We slid down on the couch, and I couldn't take my eyes or lips off of him. As his warm explored my body, they gently brushed over my breasts. His thumb lightly traced my collarbone, and his mouth devoured my neck. His arousal was hard to miss. I shifted my hips to straddle him, and he groaned. I hadn't ever been this bold. Sitting atop Tyler, I felt free, confident, and for the first time loved completely. We were only separated by our cold damp underwear. The blanket slipped to the floor.

Running his hands up my sides, he grasped my breasts tightly. It was like he was afraid to let them go. I gently rocked my hips back and forth against him. Tyler rolled his head to the side, closed his eyes, and let out a sigh. I placed my hand on his chest and sped up my movement.

Tyler let go of me and sat up. He wrapped his arms around me and rolled over so we were spooning. He snaked his hand over my hip, under the band of my lace panties, and slowly moved toward my pulsing center. I shivered, not from the cold, but from the pleasure of his touch. Slowly, he made circles around my most sensitive spot. I let my head fall back onto his shoulder. He leaned over and kissed my neck.

His hand slid down and slowly he entered me with one finger, then slipped another one in. Tyler rhythmically moved his hand and kept just enough pressure on my mound. My pulse raced and my breathing became gasps. Suddenly, I was very aware of his erection behind me. I pushed against him with my ass and he let out a soft moan; I kept it up as I rocked my hips. Grasping Tyler's hand, I held it in place, refusing to let him move from the spot he'd found. The storm intensified, and I jumped when a loud rumble of thunder and a crack of lightening hit in sync. At that moment Tyler ground his palm into me and I shuttered to a climax around his fingers. He moaned and bucked his hips as I pressed against him. Letting out a long, slow sigh, I felt wetness behind me.

"Tyler." I whispered.

"Shh." He slipped his hand over me and grabbed the blanket and threw it over us.

When we woke up a few hours later, the storm was over and the sun was dipping below the horizon. We quickly dressed, took advantage of the break in the weather, and rode for home. The horses were brushed and bedded down in the barn at our place. I finished supper, and we ate in silence. The strain of Tyler's day still seemed to be weighing on him. I felt there was more to his fight with his father, but talking about it wasn't what he wanted to do right now. The new phase of our relationship needed addressing, but now wasn't the time.

"I would have been happy to be stuck there for a few

days," I said when we were done with supper and I stood at the sink doing the dishes.

"It's a pretty little spot. It is a nice place to hide for a while," he said. "Kate, come with me, please." I followed him over to the chair. He sat first and pulled me down onto his lap. "About today, what happened in the shack… I don't want us to go backwards. I know you aren't ready for everything, but can we agree everything that happened today can continue?"

He looked like a little boy who wanted approval.

I smiled.

"I agree we need to keep moving forward in this relationship, and I have gotten too comfortable where we're at. So, yes, I will agree to continue."

"You do know I'm going to kiss you more whenever the mood strikes me, right?" he said, smiling.

"You aren't going to get a complaint from me," I said as I stood, but not before beating him to the kiss. He laughed, and I went back to the kitchen.

I went up to have a warm bath and crawl into bed. I might have liked being stuck in the cabin, but I never warmed up from getting chilled in the rain.

"You're in bed early," Ty said when he walked into our room.

"I just needed to warm up, and I haven't had much time to read lately."

"I could help you warm up." He arched his eyebrow and grinned slyly at me.

My breath quickened.

"Well, it worked in the cabin," I said, closing the book and haphazardly tossing it in the direction of the nightstand, but hearing it fall to the floor. Never taking my eyes from Tyler, I watched him walk around to his side of the bed, dropping clothes as he went.

CHAPTER 23

One day passed into the next and I made countless round trips to my father's ranch and back to my home. If they didn't need me on the Morton ranch, I would go back to my regular life.

"Katie, dear, I need to talk to you."

I stopped the work I was doing on the corrals and took my gloves off as I walked over to where Mom was standing.

"Here, have some sun tea. You have been working hard."

Taking the glass of ice cold tea, I took a drink and immediately cooled down.

"Thanks, Mom. So what's up?" I asked as I sat down on the Adirondack chair beside her.

"I hate to ask you this, but do you think you can handle things around here alone for a few days next week? I would like to go on a little getaway with your dad. It's been so long since we have done anything like that, so I've booked us into a hotel in San Antonio." She was almost hesitant to ask, but I turned to her and smiled.

"Sure, Mom, that sounds like a lovely time for you both. I

have to pregnancy check the heifers next week, but I'm sure I can handle it." Knowing how big of a job it would be, I knew I'd be in for long, hot, and messy days.

"Katie, would Tyler be able to help you out? If he can't, everything is refundable. We can choose another time to go. Your dad can't keep up this pace anymore. His back is giving out, and he needs to have that knee done. I know he will never say anything to you, but it's time we think about letting you take over everything." She took a sip of her tea and looked over at me. "You have Tyler now and I know he will help you make this place run smoothly again."

Sitting stock-still and looking at her in shock at her revelation, all I could say was, "No, Mom, you need to go. I will ask Tyler tonight what time works best for him, and we will get it done. Don't you worry about anything here. Go. You and dad have a good time, and don't worry about anything here. As far as the other, it can wait until you're back." Mom beamed and hugged me.

I COULD FEEL myself becoming worn down. There was too much to get dome on my own. I wanted to be here at my ranch and give it 100%, but I also needed to be at home with Tyler, giving our relationship that same level of work. Brian still made me anxious, and I was always on the lookout for sabotage or trouble. I couldn't confide in my parents. I needed them to think everything was going well. The worry on Tyler's face increased every time he looked at me. His brow would furrow, the wrinkle between his brows became deeper, and he would squint and his crow's feet were exaggerated. He was spending more time working from our home on the days I did office work, where he spent most of the day staring at me, looking very concerned.

A few days later, I parked my truck outside the house after another long day. I was covered in mud and manure from head to toe. I looked through the window of the kitchen and saw candles flickering, and Tyler standing at the stove with my flowery apron tied around his waist, stirring something in a pot. A smile crept over my face. I grabbed for the door handle and basically hauled myself out of the truck. I was so sore from my day of pregnancy checking heifers that all I wanted was a bath and my bed. I filled my lungs with a deep breath and walked up the steps, opened the door and walked through it.

TYLER TURNED TO ME, smiling. I followed his eyes as they looked me over from the top of my head to my toes.

"Is everything OK, Kate?" He was wiping his hands on a tea towel as he moved towards me. I couldn't help but smile at seeing him in my apron.

"That's quite a look you have going on there," I said, pointing my finger at him.

"I thought you would like it." He gave a little wiggle, arched his eyebrows and wiggled them. The stress of my day melted away, and I couldn't help bursting out laughing. "You, on the other hand, look like you have kept busy today."

"I was preg-checking at dads. It's a long day, but I got it done."

"What do you mean, 'you got it done'? Didn't you have help?" That crease between his brows seemed to be deeper than ever before.

I shook my head. "It's always just me. Everything there lately seems like it's always just me." Dejected and tired, this was the last discussion I wanted to have right now.

I could see the frustration building in him; his eyes

changed to dark blue as he clenched his jaw and balled up his fists.

"Next time you need help, you ask me to come. I will not have you working yourself to exhaustion when I want to help, and can help you. Kate, I know you have done things on your own over there for a while, but you don't have to anymore. I don't know if I can understand why so much has fallen onto your shoulders alone, but I'm here now." I hadn't ever seen Tyler like this before, so I just nodded, looked at my feet and bit the corner of my lip.

"I'm going to shower," I said as I avoided looking at him and turned towards the stairs.

"Kate, please talk to me. Why is it always just you? What is happening at your parent's place?"

"Please, Tyler; I don't want to have this discussion."

"No, we are going to have it now, because if you don't tell me what's happening, I will drive to your parent's place and ask them."

"There is nobody there to ask. Mom and Dad left for San Antonio yesterday."

"What's there?"

"Nothing that I know of but a getaway, holiday, second honeymoon... I don't know. Dad feels it's time for him to back away. He wants to have more time with mom, so they picked up and left."

I could tell there were so many things he wanted to say.

"Don't blame them, Tyler. They think now that we are married, I'd ask you for help. As far as they know, you were helping me today. That's the only way they would go."

"Other than when you needed help with that calf, you have never once asked me to spend the day helping you."

I could tell he was crushed. His shoulders slumped and he let out a sigh.

"Here I thought we had been building a relationship, trust, and being there for one another, but I guess I was wrong." Tyler turned and walked back to the kitchen. I climbed the stairs and turned on the shower.

I came back downstairs about 20 minutes later, hair wet, in some comfy clothes to a perfectly set table, candlelight, a glass of rosé and an irritated husband waiting patiently. I smiled at him and took my place across the table. We ate in silence, but I knew something was bothering him. I had been sensing it for a few days, but in typical *me* fashion, I would avoid the topic.

"May I ask you a question?" Tyler put down his fork and wiped his mouth with a napkin.

I looked over my glass of wine, which I had just brought to my lips. I set the glass down and nodded.

"What's happened? When we were in New Orleans, you were bold, made decisions easily, laughed more, were confident, and now you are a shell of the woman I saw there."

I sat there silently and shrugged my shoulders.

"Nope, that's not going to cut it, Kate. Please talk to me," he pleaded. I looked at him. He was trying to build a life with us as a couple, and I was shutting him out.

"I don't know Tyler. It's always been a struggle trying to find my place. I'm used to being dismissed, forgotten about and ignored, so it's just easier to blend in to the background. Very few people take what I have to say seriously, so I've quit trying to tell a story because I just get made fun of. Lately, I have been feeling like that all over again. As far as not asking for help, I knew you would drop everything to help me, but you have your own place to run and people to answer to. It was just easier not to ask."

I never looked up at him. I knew if I did, I wouldn't have been able to tell him what he wanted to know. Blinking quickly, I tried to hold back the tears that threatened to fall.

I LOOKED at the woman across the table from me, who'd literally shrunk before my eyes. I needed to hold her. She needed to know she was important, that she mattered. I stood from my chair and made it to her side in two strides, wrapped my arms around her and held her. At first she was tense, but in a matter of moments she relaxed into me.

"You are the most important thing in my life, Kate. I'm sorry you've been feeling invisible, but you are my light. You deserve every good thing this world has to offer, and your opinion matters to me. I will listen to anything you have to say. I love you, Kate."

I could feel her shoulders shaking; the place where her head was laying on my chest became damp with her tears. We sat on the floor in each other's embrace for an hour.

"Thank you," she whispered before we stood up.

"Kate, you are my world and shame on anyone who makes you feel second best." My hand was on her cheek, fingers entwined in her hair, our foreheads resting on one another. I could see the corners of her mouth rise in a slight smile, and she ever so slightly ran her tongue across her lips before she parted them, tilted her head and brought her lips to mine. Softly at first, but the hesitation turned into unchecked passion. Our hands began exploring each other. I pulled her as close to me as I could. My wife had let me in, had let me see her heart, and suddenly it became clear to me that this tough-as-nails outer shell was a ruse to keep people at bay and protect her heart.

From that day on, we spent our mornings together at the Patterson ranch. I enjoyed watching Kate in her element. She had a way with her cattle. She wandered through them, running her hand over their backs. I hadn't ever seen a cow whisperer before, but I felt that's exactly what she was.

"Let's go have lunch," I said in her ear as I wrapped my arms around her. Kate turned and put her arms around my neck and nodded. We finished up, closed gates, and walked hand in hand to the truck.

"Thank you for all your help, Ty. I didn't realize how much I needed it. I can't even tell you how much I'm enjoying our mornings together."

I looked down into Kate's eyes.

"It's been the best part of my day," I whispered before our lips met.

Later that afternoon, while buried under a mountain of paperwork, there was a knock on my office door. "Come in."

"So how are things over at Kate's place?" Rob asked as he walked through my office door and sat down in front of me.

I couldn't help but smile. Any mention of Kate made my heart soar. I was proud of my wife and wanted everyone to know.

"Things are really good. She's amazing with her cattle. I can see why she's able to get things done alone. She has a system. Yes, it would be easier with more people around, but she makes it work. I'm really impressed and think she needs to help rework our operation."

Rob appeared to be impressed. "How's your relationship? Is it going as smoothly?" Rob got up and poured a cup of coffee for himself before bringing the carafe over to my desk and filling my cup.

Sitting back in my chair, I ran my hands through my hair, then entwined my fingers behind my head.

"It's going well." I wasn't sure how much to say. We weren't much on talking about our relationships, but I needed to talk to someone.

"Hey, I wouldn't have asked if I didn't really want to hear the answer," Rob replied before taking a sip of his coffee.

"It has its moments. She told her parents I would help her out when they were gone, but she never asked me until I basically forced her to accept it. I want her more than I can even say, but she keeps intimacy at arm's length. I have never waited this long for any woman before. There seems to still be a lack of trust on her part, and I can't figure it out." I moved my gaze from staring out the window to looking at Rob. "I told her I loved her."

Rob's eyebrows shot up. "And? You can't keep me hanging here."

"She didn't really say anything back. She just said 'thank you'." Resting my elbows on the desk and my head on my fist, I couldn't say more. I had no words.

"That's rough. You see she loves you, right? I can see it when she looks at you. You are her only concern. She came over and asked Mom what your favorite foods were, what you hated to eat. She never stops flirting with you, but I think it's because you do the same to her. Even Jessica said something the other night about you both being perfect for each other. She might not have said those three words, but she definitely loves you."

"I know, but it would be nice to hear the words." I was pouting and Rob chuckled.

"Hang in there, brother. It's only a matter of time, and I don't think it will be a long time." He downed the last of his coffee before standing and leaving my office.

CHAPTER 24

The Memorial Day Rodeo was a big event in our town. Entry fees were taken and donated to our local Veteran Support Association. Anyone who had competed in rodeos in the past entered for this great cause.

Tyler and I were no exception. I hadn't barrel raced since last year's rodeo, and I wasn't sure the last time Ty wrestled a steer in competition. I was nervous, but then I always seemed to be before any rodeo. Ty loaded our horses and we headed out to the rodeo grounds. I exercised my horse alongside Tyler, and he coached me through a few practice runs. I was ready.

This was the first rodeo where I had let anyone help me into the arena. Tyler rode alongside me until I kicked Shadow in the ribs. She was off like a shot. I hit my strides around barrel one, tore off to barrel two and made a perfect turn. Coming around barrel three wasn't as smooth, but we rounded it okay and she flew home.

I had forgotten how much I loved riding like the wind. When you and your horse work together, it is magic. I slowed her up and listened for my time. 16.765 seconds. I patted

Shadow on the neck in praise. Tyler was waiting for me when I got off my horse, and he grabbed me and spun me around.

"That was amazing," he said excitedly and then kissed me. We were talking about the ride when we heard a commotion and yelling. Tyler and I looked up and we saw a bull heading for us at full speed. Tyler shoved me out of the way and was run over head-on by the bull. It turned and tossed him in the air like a rag-doll. Finally, it settled down, and the stock contractors and cowboys standing around did their best to get it corralled again. I ran over to Tyler, lying in a heap on the ground. I could see he was breathing, but he wasn't moving. The medical team pushed me out of the way and took over. He was carefully rolled onto a stretcher and loaded into the ambulance.

"Kate, we're taking him to the Union. You can follow us." I don't know how I found the truck, and I don't remember who unhooked the trailer, but I caught up to the ambulance. I followed it to the hospital, registered Ty, and waited. It seemed like forever.

"Mrs. Morton?"

"That's me," I said, as I jumped off my chair.

"Please come with me."

"Kate, wait." I heard a call behind me. I turned and saw Rob was sprinting to follow me. We walked into a private waiting room and sat down with the doctor.

"Mrs. Morton, I won't sugarcoat it for you. This isn't good news. He has a concussion, a broken collarbone, several broken ribs, a fractured scapula, as well as a lacerated spleen. He's going in for surgery to repair his spleen, if possible, and then we will deal with other things. You can go to the waiting room on the OR floor, and the medical team will find you when they have updates." The doctor left the room and Rob and I found our way to the waiting room on the surgical floor.

I was staring at the doors, willing them to open, when I suddenly remembered the horses.

"Rob, the horses need to be taken home. They can't stay there for the night; we didn't bring enough feed."

Rob shook his head, "Dad was taking them home and then he and Mom will come here."

I nodded and went back to staring at the door.

"What about Addie?"

Rob smiled. "I cut my date with Jessica short and had her take Addie home." I looked at Rob and smiled.

"I really like her, Kate."

"Have you told her that?" I asked him. He just looked at me like I was crazy.

"You need to, especially after this."

"Have you told Ty you love him?" The way Rob's eyes were looking at me felt like they were staring into my soul.

"What are you talking about?" I snipped at him.

"Look, I know an arranged marriage wasn't what either of you would have chosen for yourselves, but it happened. You would have to be blind not to see that you two are madly in love with each other. I know he's told you, but have you told him?"

"No," was all I could say. He was right, and I didn't like it when the Morton men were right.

Ty's mom and dad showed up a little while later. Sandra walked in like an angel and handed me coffee. "It's going to be a long night, you're going to need this." I smiled when she sat down beside me.

"Thank you." It felt like forever before anyone came out.

"Mrs. Morton?" I went to stand, but Tyler's dad got to the doctor first.

"Well doctor, what's going on?"

"I'm sorry sir, but it says here Kate Morton is Tyler's next of kin, so I will be speaking to her."

I stepped in front of a livid Brian.

"I'm Kate Morton."

"Mrs. Morton, we have repaired Tyler's spleen, and we will be watching him closely. If we have to go back in, we will have to remove it because there was a lot of damage. The orthopedic surgeon will be operating to realign his collarbone tomorrow, but he will tell you more about that. Tyler will be spending the next few days in ICU so we can make sure he is closely monitored. Here's my card; if you need anything or have any questions, please feel free to contact me. The nurses will come and get you when you can see him."

"Thank you," I said as he turned and walked away. I felt like I had gotten no real information, I was still in the wait-and-see-what-happens phase. No good news, and no bad news.

We moved into yet another waiting room. Rob called Jessica and decided he was going to head home. "Call if there is any new information."

I nodded and he left.

"We should go do evening chores quickly, and then come back," Tyler's dad said.

"Are you going to be okay here alone?" Sandra asked.

I nodded, "Yeah, I'll be fine. Go, it's okay." I sat in the waiting room alone, and for the first time, I let myself cry.

"Mrs. Morton?"

I looked up and saw a nurse.

"I'm sorry, yes that's me. Please call me Kate. Mrs. Morton sounds weird."

She smiled, "Since you are the only family here, why don't you come in and sit with Tyler? We just finished shift change so we can let you see him."

I jumped off the chair and followed her into the ICU. He was in room 5, right across from the desk. Every nurse could see him from where they sat. I knew that couldn't be good. She motioned to the chair, and for me to have a seat. I reached out to touch him but stopped. The nurse must have seen my actions because she spoke up.

"It's okay, you can hold his hand."

"Thank you," I said quietly. I took a hold of his hand and started to talk to him quietly. On all the sappy shows, they talk to people who are in comas and say life changing things to the person, and then somehow, they miraculously wake up. I must not have been sharing enough life changing information because Ty wasn't waking up. Another tear rolled down my cheek. He was so vulnerable at this moment. He didn't look like himself at all. He was puffy from all the fluids he was receiving, not to mention the swelling from his injuries, and several shades of black, purple, and an angry red covered the majority of his exposed skin. I couldn't even imagine how much that was going to hurt. I sat beside him, watching the machines keep track of his oxygenation levels, heard the hiss of the oxygen flowing through his nasal cannula, and watched the line on the heart monitor bounce with his heart beat. I listened to the IV pump as it whirred and delivered the fluids that were keeping him hydrated, and I never let go of his hand.

One of the nurses came in a while later. "Kate, Tyler's parents are here wondering if they can see him. Our policy is only two visitors at a time, so they can come in one at a time if you want to stay"

I shook myself out of the daze I was in and stood. "No, it's okay, they can both come in. I can step outside for a few minutes."

"Hey sleepy head, your mom and dad want to see you. I'll

be back when they're done." I squeezed his hand. "Tyler Alexander Morton, you better not leave me. I will not make it through another arranged marriage," I leaned down and whispered in his ear.

I left his room and walked through the doors into the waiting room, where Tyler's parents waited, and then they walked past me into the ICU when they saw me coming out. I sat on the uncomfortable plastic couch and exhaled. I closed my eyes for a moment, and felt someone sit down beside me. I was a little annoyed that in this large waiting room, they had to sit right by me. I opened my eyes.

"Gavin!" I stood and gave him a hug. "Did you just get in? How did you know? Did you come with your parents?"

He smiled.

"I chartered a flight immediately after Rob called. I saw mom and dad walking in, but they don't know I'm here. I wanted to see you before I talked to them."

"I'm happy you're here," I said as I hugged him again. We sat watching the TV that was up in the corner of the room. We couldn't find the remote, so we were stuck watching the Food Network. I wasn't complaining, the July 4th holiday baking shows were on, and I loved watching them. It fed my secret longing to be a world class home baker. Tyler's expanding waistband was proof of that.

"I have to get something to eat, want anything?" Gavin asked, standing.

"If there is a sandwich and a salad I would eat."

He nodded and walked out of the room. Brian and Sandra came back to the waiting room a few minutes later.

"They're doing some tests so we had to leave," Sandra explained. They sat down close to me, but I didn't mention Gavin. They could find out when he came back.

"Hey Kate, I hope egg salad is OK, that's all… hey Mom, Dad."

Sandra jumped up and hugged Gavin.

"I'm so glad you're here," she cried into his shoulder.

"Son, it's good to see you." Brian shook Gavin's hand.

I noticed coolness between the men and wondered what the reason for it could be. We all sat down and I ate what Gavin found in the cafeteria. The door opened and Naomi, the nurse looking after Tyler, came out.

"I can let one of you in now. We're monitoring a few of his machines, so we don't want two in the room at the moment."

"Gavin, you can go in. You haven't seen him yet."

Gavin stood and headed towards the nurse, placing his hand on her lower back, grinning from ear to ear. He walked closer to her as they walked down the hall. I could hear his laugh. I smiled. One thing all the Morton boys are good at is flirting. I giggled to myself and shook my head.

Gavin came out less jovial than when he went in, and the doctor followed him out.

"Tyler's condition is stable, for now. His blood work has come back showing good signs. I think you all need to go home and get some sleep," he said, looking directly at me.

"We'll call you if anything changes. I wouldn't send you home if I didn't think things were good."

"Doctor, can I go and say good night to him?"

"Absolutely."

"Kate, we're going to head out then. If you need anything, or if things change, please call, no matter the time." I hugged Sandra, and she and Brian left.

"I'll wait for you, Kate."

I smiled at Gavin and said "Okay." I followed the doctor

back into Tyler's room. Tyler hadn't changed; he was still lying there, lifeless, on a hospital bed.

"Well, Cowboy, I'm going to head home for the night. You better be here when I get back in the morning. Gavin is going to come home with me. Sleep well, and I'll see you tomorrow." I kissed his forehead and left. I made it back to the waiting room and broke down again. Gavin wrapped his arms around me and let me cry.

"Do you know I haven't spent a night without him beside me since we got married? I know it's crazy, but we made the decision on the day of our wedding that it was a non-negotiable."

"You've both made this situation look easy. I know it hasn't been, but you and Tyler would have found each other regardless. You fit together. It's like you've been a couple forever."

"That means a lot Gavin, thank you." We got into the truck and headed to the house.

"Hey, do you think that nurse was cute?"

I burst out laughing,

"Are you seriously trying to pick up Tyler's nurse? Stupid question, of course you are, you're a Morton! Yes, I think she's cute."

"She said she's working tomorrow. Maybe I should ask her for her number."

I didn't answer him because I knew he would. There was no chit chat when we got to the house. Gavin took his bag and went to his room, and I went to mine and collapsed on the bed.

My sleep was fitful; every time I closed my eyes all I could see was Tyler flying through the air. I heard the thud as he hit the ground and the screams and yelling trying to get the bull away from him. I walked down to the kitchen and thought maybe a drink would help me sleep. I stopped myself, because if I needed to go back to the hospital, I needed to be able to drive. My mind drifted to the hospital and I felt like I should have stayed, or maybe I should go back. I argued with myself about going back and staying home. Sitting here felt better than sitting in the waiting room, so I curled up in Tyler's chair and grabbed a blanket.

I stared out the window at the darkness and prayed that he would wake up and be alright. Sitting here was driving me crazy so I walked out to the barn and sat watching the horses sleep or eat. Just listening to them breathe was relaxing. I felt like I was being lulled to sleep. I dozed off and ended up getting a few hours of peaceful sleep.

"Kate? Kate!"

I heard my name being called and I opened my eyes. For a moment, I thought Tyler was standing in front of me. I blinked the sleep away and realized it was Gavin.

"What are you doing out here? I looked all over the house for you."

"I couldn't sleep so I sat up for a while, and then needed to get out of the house. The barns have always been a peaceful place for me. I guess I fell asleep." I pulled the blanket around my shoulders a little tighter and walked back into the house, followed closely by Gavin.

We barely got in the house when the phone rang. I rushed to grab it, hoping it was the hospital with good news.

"Hello?" I answered apprehensively,

"Kate, it is Dr. Fraser. I'm just calling to tell you Tyler had a really good night. His blood work is stable, his breathing and heart rate are normal, so the orthopedic surgeon is taking him in to fix his collarbone and shoulder. You aren't going to make it in before he goes down to surgery, so take your time getting here. He will be coming back to the ICU so you can come to the waiting room and call in to let the nurses know you're here. Do you have any questions?" I felt like I had forgotten how to speak.

"Umm, how long is the surgery going to take?" He answered my questions and we hung up.

Gavin and I headed to the hospital a short time later to wait for Tyler to come back from surgery.

"Kate, you need to go in."

Tyler's nurse, Naomi, had come out to the waiting room. I panicked and walked past her so fast she ran to catch up. I rounded the corner and saw Tyler sitting up, and he was awake.

I stopped on a dime and started to cry.

"Well I'm not sure that's exactly what I thought you would do."

I walked the rest of the way to his bed, leaned down and kissed him.

"I was so scared you were going to leave me, and I hadn't told you something very important. I love you, Tyler Morton. I don't know what my life would be without you." I kissed him again.

"If I had known all it would take was me getting all torn up by a bull for you to say 'I love you', I would have done it sooner."

"If you weren't fresh out of surgery, I would hit you."

He smirked and we talked a bit longer, but it was clear he was still groggy from all of the anesthesia and pain meds. When I saw he was starting to tire out, I squeezed his hand as I stood up and said, "I should call your parents. I'll send Gavin in while I'm doing that."

"Gavin's here?"

"He flew in after Rob called to tell him what happened. I'll call Rob, too." I didn't wait to cry again, but the tears came when I left Tyler's room.

"Gavin, he's awake. Go see him." We hugged and Gavin followed Naomi in. I made calls to Sandra and Rob, and they both said they were on their way to the hospital. Gavin came out to the waiting room a few minutes later, holding a piece of paper.

"You got it," I exclaimed excitedly.

"Well of course I did. They're moving him to a regular post-op floor later this afternoon, so I had to make my move."

y recovery was slow, and I was cranky for most of it.

I was feeling better, but I wasn't cleared for more than book work. I heard Kate come in after her day of working with the cattle. She didn't come to find me, she just went up the stairs, and the shower went on a few minutes later. I wanted to see her. Dang it. Carefully, I made my way up the stairs, but hesitated at the bathroom door. I had yet to breech this layer of privacy with her, but I needed to see her, so I went in any way. I didn't have any intentions of rounding the corner to the shower, but I could see her reflection in the mirror, and I couldn't believe what I saw.

She was standing almost cautiously, letting the water run down her front, washing the dirt, mud and grime from her face and arms. Her hair had clumps of what I thought was grass matted into it. I could feel her hesitation to turn her back into the water, like she knew it was going to hurt.

Slowly, Kate turned and let the water hit her back. She'd

braced her hands against the tile wall and didn't move. It looked like she was barely breathing, pain evident on her face.

Taking a few deep breaths, I rested my head against the wall. "What in the hell happened to you?" She didn't turn around, and I couldn't hide the anger in my voice.

"I got tossed around in the sorting pen, nothing major."

"Nothing major? Kate, your back looks like someone took a cheese grater to it and then slathered on red paint."

"Well, thanks for that graphic description." Kate said through gritted teeth. "I'm fine, Tyler. I'll be out shortly. Please, just give me some privacy."

I was so mad that I knew I'd say something I'd regret, so I caved to her wishes and slammed the door behind me. I noticed Kate's towel was still on the bed, and when I heard the running water stop, I opened the door just a crack and handed it through to her.

"Thank you," came from the other side of the door, so softly I almost missed it. I went and sat on the bed, and waited.

"Lay on your stomach, I have something that will help with the pain." My voice was controlled, but in a register I'd never heard before. I wanted answers. I wanted to know what happened, but right now, I needed to control my temper and look after my wife. Kate looked at me with tears welling in her eyes. She nodded. I carefully sat down beside her on the bed and pulled the towel down to the small of her back. I saw her tense up.

"This will help, but it will not be nice going on."

I heard her whisper, "Okay," in acknowledgment. Dipping my fingers in the ointment, I reached toward her back. I didn't know where to start, so I started at the top and worked my way down. As I applied the ointment, I could feel every flinch and every muffled sob she tried to hold back. When I was done, I walked around to my side of the bed and lay down beside her. I didn't know where to touch her, so I just took her hand in mine. She grasped mine back and whispered,

"Thank you."

"Are you going to tell me what happened?" I quizzed.

"I told you, I got roughed up against the panels by a cow or two." She yawned and could hardly keep her eyes open.

"Sleep. I'll make you some food when you wake up." I slid off the bed and went downstairs. Something wasn't adding up, so I went outside and called Rob.

"Hey, how's Kate?" Rob asked before he even said 'hi'.

"She's pretty banged up, and she won't tell me what happened. She just keeps saying she got hit by a few cows."

"A few cows? There were fifty-five in the pen, plus calves. One cow got ornery, looking for her calf, and started charging. That was enough to get them all worked up, and they all started going crazy. Things had been going great, and she was trying to cut out that calf, but she got knocked down. Too many cows in that corral and one overprotective momma."

I rubbed my forehead. "Who was in charge of the gate? Who let that many in the corral at once? We haven't had an accident around here in years. This seems crazy to me."

"Ty, it was dad. We kept yelling for him to open the gate, and he did, but he definitely didn't rush."

"He was testing her like he used to do to us?" I asked through gritted teeth.

"I think so, only this time it didn't go like it should have. Gavin and I got in there as quickly as we could climb over the panels, but she had already taken the brunt of it."

I hung up the phone without so much as a goodbye to Rob. It looked like it was time to have it out with my father. Nothing he had done up to now had risked anyone's life, but he needed to be called out on his stupid, reckless behavior.

I went up to check on Kate and found she was sound asleep, so I headed for the main house.

I walked in without even a hello.

"Where's Dad?" I asked Mom, who was in the kitchen. She looked up, and I knew she was aware of what happened.

"*WHERE IS HE?*" I yelled, slapping my hand on the table. At that moment, I didn't care that I was yelling at my mother. She'd protected him for too many years, and this time, he'd taken it too far. She never kept him from 'testing' us, but I sure as hell would not stand by and let it happen to my wife, or any future generations that come along on this ranch.

"In his office," she quietly replied, having lost all color in her face.

I turned on my heel and felt my ribs catch, causing me to groan.

"Tyler, are you okay?" she asked as she ran over to me.

"Fine, Mom. But he's lucky I'm hurt, because if I was fully healed right now, I would probably beat him to a pulp."

"You don't mean that, Tyler," she said, walking around to look me in the eye.

"Mom, you haven't seen her. It's worse than what he used to do to us." My voice barely registered above a whisper. I knew there were tears in my eyes, and I could see the tears in hers.

"I'm sorry I never put a stop to this when you boys were younger."

"I'm stopping it today." I stood as straight as I could and walked to his office.

I stormed into Dad's office, slamming the door open so hard it bounced off the wall. Dad was behind his desk, talking on the phone like nothing bad had happened today.

"Harold, I'm going to have to call you back." He hung up the phone and looked at me with what I'm sure he thought was a fiercely intimidating expression. "I know you know better than to barge into my office, son."

"Shut your mouth and listen! If you ever again put my wife in danger like you did today, I will do the same thing to you. Your only saving grace right now is I'm not a hundred percent. You have done some despicable things over the years, but this takes the cake."

"Oh please, Tyler. You are always so dramatic. She wasn't in any real danger." He leaned back in his chair and folded his hands on top of his head, clearly not having a care in the world.

Seeing red, I slammed my hand down on his desk and reached over, grabbed him by the front of his shirt and dragged him on to the desk with my one good arm. I held in a groan of pain. There was no way I was going to show him I was hurting.

"I'm warning you, old man, mess with her again and you will regret the day I was born into this family."

I pushed him back as I let go of his shirt, and he plopped into his chair, staring at me. I walked out of his office and slammed the door behind me. I took a few steps down the hall and slumped against the wall. Out of nowhere, Rob and Gavin appeared, grabbed a hold of me and took me home.

"He's lost his mind," I said as they helped me to the couch.

"We're not arguing with that one," Gavin replied, sitting down across from me.

CHAPTER 26

My back was healed from the cattle issue, and I knew Rob had been working hard, alone, while I healed. I had talked to Jessica, and she mentioned she hadn't seen him all week, so I went to find him. I found him in the barn, brushing out his horse.

"Rob, I need to talk to you."

"What's wrong?" There was a slight panic in his voice.

"Nothing, sorry. I didn't mean to worry you. I want to see if we can keep Addie for the rest of the day and tomorrow. You've been working like crazy while I've been hurt and have had no time with Jessica."

He looked over his horse, and I knew the answer was yes. He looked tired, but renewed.

"She's at the house with Mom."

"Perfect. Have a wonderful time. I don't want to see you until tomorrow night."

I turned and walked out of the barn.

With Addie picked up, we swung by Rob's place and

grabbed clothes, her teddy bear, and her blanket before walking back to our house.

"Auntie Kate, would you teach me how to barrel race?" Looking down at her, I knew I should say no, but heard myself saying, sure let's do it. Dropping her things at the door, we went to the barn, and I saddled JP for Addie before leading them out of the barn to the outdoor riding arena.

"OK, the most important thing is to trust your horse. The second most important thing is to listen to me. The second you don't listen, we are done. Deal?"

"Deal."

"You need to get used to navigating the pattern. Your speed will follow eventually. So you will walk out of the alleyway and head to barrel one. In time, you will decide if you enjoy going left or right first. Most riders take the left barrel first. You round it, head for the second, round it and head for the third. Cross in front of it and then around, then you head back home. Are you ready to give it a try?"

Addie nodded, and I walked her out of the alley and let her go.

JP was my oldest horse; a thirteen-year-old chestnut Quarter Horse. He was steady, calm, and perfect for a younger rider. I didn't have any worry about Addie riding him. A few minutes later, I felt a hand glide along my hip and then felt warmth beside me.

"She finally talked someone into teaching her."

I turned to look at Tyler.

"What do you mean, 'finally'?"

"She's been asking for two years. The excuses have been we're too busy, she's too little, nobody really knows how to teach her, and a flat out 'no' from Rob."

"Did I overstep? We can make this a one and done thing." I felt panicked, like I had screwed up big time.

"No, if anyone can and should teach her, it's you. The way you rode at the rodeo was amazing. I also did a little digging and found out you were pretty good back in the day. No, sorry, you were very good."

Shaking my head and rolling my eyes, I turned from Tyler to look at Addie. She was making another lap around the barrels. Folding my arms over the fence rail, Tyler snuggled up behind me and placed his hands on the rail on either side of me. I felt him lower his head and say,

"You really don't see it, do you?"

Turning to look at him, I furrow my brow in confusion.

"See what?"

"How talented you are. Kate, I worked with you on your turf, with your cattle, and I haven't ever seen anyone handle animals as well as you did. You make people feel at ease with very few words. Addie absolutely adores you, and so do I. You are a very special person, Kate."

I could feel the blush creeping up my neck into my cheeks. I couldn't find the words needed to reply. Maybe there wasn't any need. So I wrapped my arms around his waist and we stood there in each other's arms, watching Addie.

"Why did you quit? You were a state champion! You rode a few years at the National Finals Rodeo! This wasn't just a few rodeos here and there. Why did you quit?" he asked the question everyone asked. The question I had dodged for seven years, but I couldn't brush him off. He wanted to know, and I knew he would ask until I broke down and told him.

"I stopped caring. I stopped caring how my runs were. Every event felt like I was riding into a torture chamber. A pile of rodeos every weekend became crazy to me. I lost my competitive edge. It sounds lame, but I just didn't want to do it anymore. I was tired of the scene, tired of the games. It all ended when I caught Stephen, the guy I was dating at the time, in my trailer with a buckle bunny. We weren't just dating; we were talking about a future together. I loaded up JP and pulled out of the rodeos I had entered the rest of that year and came home. To answer your next question, no, I don't miss it. The Memorial Day rodeo once a year is enough for me." Leaning against the fence, I looked up at him.

"Well, he was a fool and obviously the stupidest man on the planet. I think you could ride again, but I won't mention it. If you want to teach Addie, I'll smooth it over with Rob."

My heart soared. Once again, my knight in shining armor came riding to the rescue. I looked back over at Addie. She hadn't stopped smiling since she got into the arena. She and JP were one.

"I also think you just lost your horse," he said. I turned to face Tyler and saw his eyes were dancing as he smiled down at me.

"He is good for her. Knows what he can and can't do, but he will always be mine." I carefully wrapped my arms around Tyler's waist, and we watched together until Addie was tired.

ADDIE WAS out in minutes when she went to bed.

"So what's the reason Rob doesn't want Addie racing?" Kate sat down beside me and cuddled up close, so I wrapped my arm around her.

"Well, Addie's mom used to ride. Rob met her at a rodeo. During the few years they were married before Addie came along, they were together all the time on the road. After she was born, Samantha was happy to be home for a while, but as soon as Rob could look after her without Samantha around, she was gone."

Kate was staring at me, waiting for the rest of the story. I looked over my shoulder to make sure Addie wasn't on the stairs.

"Rob and Addie went to Oklahoma to surprise Samantha one weekend. It was Addie's third birthday, so Rob figured it was perfect. He found her in her trailer with another guy. Turns out, Rob knew him. He was a stock contractor, and when the truth finally came out, we learned she had been seeing him since she had gone back to the circuit. Rob and Addie came home, and he filed for divorce the following morning. They did joint custody for a while, but she would be a no show more and more often. One day, Rob got a call from his lawyer saying Samantha was requesting to relinquish all custody of Addie."

Kate was silent, just taking it in.

"Poor Addie. I can't even imagine someone rejecting that little girl. I should probably let Rob know what I've done."

"I'll text him tomorrow. I don't want to take away from his time with Jessica."

Kate placed her head on my shoulder and her hand on my chest. We sat in silence for a while.

"I'm going to bed," she whispered, and kissed my cheek. I grabbed her hand, and she helped me up.

"I think I'll go as well."

We climbed the stairs hand in hand.

Lying in bed, I couldn't help but look over at Kate. She was even expressive when she read her book.

"You are at a good part, aren't you?"

Looking over at me, she smiled and nodded. It made me feel bad for interrupting her book.

"I want to say something, and please don't take this as anything other than an observation."

Her face changed to concern and uncertainty.

"You are going to be a wonderful mom."

She fidgeted and laughed nervously.

"I'm not saying we start tonight, Kate, but I just wanted you to know my thoughts. We can talk about this another time."

She nodded and went back to her book, but didn't read for very long.

"Night, Tyler." Turning her light off, she rolled over. We had been cuddling while we fell asleep lately, but tonight, my arms were empty.

CHAPTER 27

My day was busy between Addie, wanting to ride and trying to prep for family supper. I felt like I was running in circles. The other thing that was occupying my mind was Tyler's declaration about me being a wonderful mom. Being a mom wasn't something I had ever given much thought to.

"Hello, dear, what can I help you with?" I spun around and saw Sandra walking into the kitchen, carrying a bowl of potato salad.

"I don't know if I'm coming or going. I need to make burgers, so that's my next thing. Would you start the salad?" Sandra jumped into action and buzzed around, getting things ready.

I made burgers and turned the water on to wash my hands. I left the water running and grabbed my rings.

"NO!" I watched my wedding band circle the drain and slip into the pipes.

"What happened?" Sandra came running over.

"My wedding band!" I didn't have to finish. She knew what happened.

"Um, hopefully it's in the trap?" Not a reassuring hope from my mother-in-law.

"I don't want to tell Tyler. Maybe he won't notice?" I looked at Sandra with a cautious hope. She shook her head no.

"Dear, he won't care; he'll fix it." Sandra put her arms around my shoulders.

"I know, but I just wanted today to be perfect, and ripping apart the sink isn't exactly perfect." I walked out to the porch where Tyler and his dad were.

"Hey honey, I have a problem."

Tyler turned to face me and looked rather confused. I was pretty sure I had never called him 'honey' in the time we had been together. Sandra walked behind the swing and rested her hands on Brian's shoulders.

"Well, a funny thing happened. When I was making hamburgers and took my rings off, and then I went to put them back on, one fell down the drain." I got quieter as I got to the end of the story. I looked up at Tyler, and I couldn't tell if he was mad or what.

All of the sudden, Brian and Tyler started laughing. They stood up in sync, and Tyler headed for the kitchen. Brian headed for the shop, calling over his shoulder, "I'll go get the pipe wrench."

"Darlin', you do not know how many rings Dad has pulled out of drain pipes. Mom was doing this constantly. She even had one go through the garbage disposal. Don't worry about it." Tyler kissed me on the head and laughed.

I smiled and followed him into the kitchen.

We cleaned the mess up from the impromptu plumbing issue just as Rob and Jessica drove up.

"Daddy!" Addie ran to him and jumped into his arms from the top step. "I'm learning to barrel race. Auntie Kate is a brilliant teacher, even if she won't let me ride faster than a walk," Addie whispered the last part, hoping I wouldn't hear.

"I heard you're learning. That's great Addie. Let's go eat." Rob walked past Tyler and I without a word.

"He may be angrier than I thought," Tyler said, and put his arm around me.

"I'm sorry." I leaned on him momentarily, forgetting his ribs were still tender. He let out a groan, and I moved away quickly.

"I'm sorry!" I squeaked out, as I gently placed my hand on his side. He nodded, and we joined the others at the table.

We had an OK evening, filled with tension between Brian and me, and tension from Rob. I hated this. How was I going to fix it? Sandra and Brian left for their home, which left Rob, Addie, and Jessica.

"Addie, why don't you run out to the barn and show Jessica JP, and say goodbye to him. I need to talk to Uncle Tyler and Auntie Kate."

Addie jumped off the porch, grabbed Jessica's hand, and they ran to the barn.

"I'm going to say this once. Teach her how to ride properly, teach her about the sport, but no rodeos. She doesn't get entered at all. Am I understood? There will be no talk of winning and buckles."

I looked down at the ground and back up at Rob.

"Understood. Rob, I didn't mean to cause trouble."

Rob held his hand up to stop me.

"I know. I also know you had no idea what had gone on. This is something she has wanted to do for a few years now. I don't mind her learning; I just don't want her anywhere close to the competing circuit. It has nothing to do with the rodeo really; I just don't want her to run into Samantha out of the blue. I've protected her this long from that woman, and I don't need her showing up now. Addie doesn't even remember her at this point, and I don't know what would happen if she saw her."

"I promise you I would never go behind your back and do anything like that."

Just at that moment, Addison and Jessica came back to the porch.

"Well, ladies, we'd better be heading home. Addie you have school tomorrow, and Jessica is heading back into town."

"Thanks, Auntie Kate, I had a great time. See ya, Uncle Ty." We both got hugs, and then they were gone. The house was quiet again. Tyler led me to our swing, and we sat quietly together, enjoying the evening.

LATE THE NEXT WEEK, the doctor finally cleared me to work again. I was back working long hours in the office, and with the cattle. Gavin had stayed around until I was back on my feet, and it sounded like we would see more of him again since he had begun dating Naomi.

I got home after a long day of sorting cattle with my brothers and heard music blaring as I got to the porch. I looked through the living room window and I saw Kate and Addison having a dance party in the living room.

"Ty, what are you doing?" Rob asked me when he and Gavin got to the house. I motioned for them to look.

"I have to say it's been so good to have Kate here, Ty. Addison loves her, and with her mom who knows where, Kate has filled an enormous gap for her." We sat on the porch, not wanting to interrupt their party, and enjoyed listening to them laughing.

"I should go get Addie. I still have to make supper. The days of getting a meal after these marathon days are over," Rob said as he stood up.

"Yeah, it's not like Mom to not feed us," I said. We opened the door and the girls stopped mid-dance move. Addison ran over to Rob and gave him a big hug. "Come on, Squish, we need to get home."

"Aww, Dad, no. We're having so much fun!"

"Sorry, kid, I need to make supper."

"Please, stay," Kate said, before they could walk out the door. "There's tons of food."

Addie looked up at Rob with her big blue eyes.

"Okay, I can't fight both of you."

"Yes!" Addison whooped and gave a little shimmy. It was easy to find a smile when she was excited.

"Everyone, go wash up. Supper is in five minutes," Kate said, as she walked out of the living room. I followed her into the kitchen.

"How was your day?" I asked.

"Nope, sorry Cowboy, you wash up too," she said, as she pointed to the bathroom. Kate stood in front of me with her hands on her hips, making me want to ravish her right that second. I couldn't let the moment go by without stealing a kiss. Taking steps closer to her, she started to back up. The grin growing across her face guaranteed me a little teasing before I got the kiss I was looking for.

Supper was over, Rob and Addie went to their house, Gavin went for drinks with Naomi when her shift was over, so it was once again just Kate and I.

"Will you tell me about your day now?" I asked.

"It was great. I had so much fun with Addie. She has really come out of her shell these past few weeks."

"Rob says he sees a difference in her since you got here. He really is grateful for all the time you're spending with her."

"She's a great kid. He's done really well with her, and I'm happy to help when Rob needs it."

We sat out on the porch swing listening to the crickets sing and waiting for the stars to peak out for the night. This time of year was free of bugs and the heat that would drive us into the house in the evening, so we took advantage of it.

"You know, I used to think this view was the most beautiful thing about this house," I shifted in my seat to look at her, "but then you came along and changed that." Tucking a stray tendril behind her ear before palming her cheek, I said, "I can't believe I got so lucky to have you in my life."

Kate sighed, and her resolve disappeared. She took my hand and kissed it before moving closer to kiss me. Our kiss became heated and before I knew it, she crawled into my lap.

I grabbed her butt and groaned into her mouth before rolling my hips to meet hers.

"You make this so hard for me."

She let out a little giggle at the joke, which made me laugh and spoiled the mood. We went inside for a normal night, but tonight she let me cuddle her. The feel of her in my arms helped me fall asleep faster.

CHAPTER 28

I went out to the corral, got my things sorted out, and waited for the calves to come through the chute. I had been working for an hour when Brian came to see what was going on.

"Gables, take over for Kate," he shouted from behind me.

"Follow me," he demanded, as he got right up in my face.

"What do you think you're doing out there?" he said angrily as he pointed over at the corrals.

"I'm vaccinating your calves. What does it look like?" I was tired of my father-in-law already, and it had only been a few months.

"Not after the last time. You get a hangnail around me, and my son is likely to put me in the hospital. Let me tell you one thing: I brought you here because Tyler needed a wife. I didn't bring you here to be a ranch hand. Now get to your house and be a wife, Kate, a proper wife, not just a wife on paper if you know what I mean."

"So I was okay to be out helping while Tyler was laid up, but not anymore."

He turned and walked away. I had no choice but to head back to the house.

"You have got to be kidding. I have been doing this all my life and you are so afraid of my husband you are going to lose a set of hands?" Brian's face was stone. There was no way he would change his mind. I threw up my hands. "Fine, I don't need this. Standing in the blistering sun all day drawing up drugs isn't my idea of fun. See ya."

Grabbing the reins of my horse, I walked home. I didn't understand this thinking; I had always worked alongside my father, and I wanted to pitch in here when I had time. My parents raised me to help on the ranch, not to stay in the house. I was raised to work and work hard. It made my blood boil to be dismissed because I was a wife. I could work circles around that man.

WITH MY PAPERWORK done for now, I wandered out to the corral to see how Kate was doing. I looked around and didn't see her.

"Hey Gables, where's Kate?" The ranch hand looked over to where I was standing at the fence.

"Boss sent her home."

"Excuse me? He did what?"

"Look, I shouldn't have overheard, but they weren't that far away. He told her she wasn't here to work; she was here to be a wife."

I didn't wait around to hear more. I spun on my heels and went to my house. Cautiously walking in the door, I found a furious woman who looked a lot like my wife. Kate heard me come in and stopped beating on the bread dough she was kneading.

"You wanted a wife, you got one. I never pretended I was a dutiful housewife. I do the work at my place. If you wanted a housewife, you should have asked for my sister," Kate spat out angrily, almost yelling at this point.

"I don't want your sister, Kate. What happened?"

"Your *father* is what happened. First off, he tells me the only reason this marriage happened is because when my dad dies, he still gets to take my family's ranch. Then today he tells me I'm not here to help, I'm here to be your wife and I have to be a *proper* wife, if you know what I mean."

A plastic dish flew past my head and hit the wall behind me, and then a spatula hit me in the chest. I had to calm her down, fast. Her aim was improving, and the coffee mugs were the next closest thing for her to grab.

"I'm sorry, Kate. Please listen to me. A wife and a family never crossed my mind, but now I want nothing else. A doormat was never on my list of wife qualities either. I want a wife to work beside me on and off the ranch. I want so much more for this place than how it is now." She seemed to calm as I talked, so I walked closer to her with my hands raised in surrender.

"Now I have a few questions. What are you talking about when you say he will take your father's ranch no matter what?"

I could see the pain and anger in her eyes as she caved and told me what happened on the day of our wedding, which explained what I'd seen through my office window.

"I'm so sorry, baby. I will make a few calls and see how we can protect the ranch from my father."

I could see tears welling up in her eyes, threatening to fall. Closing the distance between us, I took her into my arms. She didn't resist, and she wrapped her arms around my waist. I held her until her soft sobs stopped.

"I knew he had said something to upset you the day of our wedding. I saw him talking to you through my office window. Maybe I should have asked right then what was going on. It may have saved you a lot of worry. My father is a piece of work; he always has been."

She sniffled and looked up at me. "I'm sorry. Did you really threaten to put him in the hospital if anything happened to me again?"

"You have nothing to be sorry for. This hasn't been the easiest time, and you have had to deal with the most change of the two of us. Yes, while you were sleeping after you got home that day, I went over to his office and threatened him. I told him he was lucky I was hurt, so I didn't put him through the same thing you had just gone through." I took a chance and leaned down to kiss her. Kate moved her arms around my neck and kissed me back.

As we stood together, my heart soared. He was going to help me figure things out. I never thought Tyler was anything like his father, but today I really knew for sure that he was different. In my heart, I knew it was time to take the next step in this crazy relationship; he had stood up to his father for me, promised to protect my family's legacy, and put me above anything else. I didn't want to wait; I was afraid I would lose my nerve. Looking into his eyes and without saying a word, I kissed him with all the pent up passion I'd been hiding these past months, and then I turned out of his arms and took his hand.

"Kate?"

"It's time to break rule one."

I had a sudden thought, so I halted and turned to look at

him over my shoulder. "Do you agree it's time to break this one?" I arched my brow as I waited for him to answer. I knew I didn't have to ask. The eager smile on his face said all I needed to know, but he was so adamant the night we made these rules, I thought I would tease him a bit. He wrapped his arms tightly around my waist and pressed himself as close to me as he could. I could feel his answer before he even spoke.

"You shouldn't even have to ask. The answer is yes, Kate. It will always be yes. You make me crazy without even knowing it. Sometimes, all you have to do is look at me and I want to take you right where you stand." He trailed kisses from my earlobe to my collarbone. The last thing I wanted to do was move. Tyler picked me up and flung me over his shoulder before he bounded up the stairs. "Tyler, put me down!" I lightly pounded my fists on his back, laughing at him as I bounced.

Tyler walked into our room and kicked the door closed with his foot before he gently set me back on my feet. Looking up into his eyes, I saw how much he wanted me. My breathing quickened, my heart raced, and I couldn't help but smile. I looked away and closed my eyes, taking a deep breath as my hands shook with both nerves and excitement.

"Hey, it's just me. Don't be nervous." His lips brushed mine, and I looked at him again.

"That's exactly why I'm nervous. Don't forget I have been thinking about you for a very long time." My voice was oddly quiet. His low grunt sent shivers through me. My hands were shaking so badly I struggled with the buttons on his shirt.

"Why don't you wear shirts with snaps?"

"I will only buy ones with snaps from now on," he answered huskily, as I finally got his shirt unbuttoned. Pushing it off his shoulders and sliding it down his arms, running my hands over his chest. I could smell his cologne; the woodsy, smoky, with a hint of grapefruit made me crazy. He groaned, and I smiled.

"I want you so badly, Kate. I have since the day we got married," he whispered in my ear as he nibbled at my earlobe.

"What are you waiting for then?" I whispered breathlessly.

CHAPTER 29

I didn't need any more of an invitation than that. I grabbed her legs and lifted her, and she wrapped them around my waist as I walked toward the bed and laid her down. To my delight, her shirt had snaps. I untucked it from her jeans and grabbed the middle of her shirt, yanking it open.

"See? Snaps," she said, arching her brow and smiling seductively. That smile made every hair on my body stand up. I smiled and kissed the side of her neck, trailing kisses down to her cleavage.

Her bra's clasp was in the front, and I was a fortunate man because of it. I undid her bra and freed her breasts from their confinement. They were perfectly round, perky, and fit just right in the palm of my hand. Over the last few weeks, I had acquainted myself with them often and I knew what set Kate off. I watched Kate close her eyes and let out a sigh. Shifting, she relaxed further into the bed, her beautiful brown hair spread around her. I continued my ministrations on her breasts when she opened her eyes and whispered, "Please."

I couldn't deny her. That look in her eyes had me eating out of the palm of her hand. I'd do anything for this woman. I took her nipple in my mouth, played and bit it lightly, which made Kate moan.

"Ty, please."

Her begging for me made my heart jump. Had I ever felt like this with a woman before? I didn't think so. Kate made me forget every woman that had walked through my door before her.

I made quick work of removing her jeans, and she sat up and did the same for mine. I ran my hands down her body, exploring her once again. Her skin was soft, and I had memorized every curve; the swell of her breasts, the way her chest rose and fell as she breathed, the indent of her waist and the curve of her hips. I wanted to know her body better than I knew my own. I couldn't look away. She was mine, and in this moment of complete surrender, Kate moaned in pleasure.

The sound did something to me, snapping my control. I couldn't take it any longer. I needed her. The passion was palpable, like a haze covering the room, blanketing us in a need that could only be quenched one way. Running my hand down to the junction between her legs, I bit my tongue to hold myself back from pouncing on her. Kate was incredibly ready for me. I positioned myself above her, but stopped at her entrance. I bent down and kissed her lips, teasing another moan from her delectable throat.

"Tyler," Kate pleaded, lifting her hips to pull me closer. She reached down and gently wrapped her hand around me. When she stroked me from root to tip, I groaned. Now she was teasing me, not the other way around. Kate took her other hand and placed it on my back. I slowly pressed into her, her hand guiding me.

Our eyes locked as I carefully rocked into her, moving

slowly at first, teasing Kate, teasing us both, being careful not to hurt her. She was so incredibly tight, but it felt like coming home when I finally seated myself all the way inside her. I withdrew, and she whimpered until I thrust into her again. God, the sounds she made pushed the limits of my control, but I wouldn't give in to the need to hammer into her. I needed to make this good for her. So damn good that she'd never regret taking this step with me.

Kate grabbed my shoulders and pulled me closer. When her breasts pressed against my chest, I felt my control crack. Making small motions, Kate arched her back and called out my name.

That was it. I was a goner. Her spasms came in waves, and I couldn't control anything. I gasped as I filled her and Kate's arms tightened around my neck and her legs crossed around my back.

We lay together, not moving, completely spent, and enjoying being in each other's arms. I looked at Kate in wonder. Brushing the hair out of her eyes, I asked, "How did I get so lucky to have you as my wife?"

She smiled at me and softly said, "Thank you, Tyler. You were worth the wait." Claiming her lips, I rolled over on to my back so she was in control. A few more kisses and she cuddled into me. Soon, her breathing evened out as she fell asleep.

I smiled and kissed her hair. We just gave ourselves to each other completely, for the first time in our marriage. It was perfect, and it wasn't just sex. Being with a woman I was in love with was more amazing than anything I had ever experienced before. Two people joining together mind, body, and soul. This was the woman I would have in my bed for the rest of my life. I was a lucky man.

~

WHEN I WOKE up from my nap, I had forgotten the strain of the day and the uncomfortable exchange with Tyler's father. All I knew was that I was completely in love with this man, more now than I was when we first got married. We spent the rest of the day together, making up for the months we had been married but not intimate in this way. Tyler had made me feel loved from day one, but today, at this moment, I couldn't think of loving anyone as much as I loved him.

TYLER'S PHONE RANG, and he turned it off. "You don't need to get that?"

"Why ruin today by talking to someone who isn't you?"

I chuckled at his answer before asking, "What do you want for supper?"

"You," he growled, as he pulled me back towards him. Suddenly, there was a pounding on our front door.

"Tyler, you better get this door open, right now," Brian shouted from outside.

"Was that who was calling?" I asked quietly.

Tyler nodded. "Don't go anywhere. I'm going to get rid of him."

I gave Tyler a small smile of acknowledgment as he dressed quickly and left the room. My stomach sank. This wasn't going to be pleasant, whatever was going on. Several moments later, I heard their voices raised to a decibel I hadn't heard from either of them before. As much as I wanted to hide away up here, I needed to stand with Tyler. I dressed quickly, ran my fingers through my hair to tame it, and headed down the stairs.

"Tyler, is everything okay? Hi Brian, is this going to take long? We're a little busy," I said as I walked up beside Tyler and encircled my arms around his waist.

"I don't care what goes on over at your place, missy, but it's taking away from the running of my ranch. I go to his office, and he's not there. We run a business, and I need my employees where they are supposed to be, or at the very least, answering their phones. I will not tolerate any more of these random afternoons of not working." Brian was spitting mad.

"An employee? I thought I was your son." Tyler shook his head, and I felt his shoulders slump in defeat.

Stepping in between the men, I mustered every bit of courage I had. "Brian, it was my fault he didn't go back to work." Pasting a syrupy smile on my face, I continued, "You see, I took your advice and I'm being a... *proper wife.* I think is how you put it? Frankly, if you don't mind, I'd like to get back to the job you brought me here to do." Walking away from Tyler, I ushered Brian to the door and opened it. His face turned a few shades of red as he spun around and stormed off.

Tyler looked at me, a mixture of humor and awe on his face. "Wow, I don't think I've ever seen anyone make him speechless before. Now, Mrs. Morton, back upstairs with you. I believe you had *proper wife* duties to finish tending to. A smirk at the ridiculousness of that phrase graced Tyler's face, and I turned to go up the stairs. As soon as my back was facing him, he spanked my butt, making me jump in surprise. I have wanted to do that for a long time," he growled. Turning toward him, I tried to frown, but I couldn't help but laugh at him and his antics.

Several hours later, we lay silently together in each other's arms.

"I have to confess something. The night you picked me up on the side of the road and got mad because I was out running, I was falling in love with you. Then when you came to the house and had made plans for my trip to Dallas? I fell in love with you even more. On the day of our wedding, I was already in love with you. I'm sorry I've taken so long to show you how much I love you." I rested my head on Tyler's chest and ran my fingers through the hair scattered across it.

"I love you, too. You know that, right? I knew how you felt all along, and you prove it to me every day, even if you don't realize it."

few days later, I rushed into Tyler's office with an idea that couldn't wait until he got home.

"Ty, the playground in town needs new equipment. I took Addie to play the other day, and it was terrible. The swings are broken, and teeter-totters are missing seats, just to name a couple of things." I hadn't bothered to sit down; I leaned over his desk, my hands supporting me like I was in the biggest business deal of my life. "The slide faces south and is metal. You might as well light it on fire and let the kids slide down on it. I made a call to the town office and asked what their plan was, and they said demolition was on schedule with no plans to replace it." I followed Tyler's eyes, which were locked on the V neck on my shirt. "Tyler! Are you paying attention?"

His eyes fluttered up to mine, and he shrugged and grinned.

"Okay, focus, Ty. The town office said they would keep the area as a green space, but there'd be nothing to play on. That just seems wrong. I know there are lots of people with enough money to fund the entire thing, but what if we hosted a hard times barn dance? Everyone comes in their worst clothes. We have a silent auction of donated items, and people just donate to the playground?" I suggested excitedly. "There hasn't been a barn dance for ages, and this town needs to come back together." He stood and walked around the desk to stand in front of me.

"I like the idea, let's do it."

I couldn't believe he was on board. I jumped into his arms in excitement, which made Tyler laugh. That laugh did something to my insides. Still in his arms, I leaned in for a kiss. I wrapped my legs around him and he walked over to the door and locked it, then he headed for the couch.

We christened his office, and I left with a grin on my face and a huge to-do list that included making calls, hiring Jessica, the party planner that did our wedding, and calling places to donate items. When the day was over, I had everything ready for next Saturday.

Saturday rolled around, and I was nervous. We didn't ask for RSVP s, we just hoped people would show up. The band had donated their time; we placed the silent auction items on tables for bidding, and the barn was sparkling. I paced all day. I was glad Tyler was spending most of the day with Rob; he didn't need to see me like this.

I was in the event barn looking for last-minute things I needed to fix just before people were due to start arriving. Small square hay bales lined the sides of the barn for seating. We'd strung lanterns along the beams above the dance floor, which gave off a twinkling soft light. Tables scattered around the barn were covered with red and white checkered tablecloths. There was a sweet, smoky scent of the brisket on the barbecue wafting out of the barn and it smelled divine. The catering company had outdone themselves. The atmosphere was friendly, inviting, and looked ready for a party. I was anxious, but I looked up and saw a line of cars coming up the road. Car load by car load, families were arriving, and everyone seemed so excited. In no time, the enormous barn was packed, and everyone was having a marvelous time. I couldn't believe how many members of the community had come out and supported each other. I was so busy I didn't even see Tyler until almost the end of the night when he came walking up to me.

"Well, you certainly rallied this town around each other." I smiled at him.

"I'm just so shocked by all the people here."

"You don't give yourself enough credit. People like you, and you are a wonderful person, Kate. You asked, and they know you aren't doing this for any gain for yourself. Your heart is truly dedicated to others. Now, I have danced with many women tonight, old habits you know, but all I really want is to hold my wife in my arms. So before you shut this down, please come and dance with me." I nodded at him and smiled, my heart melting just a little. There was a huge part of me that was jealous it wasn't me that had been in his arms all night. Looking over his shoulder, I scanned the room for Lona. She hadn't been invited, but I wouldn't have put it past her to just show up, anyway. Tyler holding me made me forget those feelings. I felt strong, supported, heard, but most of all, empowered. Nobody had ever believed in me the way he did.

"Do you think you reached your goal?" he whispered in my ear.

I nodded. "I think if we haven't hit it yet, we will while things are being won."

❧

SHE WAS BEAMING, and she deserved to be. This was a lot of work to have accomplished in such a short time, and clearly, it was a tremendous success. Kate was announcing the winners from the silent auction while my mom was tallying the money when things were paid for, and Kate's mom was counting donations.

"Congratulations to everyone who won the items they wanted. If you'll wait just a few more minutes, we will have a grand total to share with you all!" The crowd cheered, the band began playing again, and I was bursting with pride. Several moments later, Kate walked back to the microphone, and the crowd hushed.

"When I heard the town council had set the playground for demolition and there was no plan for replacement, it made me sad. That space has been an area for kids to play for generations. Thank you all for coming out and supporting this fundraising effort. We have the final numbers here, and thanks to all of you and your generosity, we have raised $51,957 for the new playground!" The crowd cheered and hooted and hollered. "Thank you so much for showing your support for this crazy idea. Maybe we can make this an annual event for different causes!" More cheers went up. Kate was amazing, and I was so damn proud of her.

I SAW Tyler walking towards the stage and wondered what he had up his sleeve. He reached for the microphone and I handed it to him.

"I want to just say how proud I am of this town, for pulling together for a cause the way we all have."

The crowd cheered again, but Tyler held up his hand to quieten them down.

"I would like to add a check that will match the amount given. This will be for future maintenance to the playground." The crowd hooted and hollered all over again, and whistles rang throughout the barn.

"This money has a condition, though. The condition is that our host comes up and sings a set with the band." Suddenly, all eyes shifted from Tyler to me. I felt all the blood drain from my face. My hands shook as those that knew I sang began chanting my name. They were all traitors in my mind now, especially my husband. I shook my head no, but by then, the entire barn was chanting my name. I gave Tyler a dirty look so he would know he was in trouble.

"You aren't ready to go home yet, right?" Tyler revved up the crowed, and they cheered again. Tyler held the microphone out for me to take. I walked over to him and took it, giving him a glare for good measure.

"Good thing this barn is warm, because you're sleeping in here tonight." The laughter that came from the crowd was all the encouragement I needed. Gripping Tyler's hand so he couldn't leave me up here alone, I turned to the band, and we had a quick chat.

"I will stand down in front the entire time. You are going to be amazing. I love you." Tyler loosened the grip I had on him, kissed my cheek, and left the stage. The music started, and I quickly got over my jitters and sang like I had a packed AT&T Stadium.

I watched Kate go from nervous to a born performer in moments. A few ladies came up and asked for a dance, but I couldn't take my eyes off of my wife. Just like the night in the bar when I heard her sing for the first time, she was amazing.

She walked off the stage after thanking everyone again, walked right into my arms and buried her head in my chest.

"You are something else. I can't believe you did that."

"I hear you sing almost every day, and it's one of my favorite things. It was time you got to perform to an actual audience." I couldn't help but smile at her.

It was late, and the crowd thinned out until it was just our families left in the barn.

"Well, I think our evening was a success. Kate, you are welcome to sing at my events any time you want," Sandra said. Everyone nodded in agreement.

"I probably won't take you up on that offer. I think this was a one and done thing." Kate looked over at me and frowned. Laughing, I gave her a kiss on the cheek.

"Old man, take me home." My mom elbowed my father to get him to move.

"It would be my pleasure." he replied. They both stood and said their goodnights before heading to the house.

"Yep, we're heading out too, dear," Kate's mom said as she hugged her.

"You did good, kiddo," her father said while giving her a hug, and then they were on their way home. Addie had fallen asleep sitting on Rob's lap, so he gently stood up and took her and Jessica home. Finally, it was just us left. The barn was quiet for the first time today, and Kate closed her eyes.

"We have so much cleanup to do," she moaned and pouted.

"That can wait until morning. Nothing is in here that can't be left." Cleaning up was the last thing on my mind. All I wanted to do was take my wife home and make love to her.

"I'm not sure I can make it into the house."

I extended my hand to her. Taking it, she stood. I put one

hand behind her back, bent over, and scooped her up into my arms. She immediately wrapped her arms around my neck.

"If you can't walk, I'll carry you." I leaned in toward her and devoured her luscious lips. "My love, you are the shining light of this family. I am so extremely proud of you, and I can't believe you're mine."

CHAPTER 31

"Rob is wondering if we can keep Addie for the night," I called as I came in the door.

"He has a date and doesn't want to worry about a babysitter."

Kate came out of the kitchen. "Yeah, sure, that's fine. I hope he proposes soon. It bothers Addie that she doesn't have a mom."

"She told you that?"

Kate nodded. "The day I took her to get her dress for school pictures, she said sometimes the other kids make fun of her for not having a mom. It just breaks my heart."

I was so mad I didn't know what to do.

"Ty, you can't do anything. All you can do is love that little girl like you do and be the uncle that she needs."

I nodded, but I was still mad.

"Can I ask you a question?" Kate followed me out onto the porch.

"Anything, you know that."

"In twenty years, if Rob told Addie he had found her a

husband and she would be getting married in a week and a half, what would you have to say about it?"

I looked at Kate out of the corner of my eye.

"I would be livid. It's not his place, which is what I told our fathers the day they approached me about the arrangement they had made."

"You said that? To both of them?" The shock on her face turned to appreciation in a split second.

I nodded and wrapped an arm around her as we sat on the porch swing. "Yep. I was so angry I didn't speak to my dad for days. I knew it was not fair to you, but when I saw you that day at your house, I was smitten."

"No, you were not. You were probably horrified after you'd seen me throw that cup!" Kate let her head fall into her hand. "That wasn't my finest hour. I was mad I broke my favorite cup, and embarrassed you witnessed it."

I grinned and placed my hand on her chin, turning her so I could peer into her dark eyes. "You were fiery, so angry, and so gorgeous. If I could have married you at that moment, I would have. I went home that night, jealous of any man who had ever touched you, kissed you, flirted with you. Hell, just plain looked at you. I didn't sleep, waiting for the next morning when I could see you again. That's why I was out driving around."

"When I was running?"

"I was too jittery to sit at home, so I called the guys and went out. I just needed to clear my head, and then there you were, soaking wet on the side of the road in your running shorts that barely covered anything and a sports bra." I trailed my finger from her collarbone and rounded the curve of her breast. "Let's just say sleep didn't come any easier after I got home." Her soft giggle filled me with joy. Being in love left a permanent smile on my face. I loved to see her laugh and giggle. "After that happened, every time I closed my eyes, I saw you in those shorts." I closed my eyes and smiled as big as I could. "You don't run enough anymore, by the way. I miss those shorts."

Kate playfully slapped my arm and giggled again as I continued. Looking over, I could see she was listening intently to my confessions. "Then the next day when I invited you to the house, it was so I wouldn't have to say goodbye to you in Hammond."

"All the times you called to see if I needed any help with plans or help at Dad's was really you wanting to see me?" she asked.

I nodded. "And you broke my heart every time you said you didn't need help. The day I found out you'd been here talking with my mom and didn't come looking for me, I was crushed."

"Is that why you came and found us?"

I nodded.

"I have always wondered what you really wanted to say as I left that day."

"I didn't want to say anything, I just really wanted to kiss you, but I decided it was not the time yet."

"I wish you had. It would have eased some of my fears and made me feel better about everything. I had seen you around town but always heard you were a playboy and would never settle down. It was terrifying thinking you would keep those ways up after our wedding. I didn't want to be a laugh-ingstock, and I didn't want to be hurt." Her eyes showed how much she had been worried about my past.

"I wish we had talked more about past relationships during that week and a half. We spent a lot of time together and talked plenty, but we missed out on quite a bit of getting to know each other a little better. Maybe things wouldn't have been so awkward at the start if we had talked about more things that mattered."

"I'm not sure we could have known those things. We didn't know each other's day to day, and there was no way we could have. We didn't have the time," Kate said, looking off towards the barn and unconsciously pushed her foot against the floor, making the swing move. "Is there anything you wish you could have done differently?" she asked quietly.

I looked at Kate and smiled. "I only wish I had opened my eyes and realized I needed you in my life much sooner."

"I always wondered what was wrong with me."

Quizzically, I looked at my wife, wanting to know more, hoping she would explain what she just said.

"You went through basically the entire town but steered clear of me. Not that I wanted to be a notch on your bedpost, but back then, it would have been nice to know why I wasn't."

"You want to know why I didn't try? You were too good for me. I didn't want a forever, I just wanted a right now, and I knew you would be a forever." I leaned toward my wife and millimeters away from her lips, I whispered, "You are my forever." Our lips met and as the passion increased, we were interrupted.

"Uncle Tyler, Auntie Kate, I'm here."

We looked at each other, smiled, and looked over at Addie. I loved my niece, but her timing right now was terrible. All I wanted to do was take my wife inside and do unspeakable things to her.

"You two need me to find another sitter?" Rob asked, looking at us with an arched brow.

I looked at my brother and made a 'well' face and Kate slapped me.

"Addie, I've been waiting for you to get here. I need

backup, your uncle is annoying." Rolling her eyes, she looked at me and smiled. I chuckled and stood from the swing.

"See you in the morning, Squish. Love you," Rob said as he and I walked off the porch.

"Bye, Daddy, say hi to Jessica for me."

"I will," he called over his shoulder. The girls went into the house, and I walked Rob to his truck.

"Things are serious between you two."

"Ty, I really think this time it's right, but I'm so worried about getting hurt again. And then there is Addie to think of." Rob's voice trailed off.

"I think you'll know when it's time, and when you are ready. As far as Addison goes, she just wants you to be happy, and to have a mom."

I hadn't meant to say that last part, but the talk I had with Kate was still in the back of my mind.

"Rob, I didn't mean…"

"I know. She tells me that, and I know she's told Kate, so I'm guessing Kate has told you. I want to give her that, but I also want to thank you and Kate for being so willing to help. Kate is there the instant I need her, and I know whatever happens between Jessica and me, Addison has a wonderful backup. I don't know how you missed her all these years, but I'm glad she's here now."

"I was a fool. I don't know how I survived without her." Looking through the window at Kate, I couldn't remember what life was like before her. Shaking myself out of my haze, I turned back to Rob.

"Have a good time. You don't need to hurry to pick Addison up in the morning."

Rob looked at me and grinned. "See you tomorrow, brother."

Rob climbed into his truck and drove off.

I turned and walked back into the house where the girls were cuddled up on the couch, and Kate was introducing Addison to The Little Mermaid.

"I'm going to go do some work. I will be in the office here," I whispered into Kate's ear.

"I'll bring you some popcorn soon."

I leaned down and kissed her, then went to get a little work done. Kate arrived with the bowl of popcorn, as promised, not too long later.

"Where's your shadow?"

"She fell asleep about ten minutes into the second movie, so I tucked her into bed. That means we have the rest of the night to ourselves." Kate slid between my desk and my chair, perched on the edge of the desk. Running my hands up her thighs, I groaned.

"Give me ten minutes, and I'm all yours."

She made a face at me and got off my desk. "Ten minutes, that's all. Then I have other plans for you."

I finished typing up the email I needed to send off as fast as I could, shut everything down, and went to find Kate.

"You're lucky, you only had two more minutes, and then I was going to bed, alone."

"What was your plan in the office?"

"Come with me and find out." Standing up from the couch, Kate grabbed my hand, and we went upstairs.

I HADN'T REALLY THOUGHT this through, but I walked over to the big chair in the corner and pushed him down into it. Walking over to the Bluetooth, speakers I quickly set up the playlist I had found while waiting for him to be done in his office. I walked across the room into the bathroom and quickly changed into my raciest lingerie. The music started, and I opened the door and slowly and seductively walked over to him.

Gently I placed my hand on his shoulder, and ran it down his chest, inside his shirt, behind his neck as I walked around to face him. I could feel his breathing becoming faster. Standing beside him, I swung my leg back and straddle his thighs.

Frantically, I searched my brain for what I'm supposed to do next. I should have read the article more than once. Slowly, I swayed my hips from side to side as I lowered down to sit on his lap. His hands crept up my thighs.

"Oh no sir, *no touching.*" I leaned over and whispered in his ear, taking his hands and placing them on the arms of the chair. There was mischief in his eyes but also hunger. I stood and moved away from his lap.

Grasping the clasp on my outfit, I let the top fall to the floor. Tyler gasped, and his eyes doubled in size. Turning away from him, I danced back towards him and took a seat on his lap again. Pressing my butt into him, I knew I was having the desired effect. One of his hands snuck around and grasped my breast.

"No touching, Mr. Morton. That will cost you extra."

I stood and again walked away from him. Before I turned back around, I heard the ripple of snaps being ripped apart and knew he had removed his shirt. Facing him again, he was standing and walked over to me.

"Kate, this is amazing but I'm about to lose it here." He grabbed me and pulled me to him. Our lips met in unbridled passion. He unzipped his pants, and they fell to the floor with a thud because of his belt buckle. We both froze, waiting to see if the sound woke Addison.

"I think we are safe," I whispered.

He attacked my mouth again and lifted me so I could wrap my legs around him. Backing up to the bed, he sat down and slipped his hand between us.

"You are more than ready for me, baby." He lifted me, lowered his head, and attacked my breasts. I let my head fall back, enjoying the feeling of being the one in control.

"Tyler, I need you now." I was almost growling in his ear. He shifted me on his lap and slowly entered me.

"Alright, what's your plan now, you little vixen?" Tyler asked between kisses.

I pushed him so he was laying down and ever so slowly started moving my hips. His hands roamed my body and slid down between my legs. He found the exact spot he needed to push me over the edge. My pace increased, and he met me with increasing thrusts. We rode together at what felt like breakneck speed. Deep from my core, the heat and intensity built. I placed my hands on his chest and rode him through shuttering ecstasy.

Lying down on his chest, he wrapped his arms around me, "You know I am more than happy to work late if this is what waits for me when I'm done."

"You should have seen what you were going to get if you had closed your computer in the office." I looked up and him and he started laughing. We rolled over and spent time in each other's embrace. I felt connected to him more than I had ever felt before.

ADDISON WAS up with the sun and came flying into our room.

"Auntie Kate, let's make breakfast," I groaned in disapproval. Tyler and I had only gotten to sleep a few hours prior to her wake up call.

"Who needs an alarm clock when you're here?" Tyler asked, tickling Addie.

"Uncle Tyler, stop!" We managed to hear through her giggles, and Tyler stopped.

"Well, what do you two want for breakfast now that you have woken up the entire house?" I stood at the edge of the bed with my hands on my hips, trying to be mad at them both, but it wasn't working so well.

"Pancakes and bacon," Addie yelled.

I rolled my eyes and hit them both with my pillow as I turned to leave the room. I saw Tyler grab the pillow and aim it to throw it at me through the mirror, so I dodged out of the way and the pillow hit the floor and I just stepped over it.

"You are going to have to be sneakier than that."

"Just you wait, I'll get you."

Our morning flew by. Tyler had gone into the office for a bit to finish up what he hadn't gotten to last night. Rob and Jessica came and picked up Addie, and then it was just me. Cleaning up from last night and this morning, I realized Addie needed her own space here. Even if Rob and Jessica had a future, she would still spend time here. I wanted to talk the idea over with Tyler, but it wasn't something that I needed to interrupt his day over. Hopefully, he would be home soon, since it was Saturday. A ride out to the trapper's cabin seemed like the best thing to do today, and it would give us time to talk and be together, with no interruptions.

CHAPTER 32

I heard the front door open and close and turned to see Tyler standing in the living room.

"Hey, you're home early, which is good because I have an idea that I know you can't refuse." I called from the kitchen.

He walked over to where I was standing and wrapped his arms around my waist.

"I'm just home to grab a few things, and then I have to head to Montana for some business. The land deal I've been working on for what feels like months is hanging on by a thread, and the investors are tired of phone calls and emails. They're demanding an in-person meeting."

I leaned into him and rested my head on his shoulder, letting out a sigh. "How long will you be gone?"

"All week," he replied, seeming as glum about being separated as I was.

I spun around to look at him. "All week?" He nodded, misery at the situation plain on his face. Complaining would not make his mood, or this situation, any better.

"We still have some business up there to finish, and I need

to go look over the books and make sure things are running smoothly. I wanted to ask you to come with me, but I'm afraid that with me being gone, Rob will need help with Addie."

"Of course I'll help. I can't leave now, anyway. I need to get dad's cattle moved so they don't starve down south."

"I forgot about that. Do you want me to put off my trip for a few days?"

I shook my head as the words were coming out of his mouth.

"No, you need to do this, and the plans are made. I'll see if Rob has half a day to help if I think I need it." I really tried to mask my disappointment. We were in a great place in our marriage, and now he was going. I moved as close to Tyler as I could. I knew this week would be long and hard without him, but he had responsibilities he needed to handle.

Tilting my head up to look at him, he brought his lips to mine. We stood in the kitchen, kissing and hugging, neither of us wanting to let go.

"What was this idea you were pretty sure I couldn't say no to?"

"Oh, nothing important. I just thought we could head to the trapper's cabin for the rest of the weekend."

He almost growled with disappointment and pulled me tighter to him.

"When I get back, you better have everything ready because that's where we'll go for a week."

His phone broke up our moment by ringing. Just this once, I wished he had ignored it instead of answering.

"The plane is ready. I need to grab a few things," he said as he hung up and ran up the stairs, coming back down a few minutes later with his suitcase. I secretly hoped he was going to come back down with mine also, but it didn't happen.

KᴀᴛE ꜰOʟʟOᴡED me to my truck, a smile pasted on her face and, if I was reading her correctly, sadness in her eyes.

"I'll be back by Saturday evening."

"I'll be waiting, husband," she whispered before we kissed goodbye.

"I'm going to miss you. I promise to make this up to you when I get back." Looking deep into her eyes, I hoped she felt how sad I was to be leaving her.

"I'll miss you too. See you Saturday." She smiled and nodded. I brought her as close to me as I could, placed my hand under her chin, and lifted her head. We kissed like we wouldn't see each other for years.

She backed away from the truck and I hopped in.

"I'll call you when I land." She nodded and waved as I backed away from the house. I had made this trip many times, but this time, I resented having to go. It made me angry having to leave my wife alone to get her work done by herself. It made me mad she had to work so hard without help. I would fix that when I got home. I watched the rearview mirror until she was out of sight. This week needed to go by quickly.

I ᴄOᴜʟDN'ᴛ ʜEᴀR his truck anymore, so I went back into the house and flopped down on the couch, looked at the clock and decided I would let myself have a pity party for half an hour. When the time was up, I called Rob.

"Hi, Tyler said you might need a hand with Addie. Would you like me to come get her?"

I instantly heard relief in his voice.

"Yes, Kate, please. I'm trying to get some fencing done.

Jessica got called into the office and with Ty gone, it will take twice as long."

I ran over to Rob's house and packed a bag for Addie and then went to pick her up from the pasture.

"Addie, I have a plan. Want to go shopping?"

"For what, Auntie Kate?"

"For your room at our house. I want you to feel as comfortable at our house as you do in your own, so let's run to the city and get what you want."

"Oh, Auntie Kate, really?"

I nodded yes, and we ran to the truck.

Addie chatted about how she wanted to decorate her room, and I didn't question it. We got to the city and started our search.

Several hours later, with everything checked off our list, we decided we deserved a break, so we went to grab fast food for lunch.

We were walking back to the truck after our lunch, Addie talking excitedly about how amazing her room was going to look, when I suddenly heard a voice behind me.

"Well, isn't it something that we ran into each other again?" I turned around and saw Lona sauntering towards Addie and I.

"Lona," I said as nicely as I could.

"I heard Ty headed out for Montana today."

"I'm sure you did."

"I am heading to Montana this afternoon, actually. My sister lives there, and I'm due for a visit."

"I am sure you are," I mumbled under my breath.

"Well hello miss Addison, have you missed me?" Lona asked as she tapped Addie on the nose.

Addie looked up at me and back to Lona, turned up her nose, shrugged her shoulders, and shook her head no.

"What a rude child," Lona huffed.

I looked down at Addie, gave her a sly grin, "No, she's just an excellent judge of character."

Lona looked at me and frowned. "Well, I best be on my way. I would hate to miss my flight."

"That would be terrible," I replied in a sarcastic tone.

"Hopefully, I'll run into Ty." She smiled and wiggled her eyebrows.

"I think it would be best for you if you didn't."

Lona waltzed away with a 'toodles'. I was glad we had finished our shopping so we could head home. I made a mental note that I was going to have to go to a different city to shop from now on.

Addie and I got home and put her new bed together. She had picked out a white canopy bed and a dresser to match. The comforter was pink, fuzzy, and warm. A faux chandelier replaced the standard square glass shade, soft pink curtains hung to the floor, and a small white rocking chair sat in the corner next to her bookshelf.

"Auntie Kate, it's beautiful!" I watched Addie with her enormous smile and gigantic eyes. She ran over and wrapped her arms around my waist and held on for dear life. "Thank you very much. This is the best day ever!"

I hugged her back, and my heart soared. She was right; it was a great day. There was a knock on the door, and Rob walked in.

"Daddy! Come with me. I have something to show you!" Addie ran down the hall, dragging Rob behind her. "Look what Auntie Kate did for me!" Rob looked around the room and over at me and smiled.

"Hey Addiekins, why don't you go grab your toys from the living room and get your boots on?" Addie ran out the door and down the stairs.

"I hope you don't mind, I probably should have talked to you first."

Rob shook his head no. "Kate, it's okay. I appreciate you making her feel at home here. I can't tell you how much it eases my mind that when she needs a woman, you're there. Yes, Mom is always around, but that relationship is different, and I don't want it to change." Rob looked around the room again and smiled.

Rob and Addie left for their place, and once again, I was alone in my home. I wandered into the kitchen and stared into the fridge. Nothing looked appealing, and I didn't feel like cooking an enormous meal for only me, so I grabbed the cheese and salsa and closed the fridge. I walked to the chip cupboard and grabbed the taco chips. Tonight's supper would be nachos.

I hadn't talked to Tyler all day, so I decided to call him. It was late, so I figured he would be done with his meeting. With my supper made, I walked into the living room, picked up my phone and dialed his number.

"Hello?"

"Hi, how's your day been?" I could hear lots of background noise.

"I'm in the middle of a supper meeting, Kate. Can I call you back when we're done?"

"Sure, bye." I heard a woman laugh in proximity to Tyler's phone, but I figured she was part of the business team. The line went dead, and I went back to my supper and turned on the TV.

My phone rang, and I looked down, expecting it to be Tyler. "Delaney, what's up?"

"Have you been on social media at all tonight?"

"No. Addie was here for the day and I just sat down to eat

some supper." My phone buzzed, and I saw a text from Delaney.

"Really? You're already talking to me but you had to text as well?" I turned the speakerphone option on and opened the text.

My heart dropped to my feet.

There it was, all over social media, a picture of my husband with Lona draped all over him. She was wearing the same clothes I had seen her wearing in the city earlier today. She would have had to go straight to the airport after seeing me to be there already. I would have been comforted if he had looked appalled, but he looked happy, like he was having fun. Then I recognized the woman's laugh I'd heard on the phone earlier. I had heard it before. It was Lona's. Tears instantly filled my eyes and fell onto the screen of my phone.

"Kate? What do you need from me?"

"I'm coming home. I'll be there in about half an hour; I just want to pack a few things." A million thoughts ran through my head, but the one that was at the forefront was how much of a fool I had been. How I had let Tyler say all the right things and let him do all the right things and missed the signs of this side relationship; the random phone calls that were always business, the emails at crazy times in the night. I should have known better. No man could go this long without sowing wild oats, especially when he wasn't getting what he needed at home for so long. Had I driven him to this, or was it something that had never stopped?

CHAPTER 33

he front door swung open and Rob, Sandra, and
Brian stood in the doorway. They looked at my
packed bags and all started talking at once. All three were
making a case for Tyler, saying that I shouldn't jump to
conclusions, and that I should call him. Maybe even just go to
Montana. I shook my head.

"Maybe if this had been the first red flag I would, but it
isn't. You know, maybe if he wasn't getting pulled into the
office with random phone calls from you, or goodness knows
who." There was no way I would break down in front of
them. With sheer determination, I gritted teeth and continued
my tirade. "Maybe if he wasn't always here at home in his
office, sending emails. Heck, maybe he wasn't even working,
but was fooling around. I don't know." I walked directly in
front of Brian. "All I know is, you got me into this. I have
upheld my end of the deal, but nothing says I have to stay
here and put up with this crap. I have ignored that this could
happen because I hoped Tyler had told me the truth, but I
won't sit by again and be the fool. I'm going home." Pushing

217

past them, I threw my bags into the back of my truck and climbed into the driver's seat.

Tyler's family had followed me out of the house and were still trying to make a case for him at the truck. Brian looked like he was going to spit nails. He turned to Rob.

"I called the airport. I got you on a flight that will leave in half an hour from the private airport. We'll keep Addie. Go and find out what the devil your brother is up to. Make that woman go away. I don't care how or what you do, Rob."

Sandra's head snapped toward Brian and back to Rob. I felt like I had missed something between the family, but I couldn't make a compelling argument to change Brian's mind.

"Bring or send him home, son," was all she said.

I slid to a stop in front of my old house. When I moved out, Delaney moved in. It was easier for her. She didn't have to look for a place right now, and she would be around to help dad. Delaney swung the door open. Just as I was about to get out of the truck, my phone rang. I looked at it, and Tyler's face stared back at me. I threw the phone back onto the seat of the truck and closed the door. There was no way I wanted to hear what excuse he had for me, or how he was going to talk himself out of this mess.

"Here, you look like you need this," Delaney said, as she handed me a margarita. I walked into the house and saw Beth, Jane, and Sarah. I gave them all a half a smile and immediately broke down. The four of them gathered around me and wrapped me in a hug and let me cry.

"You know, Kate, this is Stephen all over again, and you deserve so much better," Jane commented.

"That two-timing swine! What is it with me and men? The ones I pick and the ones that are picked for me. It must be me."

There was a chorus of no's and protests. Staring out the

window into the darkness, I thought back to the only other man I had let get this close to me. His betrayal had cut deep and made me reconsider loving anyone; but what Tyler had done hurt me more than that. He knew my history, and he still fooled around on me.

For the rest of the night, we drank, I cried, and we planned out how we would carry out every terrible thing we could think of to hurt, maim, and torture Tyler.

THE BUSINESS SUPPER had gone well. I managed to salvage the mess that had been created by Mike. I finally managed to get to my room and fall into bed, completely exhausted, around midnight. What felt like minutes later, there was a pounding on the door, pulling me from a dead sleep. The clock read 1:00 am. Why would anyone be out at this time of night? I walked over and opened the door, ready to rip someone's head off. A right hook met me from someone who looked a lot like Rob. I held my jaw and clenched my fist, meeting his face with it in return. The fight was on. I caught a glimpse of my opponent and saw that it was indeed Rob. The unannounced, unexpected visit and the instant fight made me mad. I connected a blow to his stomach, and his next punch hit me in the eye.

"Stop, hey knock it off *Rob, enough!*"

We both sat on the floor, panting and staring at each other.

"What on earth are you doing here? And what did I do to deserve that for a hello?"

"Where is she?" Rob asked as he got up off the floor and wandered around the house.

"She? Who are you talking about? *Who* is supposed to be *here?*"

Rob was checking my room and heading for the other rooms in the house.

"Lona," Rob yelled, as he turned and stared at me. "She has posted pictures of the two of you together tonight all over social media. She's basically draped all over you. I know what your next thought is going to be, and yes, Kate, you know— your *wife*—has also seen them. She's moved out. She had her bags packed when we got to your place ready to fix this, but she headed out."

"We?"

"Mom, Dad and me. We went to see if she knew what was going on, and well, yep, she does."

I opened my phone, and there were a dozen pictures of Lona and me together.

"Rob, it's not what you think. She showed up at the restaurant during the meeting, sat down, had supper, charmed the investors, then I ditched her. I know that's not what it looks like." I ran my hands through my hair, frustration and anger eating at me. "What am I going to do?"

"I suggest you call your *wife*," Rob replied.

"I have been trying to all night, but there's no answer. Now I know why. Do you know where she went?" I looked down at my phone and dialed Delaney's number.

"Hello?"

"Delaney, it's Tyler. Is Kate with you?" I basically hollered into the phone.

"Like I would tell you, you lying snake."

"Laney, is it him?" I heard a voice yell in the background.

"Yeah it is. He wants to know where you are," Delaney called back, but also yelled into the phone. I had to smile. Delaney was obviously drinking or she wouldn't have just given away where Kate was.

"You can tell him the divorce papers will be waiting for

him when he gets home on Saturday." Delaney must have put it on speaker mode, but it wasn't Kate's voice that said it.

"Kate, no, you don't need to talk to him. He doesn't deserve your time," someone called out.

"Delaney, give me the phone," she said.

"Kate, please, this is all a…" The line went dead.

I hit the redial button, but this time it went straight to voicemail. I threw my phone across the room and it clattered to the floor.

"Rob, what am I going to do? Lona approached Kate shortly after our wedding and told her we were together behind her back, and I was figuring out how to leave her to be with Lona. She's going to think I have been fooling around for months and lying to her our whole marriage."

"You need to figure out how to get home pal, fast."

I called every airline, and I found a flight that would get me to Las Vegas and then back into Dallas by 6:00am, and then I would be back to Kate by 9:00am. Frantically, I left Rob the notes about what had to be done and ran out the door. I kept trying to call Kate, but there was no answer. I couldn't blame her, either. She had finally opened up and let me in. These last few weeks had been fantastic. I loved my wife more than anything in the world. I just needed to make her see that.

I stumbled out to my truck and opened the door the next morning to see a hundred missed calls from Tyler showing on my phone. There were ten voicemails too, but I didn't want to listen to any of them. I put the phone back on the seat, grabbed my bag, and went back into the house. Everything was spinning, and I knew from the way I was walking that I was still quite drunk, but really, what could I expect when we only quit making margaritas at 5:00am?

I hadn't been back in the house for five minutes when there was a knock on the door. I was the only one up; the other four were passed out on the floor. I chuckled. We hadn't had a night like this since way back in our younger rodeo days. I staggered to the door and swung it open, expecting to see one of their husbands. What I hadn't expected was to see *my* husband. I blinked myopically, scrunched my eyed closed tight and then opened my eyes again. He was still there, and thankfully, he'd stopped spinning.

"You look terrible. What happened to your face?"

"Rob happened."

"Good, you deserved it." I pushed him out of the doorway, walked out of the house, and closed the door behind me. I didn't need one of the girls waking up because they probably would have fought him, too.

"What are you doing here?"

"I called every airline last night and got a flight. Kate, those pictures were a lie. Nothing happened between me and Lona. She showed up in Bozeman and made herself welcome at supper. I made it clear that she was not welcome, but one of the business partners objected and let her stay. She made a fuss over them and suddenly the deal was so close to complete. I knew I should have left, but I needed this to get done. Come home, we can both sleep, and then we can talk."

"I think I'll just sleep this off here. I might come over later."

Looking up into his eyes, I hoped to find the truth, but I only found his tired eyes staring back at me. I turned and walked back into the house, and closed the door behind me. I leaned on the closed door and once again let tears roll down my cheeks. Walking into the living room, I put blankets over the girls and walked to what had once been my room and climbed into bed. With the blankets pulled up around my face, I drifted off to sleep.

"Kate? Kate! You need to wake up!" I could hear Delaney calling my name and feel her shaking my shoulder.

"Leave me alone," I whispered, because anything louder than that was seriously going to hurt my head.

"Kate, get up. Tyler's outside, sitting in some random car."

"Do not get all lovey-dovey on me, Laney. I already talked to him and he had little to say… From what I remember." I frowned and held my head.

"When did you talk to him?" Delaney flopped down on the bed.

"When you and the other girls were passed out this morning. He showed up here about 9:00. He flew all night and then came straight here from Dallas or something." I pulled the blankets up over my head but caught a whiff of my breath and decided that wasn't the best plan, so I moved them back down.

"Come on Kat, hear him out."

"Laney, last night you were ready to cause him bodily harm. What's changed in a few hours?" I lay there staring at her, waiting for the answer.

"I'm sober?"

"Is that a statement or a question?" I looked accusingly at her.

"Statement." She held her head high and looked very confident.

I shook my head and threw my feet out of bed, and walked to the bathroom to brush my teeth.

I threw my things back into my suitcase. "You are hard to figure out Laney. Last night you wanted me to divorce him. Today, I have to hear him out. But thanks for making me forget for a few hours. You are the best sister a girl could ask for."

Delaney grabbed me in a hug.

"Kate, he's not Stephen. Tyler is here. Whatever happened in Montana, he's here to own. That other schmuck didn't even try. I think your husband is a good man, Kat. Just talk to him." I nodded and walked out to the car Tyler was in. I looked in the window and saw that he was asleep, so I put my bags in my truck and went back around to his window and banged on it with my fist.

Startled, he blinked a few times and looked at me. "I'm going to the house. We need to talk and we aren't doing it here." Turning away from the window, I walked back to my truck and drove back to our home.

CHAPTER 34

We pulled up to the house in our separate vehicles and he got out, but I stayed in my truck. He walked over and opened the door, but said nothing. Climbing out, I reached for my bag, but he took it from me. Our home felt different. Gone was the wanting and longing that was here when he left. The playful, flirtatious atmosphere dissolved, and anger and tension had replaced it. I needed coffee, and I suspected he did, too. I walked into the kitchen and made us each a cup and went back to the living room. He was sitting on the couch with his head in his hands. He was a shell of the man I had known a few days ago. His shoulders were hunched over, and it seemed like he had gone grey overnight. The black eye and fat lip didn't help his look.

"Tyler," I whispered.

He looked up, and I handed him the cup of coffee. Our hands briefly touched as the cup exchanged hands. The same little touches I once had longed for, the ones I had made happen during our first days as husband and wife, the touches that sent thrills through me and sparks to my core, now brought pain and a sense of loss. I was angry at my body that his touch could send me into a teenage girl tizzy right now. How could you be so angry at someone, yet long for their touch and long to be held by that person? I didn't dare sit next to him because the traitors that were my hormones would take over, and I knew we would end up in each other's arms, so I sat on the couch across from him.

❧

"KATE, I'm sorry. Nothing happened beyond those pictures. I didn't even know they'd been taken. I would never, and could never, do that to you. Things look terrible, but please, you have to believe me that there was nothing going on." Tears falling and hands clenched to control my temper, I looked up at Kate, who sat strangely still and silent. If she hadn't blinked, I would have sworn she was made of stone. "Kate, please say something."

"I ran into her on Saturday in the city when I took Addie to get things for her room here. She knew you had gone to Montana. How did she know that?"

"Mike, our business manager in Montana, called her and told her. Apparently, he has been keeping her apprised of the dealings that have been happening there. A year ago, she had been interested in buying shares in the Montana ranch, but I just figured when we broke up she would find something else to invest in."

"Mike is being removed from his position, I would hope," she said stoically.

I nodded. "Yes, as we speak, actually. Rob is firing him." I watched her look past me, out the window.

The frown line between Kate's eyes deepened as she looked back at me.

"Tyler, I don't know if I believe you yet or not, but you have definitely broken the trust we had built. If it comes out that there was more going on than these pictures, you will find divorce papers on your desk. I will not be the wife that looks the other way. If it is only the pictures, we will need quite a while to rebuild the trust we had, or rather the trust I had in you."

She set the cup of coffee down on the table in front of me.

Taking a deep breath, Kate continued. "Until then, I will take the room down here, and we will be married in name only. No touching, no kissing, and we will spend only necessary time in each other's company until I can be sure nothing happened." Looking into her eyes, I saw heartbreak. When she stood to go, I grabbed her hand. She turned to look at me. The look on her face cut me to the core. She was disgusted with me, maybe even repulsed at the thought of me touching her. I had never felt a heavy sadness in my soul like this.

"No, I don't accept those conditions. There is no way I will not pretend I'm alright not touching or kissing you, but for now, fine, but we will spend time together. I don't want to be roommates. I agree to separate rooms, for the time being. I have never and would never fool around on you. Please believe me."

Kate looked at me, and I could see tears welling in her eyes. She pulled her hand away and walked to what was now her bedroom.

The ringing of my phone made me look away from her closed door.

"Rob, have you found anyone to vouch for me?"

"Well, she's a tough nut to crack, Ty. She is adamant that

you were a willing party to anything that happened the other night. I still have to talk to a few people, so I hope one of them comes through." I hung up the phone, more convinced than ever I had to figure out how to prove I was not a cheater.

THE WEEK HAD BEEN LONG, and I had spoken very few words to Tyler. While spending our agreed upon time together, my phone rang.

"Kate, you need to get to the hospital. Dad took a fall off his horse and things aren't looking good. He's in the ambulance, and Delaney and I are following. Please hurry." Mom was on the verge of crying.

"Mom, I'll leave right now. I love you."

"I love you too, dear."

"What's wrong, Kate?" Through my tears, I told him what my mom had said.

"Let's go." Tyler stood and held his hand out to me.

"Don't worry about coming with me. I'm fine going alone." I stood without taking his hand and I walked towards the door.

"Nice try, Kate, but this isn't something you get to push me away from." Tyler grabbed our coats and ushered me out the door.

Sitting with my mom, sister, and husband in the same waiting room where I waited for Tyler to wake up was almost too much.

The doctor came out a while later, "Mrs. Patterson, I'm afraid the news isn't good. Your husband has had a severe stroke that most likely caused the fall from his horse. When he fell, he hit his head on a rock, which caused further brain bleeding. We'll run a few more tests over the next few days to determine the severity of the damage." The doctor left the waiting room after delivering his awful news.

"Kate, Delaney, your dad and I have discussed this. He doesn't want machines to keep him alive. I will decide to stop treatment if the doctor says there is no hope for any recovery."

I put my arms around Delaney, and we cried together.

"Mom, you know what he would have wanted, and we will support your decision."

Delaney nodded her approval. Tyler sat holding my mom's hand while we waited for further information.

The doors to the ICU swung open and Naomi came out. I smiled at her, and she came over and hugged me. "My shift ends soon if you need someone to sit with you."

"Thank you. I may take you up on that." I glanced at Tyler, who had kept a safe distance across the room.

"Is that a good sign he's here?" Naomi quizzed, motioning over to Tyler.

I shrugged, "He wouldn't let me come alone, and I didn't feel like arguing."

Naomi put her arm around my shoulders and gave me a hug. "I better get back in there. If anything changes, I'll make sure you know." Her half smile didn't fill me with confidence.

"Thank you." I watched her walk back through the doors.

It was a long night of watching medical personnel walk in and out of that forbidden part of the hospital. They couldn't get dad stabilized enough to let us see him. The doctor made countless trips to keep us updated. I had propped my head up with my coat and snuggled into a corner, hoping to get a few minutes of sleep. The bench flexed as the seat next to me became occupied. I didn't have to open my eyes to know who had sat down. His gait, his breathing, the cologne, and his entire presence were etched into my brain, as was my longing for him.

"Your mom thinks we should take shifts, and then nobody will get exhausted." His voice was quiet, calm, and quite frankly, annoying right now.

"I'm not leaving, Tyler. If you want to, go right ahead, there's no reason you need to stay." I didn't open my eyes, but he didn't move.

The days passed by and my father was moved out of ICU to the neurological wing. We painstakingly made a schedule, so he was never alone. If he woke up, we wanted someone to be there. Delaney took the evening and half of the night shift before mom came to relieve her. I would send Mom off after I was done with the morning chores. Tyler would arrive mid afternoon and sit with me for as long as I stayed. Most days I left, and he waited for Delaney. The exchanges between Tyler and me were short and to the point. When I would say goodbye to my dad, he always walked me to the elevator. No words were ever spoken, but when the elevator would arrive, he would say 'see you at home'. The doors would close and I would cry.

With taking shifts at the hospital, I had avoided spending much time alone with Tyler at home for almost a week and a half. Today, Delaney decided she wanted to come in early, so I came home. I watched a thunderstorm roll in and wondered how spectacular this would have been, watching it with Tyler in our room. I hadn't thought about us together in that room for a long time, but I missed him. Lightning cracked across the sky, the rain pelted against my window and sent shivers through me. I drew my covers up around me a little tighter. Would Tyler let me crawl in beside him if this storm got any worse? At almost 37-years-old, I still wanted to run and hide during a terrible storm, and that's all I wanted to do now.

Sleep didn't come easy. I felt like it was the universe telling me it was time to make a change. But what change?

My phone buzzed, which was odd, because I usually had it turned off. I opened my text messages and saw a text from Tyler.

Ty: You OK down there?

I couldn't help but smile. Since the storm at the trapper's cabin, he always made sure I was alright during thunderstorms.

Me: Yeah, I'm fine.

It was a lie. I wasn't fine. I wasn't fine because of the storm, and I wasn't happy living separate from my husband.

Ty: You know, I could meet you in the kitchen for a glass of hot chocolate.

My room was lit up with a sizzle of lightning. That one hit a little too close for comfort. I didn't have to reply. I heard Tyler stomping down the stairs, and my bedroom door flew open. There he stood, like a knight in shining armor. Well, a knight in his boxers and no shirt. He looked so good I wanted to reach out and run my hand along his chest. I wanted his arms around me, but every time I thought about him holding me, I saw the pictures of him and Lona.

"Come on, let's go to the kitchen."

He stood there, holding his hand out for me to join him. Throwing my legs over the edge of the bed, I scooted off and stood. I heard Tyler take a deep breath, and his eyes scanned my body. The night gown I was wearing was thin silk, and it had ridden up as I got off the bed. A flush of red crept across my cheeks. I pulled at the hem to get it back into position.

"I've missed that view," Tyler admitted, arching his eyebrow and grinning slyly. Shaking my head, I walked to the door and went to slide past him. His arm swung up, and he braced himself against the door frame, which made it so I couldn't leave. Stopping centimeters from his arm, turned and looked at him. "I miss you. I miss holding you and burying my nose in your hair when I fall asleep." He dipped his head close to my ear and almost growled, "I miss having you in my bed."

Suddenly aware that we were jammed together in the doorway, I felt my breathing quicken and my resolve fading. We were pressed together. Tyler was not hiding the fact he had missed me. He moved and pressed his hips toward me. My body was betraying me. Feeling the growing dampness between my legs, I knew I needed to get away or I would ride out this storm in his bed. I ducked under his arm and walked to the kitchen.

CHAPTER 35

Four weeks went by and there was no change. Glimmers of hope were just wishful thinking. The doctor called a family meeting.

"Mrs. Patterson, I'm afraid the news isn't good. We had hoped as time passed and the swelling decreased, that his brain function would improve. But every test is leading us to the same answers. He is brain dead. I don't know if you ever discussed what his wishes would be in this situation, but it is something you need to decide now."

Tyler had gone to stand behind my mother while the news was being delivered. At this moment, I was more focused on watching him than my mom. He was the strong one. My mom leaned in to him and he walked her back to a chair.

"Doctor Frasier, is there any improvement at all?" Tyler questioned. "Money is no issue. We can fly in more specialists."

The doctor shook his head no. "He will always require a machine to breathe to keep him alive."

My mom spoke up, "He wouldn't want this, Doctor Frasier. Please turn them off."

The doctor excused himself so he could get the necessary papers necessary for terminating dad's care. Mom signed the paperwork, and while the doctor pressed buttons, Delaney and I sang Amazing Grace like we used to when we were little in church. It was dad's favorite and he would always ask us to sing it.

I thought back to a few weeks ago when I went to see my dad. I drove in the yard and Mom was out working on her flowers.

"Hi, Mom." I called as I walked toward her.

"Well hi; what brings you over here today?"

"Well, I want to talk to you and Dad. Do you know where he is?"

"Last I saw him, he was in the barn. Let's go check." She put down her pruning shears, and we walked over to the barn.

"Hi, Dad," I called when we saw him.

"Well, girlie, I thought this was your day off from this place?"

"Could you stop for a few minutes?" Dad walked over and put his arm around my mom. I smiled. Their marriage was one to admire.

"I just wanted to say thank you. It's not a shock that I wasn't happy when you said I was marrying Tyler, but I really want to tell you I'm very happy with him. I couldn't imagine being happier. I want to tell you I'm sorry for what I said in anger, and I know you were only thinking of what would be best for me."

Mom was crying, and Dad was beaming.

"He really is a good man, Katie. We knew very early on that he was in love with you. I knew it would take you a while to figure it out, but I knew you would get there."

I hugged my parents.

"Now, I have to get back to work," Dad said as Mom and I walked back to the house.

"Can you stay for a bit? I want to dig a few of these flowers out for your flower bed. You could take them with you today." I nodded, and we both started digging.

TAKING one last look at my dad before the machines stopped beeping, I whispered in his ear, "I love you, Daddy." I stepped back and the machines all stopped. It was eerily quiet. The doctor pronounced death at 6:32 p.m. Delaney and I held onto each other, with tears streaming down our cheeks. I looked over at Tyler, who wrapped his arms around my mom and held onto her while she wept. We all walked out of the hospital together.

"I'll come over tomorrow, Mom." She nodded. "Delaney is going to stay with you tonight. I can stay tomorrow night."

"Thank you, girls. Tyler, I don't know what I would have done without you today. Thank you for being here."

"I wouldn't have been anywhere else, Julie." They hugged goodbye, and it was clear just how much Tyler meant to my mom, and just how much she appreciated him.

AFTER HUGGING JULIE, I pulled Kate to the side. "Darlin', I need you to sign this. It's for the ranch." I hated that I was doing this now, but it needed to be done. The look she gave me was of pure disdain. "I can't believe you brought these here. Couldn't this have waited?"

She grabbed the papers out of my hands, picked the pen

up, and signed where I showed her. Slamming the pen down, she walked out of the hospital.

"Tyler, go after her. She won't understand now, but in time she will." I looked into Julie's eyes. They were the same as Kate's. All these months, I thought she was the spitting image of her father, but she had more of her mom in her than just her eyes.

I RAN out to the parking lot, but her truck was gone. Hoping she went home, I headed that direction.

"Kate? Kate! are you here? I found her in her room, packing her suitcase. What are you doing?" With every piece of clothing she packed, the pit in my stomach grew.

"Well, since he's gone, there isn't any reason for me to stay. I'm going to go home to my mom." Her face changed in an instant. "I can't go home. It's not mine anymore."

"That's what I need to talk to you about."

"Tyler, you are correct. We need to talk about the Patterson ranch." I turned and saw that my father had walked into our house with my mom at his side. "Let's have a chat out here in the living room."

I held my hand out for Kate to take, but she slapped it away and brushed past me.

"We are so sorry to hear about your dad, Kate." As much as he tried to sound sincere, my father's words fell flat.

"Dad, what has to be said now that can't wait?" I needed to talk to my wife, without him around.

"I'm wondering when you think your mom could clear out. Now I'm not saying it needs to be tomorrow, but I have plans for that place." He leaned back in to the couch, looking very pleased with himself. Tears rolled down Kate's face.

Standing, I walked to my office and grabbed an envelope.

"Hold your horses there, Dad. These papers took effect today." I pulled out three copies and handed one to dad, one to Kate, and kept one for myself. "If you read these, you'll see it's a Bill of Sale that states the Patterson ranch is now owned by Kate Morton."

I heard her gasp, and my father was turning a few shades of red. Clearing my throat, I continued. "When you arranged the deal with Ben, you failed to put a lien on the property, which let me buy the ranch for Kate. I worked the deal with Julie after Ben's stroke. Knowing that even if he had pulled through, life was going to have to change."

"This will not hold up in court. I will sue!" My father jumped up from his seat.

From behind him, my mother's voice was quiet and confident. "Brian, if you do that you will be one lonely and very broke old man." All our eyes shifted to her, including my father's.

"Sandra, I'm doing this for our family," he spit out through gritted teeth.

Standing, my mother stood toe to toe with my father. "So am I. Kate is our family, and we are lucky to have her."

"You don't talk to me this way!" Dad said, glaring at my mother.

"Maybe I should have been talking like this to you the entire time. Brian, how can you not see the problems you have caused over the years?" Mom looked back at me as if she needed my strength. She took a deep breath and turned back to Dad. "Our boys hate you, Brian. They have had to deal with all the crap you did to them because you were *making them men*. They became fine men on their own, despite your treatment of them. They were and are determined to be nothing like you."

My father's lips were pursed, the vein in the middle of his

forehead popped and I could tell he was clenching his jaw. Suddenly his jaw slacked, and his eyes shifted to me and fell. I think, for the first time in his life, he realized the truth. His sons couldn't stand him.

My father turned and walked out of our home, leaving my mom alone with us. "Kate, I truly meant what I said. You are part of this family, and I am thrilled you're here. I know the heartache you're feeling from losing your father. It will take time, but you will be able to look back and think of him without tears."

The two most important women in my life embraced, and mom let Kate cry.

"Let me tell you both something, I have never seen in my life; a love like yours. Neither of you knew each other past being acquaintances, and you definitely didn't know all you needed to know before you got married." Mom brushed hair away from Kate's face, and smiled at her. "And you, Kate, had no basis for trust, especially given Tyler's reputation. You had no experience with the difficulties of being a couple. You are struggling right now, but like most struggles, they will pass and new ones come along. Work together; build a rock-solid foundation that won't crumble."

I snorted. "It's pretty crumbly right now, Mom."

She smiled and patted my cheek like when I was a kid. "Sure, your current foundation has taken a little beating this past month thanks to that woman, but you both are still securely standing on it. Life on this ranch isn't easy. You've seen it time and time again. It's one of the driving forces behind Rob's marriage breaking up. Your dad wanted Rob around all the time, which gave Samantha her freedom at rodeos to find someone else to lean on. Brian isn't an easy man to handle, but both of you are doing the most amazing job of it. I am thankful every day that my boys seem to have somehow avoided his pitfalls. Kate, you are the light this place needed, that I needed." Sandra reached up and wiped the tears that were slipping down Kate's cheeks. She leaned in and whispered something I couldn't hear, but it made Kate smile. Walking her to the door, I hugged her goodbye, and then Kate and I were alone once again.

"So my family ranch is my ranch now. Is this where you tell me I'm no longer bound to the deal made by our fathers and I can go back to my regular life?" The words came out of my mouth with more hatred than I had intended. I could see I hurt him. His shoulders hunched, and he closed his eyes.

"Kate, I didn't do this, so you would leave. I did this, so you have the option to go or to stay and choose me. There will be no surprise on which option I hope you choose, but maybe you will be able to finally see how much I love you. There is nobody else for me in this world." He closed the distance between us and took my hands. "Please, Kate, choose me." His last words were whispered like they were a thought that wasn't supposed to be heard. "I'm going to sit on the porch for a while." He walked into the kitchen, rummaged around, and walked out the side door.

I took the time in his absence to read the contract I had signed at the hospital, and then I headed out to the porch.

"I thought you might like some sun tea," he said, holding up a glass. "Tea and talking on the swing was how we connected the first time." I smiled and joined him. This was the closest we had been all month. He reached for my hand, and I didn't pull away.

"I want to make new terms for our relationship, Tyler. I would like to go back to the way we were when we got married; learning to trust each other." I couldn't look at him; instead, I looked down at my hands, which I was unconsciously wringing.

"So that would mean sharing touches, sharing a room, and kissing when the mood strikes?" Tyler asked as he looked into my eyes.

I nodded yes.

"When do these terms begin?" His eyes danced, and the mood around us lightened.

"Well, I was just assuming they would start today. Now."

He was off the swing so fast it was as if someone had pushed an eject button. "I'm going to move your stuff back to our room!" he yelled, as he sprinted through the living room to the bedroom I had been occupying.

Tyler made countless trips up and down the stairs. I was sure I hadn't moved that much stuff, but I sat on the swing and waited.

Flopping back down beside me, he looked over and smiled. "I moved all your stuff back in. I hope I put it in the right spots."

"I'm sure it will be fine." I laughed and thought once again that I'd be getting in trouble because of that smile.

With supper finished and the dishes done, I sat across from Tyler to watch TV for the rest of the evening. As the hours passed, I got more and more nervous. I needed to get it together. "I'm going to shower and go to bed," I said, the nerves plain in my voice even though I'd tried to hide it.

"I'll be up shortly." He looked up at me and smiled. As always, I knew that smile would get me in trouble.

CHAPTER 36

She walked into the bedroom much the same as she did on our wedding night, wearing the same sleep set, if I wasn't mistaken. The last month had taken its toll on her. I figured she had dropped about ten pounds, judging from how her clothes fit. She had been running daily again. She needed to feel normal, and like she had said the first time I found her out running the road, running was her therapy. Ashamed that she needed that time daily because of me. I had hoped that with our life looking like it would go back to normal, she wouldn't need that daily escape. I worried about her, and I became determined to get her back to her regular self in every way. She seemed startled that I was in bed waiting for her, so I smiled and threw back the covers.

"This seems like a little déjà vu." I thought back to our wedding night and how unsure she was when she walked into our room. She climbed into bed, pulled and fluffed the covers, then turned to look at me.

"Tyler, please, just hold me." Her voice was soft, pleading.

We both turned our lights off and cuddled into one another and slept.

Waking up in each other's arms seemed to be a dream. I opened my eyes to find Kate staring at me.

"Do you do this all the time?"

Bursting out laughing, she playfully slapped my arm.

"How did you sleep?"

"The best I have slept in a long time. How about you?"

"I don't know if I have ever slept that well." Her smile was contagious, and I brought her closer to me and we dozed off again.

"I have to go to mom's tonight. Delaney needs to get some work done." She was almost whining, and it was cute.

"Fine, I will be over when I'm done here."

I was done with work; I went to Julie's. Walking in the door, I found the girls in the kitchen. Julie was sitting at the table, crying. Delaney was sitting beside her. I looked around the room for Kate. Delaney saw me and motioned to the stairs with her eyes.

I climbed the stairs and found Kate in the last bedroom.

"Hey," I whispered when I found her lying on the bed.

Tears streamed down her face. Her eyes lit up when she saw me walk through the door. Sitting on the edge of the bed, I lay down beside her and took her hand in mine.

"What's up?"

"Mom and I fought. I lost my cool, and it's my fault." Kate rolled onto her side and wrapped her arm around me, getting as close as she could.

"You didn't throw anything, did you?"

She looked up and glared at me.

"Kate, everyone's on edge. I'm sure it wasn't that bad. My mom sent supper over, so why don't we all eat? I'll help where I can, and then we can cuddle up here for the night."

"Seriously, Tyler, is that all you think about?"

"Supper? Yep, most of the time."

Kate wiped her tears and laughed.

"Oh, you mean you and I alone together. Yep, that's pretty much it. Can't blame a man for loving his wife, can you?"

Kate leaned over and kissed me.

"I don't know what I did to deserve you, but I'm glad I have you. Also, you are the first boy ever allowed in this room, so don't do anything that will get you kicked out." Kate kissed me again and sat up.

"Well, where is this supper you promised?"

"Nope, not until you tell me what you and your mom were fighting about." I playfully spanked her rear end.

"The books. I admit it's not my forte, but this ranch is in terrible shape and she's refusing to see it. Even with the amount you paid her that still doesn't cover the debt." Kate laid her head on my chest.

"I will look after supper." I knew the finances had been a struggle, but I was worried now.

We walked downstairs and things appeared to have settled down.

With supper over and the dishes done, I looked over what had caused the fight between Kate and her mom.

"Julie, I have to say, the books are a mess. I don't mean to speak ill of anyone, but it's not much of a surprise my father was involved."

Julie was crying again.

"Please don't feel like I'm overstepping, but Kate, but I'm taking over the finances. I will get them figured out. There will be bank and insurance tie ups for a while, but I can navigate them."

"I'm going home, I have to get some work done." Delaney stood, hugged her mom, and walked out of the house.

"I'm going to bed. Goodnight," Julie said as she stood from the table.

Kate and I both echoed our goodnights and stayed in the kitchen.

"Thank you. You already have so much on your plate; you didn't need this too." Kate slid her chair back from the table and stood up and walked to the sink. I followed her.

"Kate, this is your problem now and I will do anything for this family and more importantly, anything for you." I wrapped my arms around her shoulders and held her tight. "Come on, let's go to bed." I stood at the stairs while Kate turned the lights off. We climbed them hand in hand.

"How are you really doing?" I asked as I climbed into bed. Kate sat on the edge of the bed and didn't move; she just let out a sigh.

"I have navigated the last month alone because of my stubbornness and pride. Everyone else leaned on you except me. My father is gone, and I pushed you away. I have been such a fool." She dropped her head into her hands and cried.

I moved across the bed, sat up behind her, and wrapped my arms around her. "You didn't push me away. You were hurt, and I didn't know how to fix things. Kate, I'm going to tell you something I have learned about you over these last few months. You, my love, are too hard on yourself. There's never been a time when you give yourself a break." Her tears stopped, and she turned her head to nuzzle into my neck. "Kate, the rest of the week will not be any easier. Trying to get things sorted out around here will take some time, so I want you to promise me you will give yourself some grace." I felt her nod.

"Tyler, what about my mom? She might hear us." Kate protested as she tried to push me away playfully.

"She's on the other side of the house, there's no way she

will hear us. Well, unless you get wild." I snaked my hand from her neck down across her breast to her hip and slowly dragged my fingers to the apex of her thighs. "Kate Morton, you naughty girl."

I had found she wore no underwear beneath her nightgown.

"Well, you can't blame me for hoping." Her brow arched, and she reached down my side and took hold of my package. "Hmm, it feels like you were hoping for something too."

"Oh Kate, have we been apart so long you forget I don't wear anything to bed?"

"Nope, I haven't forgotten." She pulled me down to kiss her.

Teasing her a little more, I grabbed the hem of her pajamas and slowly raised it to her shoulders, never losing eye contact with her. Kate sat up and ripped off the satin gown. I reached out and flicked her taut nipples. Her head fell backwards, and she let out a soft moan. Knowing that this was her kryptonite, I kept it up for a few minutes, alternating from left to right. Kate's breathing increased and her moans became more frequent and louder. Her hand closest to me, reached for me but I made sure I stayed just out of her reach.

"Tyler, you are mean," she groaned.

As much as I enjoyed this, I needed her. I gently pushed her back down on the bed and positioned myself above her. Slowly entering her was the most difficult thing I had ever done, but I didn't want this moment to end. Kate raised her hips, trying to make me hurry.

"I'm in control now baby."

"Tyler," she hollered.

"Shhh we are going to get caught," I growled as I pushed the rest of the way into her.

Kate arched her back and gasped, "This isn't fair."

Like she was able to read my mind, she clamped her hands on my ass and wouldn't let go. I had no choice; I began to make small riding motions and Kate loosened her grip.

We rode together in sync until her panting became desperate; I shifted my hips, and she moaned my name. It was all I needed. I grabbed her breast and slowed down my thrusting, but increased the force.

"Tyler, Tyler, I'm…" She didn't have time to finish her thought. She raked her fingernails across my shoulders and threw her head back one more time, and convulsed around me.

It was too much; I couldn't hold back anymore. A few more good thrusts and I collapsed, gasping for air. Kate's arms were wrapped around me tightly. I rolled on to my side, taking her with me. With my free hand, I ran it behind her head and drew her in for a kiss.

"Never make me go a month without you again," Kate whispered through the darkness.

CHAPTER 37

The days leading up to the funeral were filled with laughter and tears. We went through photo albums to find pictures for dad's video tribute. Phases of teen years I had hoped Tyler would never see were met with laughs and a lot of pointing. Tyler worked alongside me to get chores completed.

We went up into the loft one evening and watched the sun set over our ranch.

"I'm not sure it will ever feel like ours, Ty. Everywhere I look, Dad's here."

He wrapped his arms around me tighter.

"One day, I'm sure it will."

"I have never asked how you managed to pull everything off, but maybe I don't want to know." I looked up into his eyes.

"There's no marvelous story, Kate. When your dad was first in the hospital, I called my lawyer and had him look into the deal Dad had made with him. It was really very easy once I got your mom involved. He leaned down and kissed me, and then continued. One of the days I was at the hospital with Julie, I put forward the proposal. She was on board before I even finished talking. That was one of the days we thought your dad moved his hand. Your mom and I went to the lawyer's office and had the paperwork drawn up. I had to have you sign your portion as soon as I could so it wouldn't be challenged. I felt horrible making you sign the contract that day, especially since you didn't know what you were signing. It never crossed my mind that you wouldn't read it."

Bringing his hand to my face, he lightly grazed it.

"I can never repay you for what you did. You gave mom more than fair market value and assumed the debt. Are you sure you can cover all this?" I turned in his lap and faced him.

"Baby, I told you in this very barn that you never had to worry about money again, and that includes this. Over the years, I have invested well. The Montana ranch has been quite successful. I can be completely independent from Lone Star Ranch if you say the word."

Tyler was willing to give up everything for me.

Straddling him, I shifted as close as I could to him. "I don't want to rip apart your family. Yes, there are problems that will need to be sorted out, but family is so important. We have managed all these months to run two places; I don't see why that has to change."

Wrapping my arms around his neck, I smiled.

"There are going to be a few changes around here, Mrs. Morton." Every time he called me that, my heart soared. "You are going to have help, and by help, I mean me. There is no way you are doing all the work yourself anymore. OK?" I nodded and kissed him to make sure he knew I agreed to the new plans.

Sleep didn't come easily that night. Tomorrow, I would have to say my last goodbye to my dad. I tossed and turned.

Suddenly, Tyler's arms were grabbing me and he pulled me close.

"I don't care if you lay here awake all night, but I'm getting seasick with your bouncing around." He made me laugh, and I relaxed and cuddled into him.

The morning sun shone through the window. I had fallen asleep for a few hours thanks to the powerful arms around me. There was no reason to get up and start the day earlier than I needed to. It wouldn't make it go any faster.

"Don't get up. You don't need to, and I have a month of mornings without you in my arms to make up for." His sleepy voice was seductive, and he wrapped his arms tighter around me, so I had no choice but to stay where I was.

The hours ticked by, and mom's house was abuzz with activity.

"Patterson women, you need to get out the door now." His voice rang through the house. Mom, Delaney, and I turned to look at Tyler. Mom walked over to Tyler and placed her hand on his cheek, and smiled.

"Girls, we need to go." She walked out the door to her car, and Delaney followed.

"Dad used to yell that when we were running behind schedule." Looking at Tyler, tears welled up in my eyes and I collapsed onto the chair behind me. Tyler knelt down in front of me. His face was concerned. I wrapped my arms around him and cried. "He's gone, Tyler. What am I supposed to do without him? Our kids will never know him. He isn't going to be here to give me advice."

My cries slowly turned into sobs, and Ty just held me. I sat up and he ever so gently wiped the tears from my face.

"Our kids will know him through your memories, your mom, and Delaney. I don't know what you will do without him, but I'll be here. You come to me for help. I will be your strength, like you're mine. There is nothing you have to face alone. His lips brushed mine ever so gently. We have to go." I nodded, and we walked out to our truck, hand in hand. It didn't matter what the rest of our life held. The man sitting beside me would be here to support me, guide me, and love me.

~

OUR LIFE RETURNED to normal over the next weeks, There was a knock on my office door.

"Come in."

To my delight, Kate walked through the door. I stood and walked over to her. Leaning down, I kissed her. Her arms wrapped around my neck, and she returned the kiss passionately.

"I've missed your lips." I arched my brow, smiling at my beautiful wife.

"I've missed yours too." She ran her thumb across my lips. "Do you have a few minutes to talk?" I hated how she sounded, but I kept the smile pasted on my face.

"Sure, let's sit over on the couch."

Leading her to sit. "Tyler, I spoke to the lawyer this morning." Her face hadn't changed. She looked me square in the eyes. My stomach sank.

"Kate, please, things have been going so well." I couldn't muster more than a whisper. She turned and pulled an envelope from her purse and handed it to me. Opening the flap, I pulled out the papers.

"As you will see, I have placed tabs where you need to sign." She was looking down at her hands now.

Frantically, I flipped through the papers and looked at Kate. "You added me to the titles of your ranch?" A smile spread across her face, and she nodded. I looked back down at the papers.

"We, you and I, now own my father's ranch. I know you did it to secure my future, but I don't want a future without you. I choose you. So, are you going to sign them?" She dug through her purse and held a pen out to me.

I tossed the papers onto the coffee table in front of me and grabbed her by the waist. Pulling her onto my lap with a laugh, she squealed before I kissed her.

She chose me!

Breaking the kiss with a grin, I grabbed the pen from her slack fingers and signed where I needed to. Tossing the pen onto the papers, I pulled Kate to me for another kiss.

"Let's go home. I have plans for you that I don't want to carry out here." Running my hands through her hair, attacking her neck with my lips, I ushered her out the door toward home.

EPILOGUE

I walked into Tyler's office and found him on the phone; he motioned for me to sit and wait.

"So, what's up? You don't normally just show up over here these days."

"Well, I umm, hmm." This didn't seem so hard when I practiced in the mirror. "Tyler I, well, we're going to have a baby."

I sat there, waiting for a response.

He looked shocked, but a smile crept across his face. "Are you sure?"

I nodded.

"I took three tests, and all were positive." He leapt from his chair and came to where I was sitting, kneeling on the floor in front of me.

"I can't believe it. I'm going to be a dad!" The wonder in his voice made me smile. We kissed, and he put his hand on my stomach. Butterflies still flipped inside from his touch. "How far along do you think you are?"

"I'm not sure. Six to eight weeks. Maybe." I could see him searching his brain, thinking back to those weeks.

"We have had some very fun nights in the last few months," he said, grinning from ear to ear.

"Apparently so. I called my doctor and I'm going to see her in a few days."

"Are you feeling, ok?" he asked.

"I'm tired, and nauseous all day. That's why I took the test."

"I'm so happy." He pulled me up and spun me around. The smile that had gotten us into this situation spread across his face.

"You're sure? We hadn't really talked about it." Hesitancy laced my words.

"Kate, I am ecstatic." He leaned towards me, and we kissed again.

SHE COULD HAVE KNOCKED me down with a feather when she told me she was pregnant. We hadn't really discussed a family. We both wanted kids, but we didn't set the timeline.

Walking back to the house that night, I felt like I was on cloud nine. I loved coming home now. I found Kate in the kitchen making supper, music blaring from the stereo, and my wife putting on a concert to what I could only believe was a packed house screaming her name. The nights I would come home to an empty house had quickly faded out of my memory. She would immediately stop when I walked in, but those days I could sneak in and watch her were perfect.

"How long have you been there, Ty?"

"Long enough to know that the crowd loves you." The dishcloth hit me square in the face.

"Your aim is improving." I laughed.

"How was your day?" I asked her.

"It was good." She sighed and rubbed her lower back.

I walked over to her and rested my hand on her very pregnant stomach. I could feel our child doing what seemed like backflips. It always amazed me that Kate just carried on with whatever she was doing when this little one was this active. I imagined her insides were all black and blue.

"It smells amazing in here. What are you making?" I peered over her shoulder.

"Remember our cooking class in New Orleans? I decided it was time to relive that meal."

"Jambalaya? Well, that sounds so much better than spaghetti. I spun her around to face me, then leaned down and kissed her. Can I help you with anything?"

"Yes, the shrimp is in the fridge. Please grab it." Turning to get it before I could even think of what she was up to, my butt cheek once again stung from the slap of the spatula. I spun around, and there was no coy smile this time.

"Katherine Morton, you little… She took off running through the house. I caught her in the living room and turned her towards me. Backing her up to the wall, I playfully pinned her against it. You are a troublemaker." I pressed my lips to hers.

THE NINE MONTHS flew by and suddenly I went into labor. I called Tyler's cell phone, but there was no answer. I called Rob, but he was with Tyler, so also no answer. Delaney was already in town, working at the school. Mom had gone to lunch with friends. My next call was to Sandra.

"Hi Kate, how are you today?"

"Sandra, I think I'm in labor and I can't get a hold of Tyler. I don't know what to do."

"Oh dear, I'm in the city, and I'm fairly sure the boys had to go chase some cattle down South. Let's see, Brian's home. I'll call him. Get your bag together he will be right over. I'll also have him send Gates to find the boys." She hung up before I could protest Brian coming to get me. A contraction hit and I tried to walk it off. There was no way I was going to spend thirty minutes alone with Brian. I had to come up with another plan. The latest contraction was over, and I finished getting my bags to the door.

In less than 5 minutes, he was he was shouting as he ran through the door. "Kate, we need to go."

"You have to be kidding to think I am going anywhere with you. I will drive myself." No sooner had the words came out of my mouth, I doubled over with pain from a contraction.

"Look, you don't have to like me to ride in the same truck, but by my guess you don't have much time before this baby arrives and as much as you hate me, I'm pretty sure you don't want me delivering it. Cattle I can handle, people, not a chance. Do you really think you can wait it out for someone else to show up?"

I hated letting him think he was right, but I had no choice. Waddling toward the door, I handed him my bag as I walked by him silently. He threw it over his shoulder and then took my arm.

"The sooner we get there, the sooner I don't have to deal with you." I mumbled through gritted teeth. We left the house and before I got down the stairs, I grabbed onto the railing with one hand and gripped Brian's arm with the other, waiting out another contraction.

"Okay, let's get you in the truck." He tossed my bag in the back seat and helped me up into the passenger side.

"Did Gables go to find Tyler?" I managed to get out through gritted teeth while breathing through a contraction.

"Yes, I sent him. Hopefully, he can find them right away. Just keep breathing Kate, it's all going to be okay."

We arrived at the hospital in thirty minutes and Brian got me a wheelchair. I was admitted and in a room before I realized what was happening. Sandra and my mom showed up soon after they admitted me. When they got there, Brian stepped out. My contractions were fast and fierce. I had never been so happy to see a doctor with a needle before in my life. He made quick work of the epidural, and I was happy once again. I asked about Tyler again, but nobody had any news. The doctor walked in a short while later, tying up her mask, and said, "It's time, Kate. Let's have this baby."

"No, this can't be happening now! Tyler isn't here. I can't have this baby until he gets here." I was in full-blown panic.

The doctor walked up to the head of my bed, leaned in, and calmly whispered, "Kate, you need to calm down, regardless of who is here. This baby is ready to make its arrival."

I wanted so badly to stop and wait, but I knew that's not how things worked. Closing my eyes and taking a deep breath, I refocused and pushed when I was told to, and then suddenly, a large, rough hand took hold of mine. I opened my eyes and there he was, standing beside me in his cowboy hat, work coat, and dirty chaps.

"Ty! You made it!"

"Of course I did. I wouldn't want to be anywhere else." He leaned down and kissed my head.

"Okay Kate, one last really good push and this little one will be ready for the world." I gripped Tyler's hand as tight as I could and pushed with everything left in me. "It's a boy!" the doctor called out. I looked up at Tyler, and he was beaming. The nurses cleaned him up, wrapped him in a blanket, and placed him on my chest. In a split second, our lives went from just being him and me, to being the three of us. Tyler kissed me as tears glistened in his eyes and a proud smile lit up his face.

"Good job, Momma," he whispered as we gazed at our son.

"I'm so glad you got here in time."

"I wouldn't have missed this for the world." He leaned down and kissed me again. Forever a family, the start of our own legacy, the beginning of another generation of Texas rancher.

THERE WAS a knock on my hospital room door. Kate and I looked up and saw it was my dad. "Come in, Dad. Here, why don't you hold him for a while." I handed Tyler Benjamin Morton Jr over to him.

"Oh no, Tyler, I haven't held a baby in ages." He tried to back away, but I set TJ in his arms anyway, knowing he wouldn't let anything happen to him.

"It hasn't been that long, Dad. You used to hold Addie all the time." I looked over at Kate, who was smiling at us.

"I came here to apologize for my behavior, and for how I've treated you, Kate. I never gave it a second thought when I organized the business deal with your dad. The only thought I had was what I would get out of it." Brian shifted TJ in his arms and sat a little straighter in the chair. "I have treated you terribly, and I am so very sorry. You have brought more to this family than I ever imagined." He looked down at TJ, then up at Kate.

"I accept your apology, Brian," she took my hand and looked up to me, then over at the baby in my father's arms. "But I want you to be fully aware that if you ever treat my son the way you treat your own, I will be the one you have to deal with." Dad nodded, and I was sure I saw the color fade from his face.

"Son, I also need to say sorry to you. I tried my best to make men out of you boys when all I should have been doing was teaching you how to be good husbands and fathers. I should have been better to you three." Tears slipped down his face. Never once had I seen my father cry. "Seeing you with your son made me realize all the years I missed out on." He stood and handed TJ back to Kate. "Tyler, can you ever forgive me?"

"Dad, be that kind of grandfather to our children, and it will start the forgiving process. I don't hate you, Dad, that's not who I am, but I want better from you for our children than what I had from you." I walked over to him and gathered him up in my arms. For the first time in as long as I can remember, my father hugged me back. Something I had longed for most of my life.

Brian was born to be a grandpa. He doted on TJ, and it thrilled Sandra to have a grandson. Addie was the best cousin around. My mom was over a lot and was always up for babysitting when ranch work was too dangerous to have TJ hanging around.

One night, months later, while lying in Tyler's arms, with the sounds of crickets in the yard and the coyotes barking in the distance, I knew that had it not been for an arranged marriage, I wouldn't have this life.

"You're thinking about something, I can tell," Tyler said.

I smiled. "You know me too well. I was just thinking about our situation. A year and a half ago, we were dealt a hand neither of us really wanted, but look at us now. I'm more in love with you now than the day you first took me to the trapper's shack. We have an amazing life; we get to raise our son in the wide open. I couldn't have asked for a better husband or father for our son. If I had to do it all over again, I would."

"Same Mrs. Morton, same."

I kissed Tyler, and we fell asleep in each other's arms.

SUN TEA RECIPE

261

1 gallon water

    4 orange pekoe tea bags

    1/2 c. lemon juice

    1/4 c. white sugar

    1/4 c. iced tea mix

Fill a one gallon jar or jug* full of water, toss in the four tea bags and place out in the sun until the tea has steeped to your desired strength.

Mix in lemon juice, white sugar, and iced tea mix and refrigerate. When cold pour over ice and enjoy.

*A gallon pickle jar works well for this!

THE ATONEMENT

The week flew by and I had been on and off the Morton ranch probably fifty times, or at least it felt like that many. Every time, it disappointed me when I didn't see Rob. He probably steered clear of me on purpose, and I wouldn't blame him at all. Running away from him the first day back on the ranch reminded me of the horrible things, and walking away from him that night we broke up was the ultimate betrayal.

I parked in front of the barn and sat mentally preparing for the day, listening to the song playing. It was George Strait; You Look so Good in Love. Closing my eyes, I was thankful that after tomorrow, my time here would be over. I could build a business and move on from Rob. Obviously he wanted nothing to do with me, and as much as I wanted to try again, it would be easier than not watching for him around every corner. I took a deep breath and readied myself to get out of the car. The passenger door swung open and someone sat down in the seat. I was staring into Rob's eyes, five inches from my face. I stopped breathing. My eyes felt like they were going to pop out of my head. So many thoughts were running through my head, but I couldn't think fast enough to make sense of them. I had wanted to see him and now he was here and I didn't have a clue what to say.

He smelled the same, like a walk in the woods, of cedar, surrounded by lavender and the sweet scent of honeysuckle. It felt like coming home. I used to long for my clothes to smell like him at the end of the night. Smiling, I thought back to the pull over jacket I stole from his room just because it smelled like him. It was the one thing of him I took to New York with me and until I met Jeremy; I curled up with it every night.

"So is there a reason you run away every time I try to get close enough to you to say hi?" His smile was the same crooked smile he always reserved for me. For others, he just gave them a quick smirk but for me his face lit up. His eyes, an indigo blue that danced when he looked at me. My heart raced, and I thought of how easily I could get lost in that sea of blue. The last eight years had been good to him. "Don't be nervous. It's just me."

"I'm not nervous." I hoped I was convincing because I was sweating like a liar in church. He may need to call for CPR if he keeps looking at me like that. I licked my lips and tried to slow my breathing.

"You always bite your lip when you are nervous. I'm glad to see that hasn't changed. Hi Jess, how are ya?"

"Hi. I'm good. How are you?" I fidgeted with my keys.

"I'm good. So are you going to answer my question?" He hadn't changed, still relentless as ever.

"Well, the first day I was here, I was tired from my drive, and I didn't want you to see me like that. And the rest of this week I haven't exactly been hiding, so who's fault is that?"

His warm-hearted, full of joy laugh reverberated through my car, and my heart skipped a few beats. That laugh haunted my dreams when I was lonely those first months in Manhattan. Then, when life crumbled with Jeremy, I started hearing it again. Now sitting here beside him, I knew I was a goner.

"Fine, I will admit when you drove away without even so much as a wave, I was hurt. I wanted to welcome you home. Talk to you and see how you were. I figured you were still angry with me, so I stayed away." Rob looked down. He brushed an imaginary piece of lint off his jeans before looking at me again.

"I'm not mad, Rob. To be honest, I never was." I could feel tears filling my eyes. Being open with him had always been easy until our fight about me leaving.

He cleared his throat and changed the subject. It wasn't one either of us wanted to dive into at this moment.

"You've been busy. I'm not sure I've ever seen this place look so good."

"Ha, your mother has hosted so many events and had famous planners and decorators over the years. I don't even think this would make the top 50." I shook my head and stared out the driver's side window.

"Hey, look at me."

I turned my head slowly towards him.

"Talk to me."

I didn't know what to say.

"Jess, it's just me. Come on, we've never had a problem talking."

"No, that was something we were usually ok doing. Have you had a busy week?"

"Ya, it has been busy. There's been so much to help Tyler with. How about you? Are you ready to have this week over?"

His face didn't match his calm demeanor. His eyes were searching, hoping I gave him the answer he wanted.

"I will be happy to breathe again, but I will miss being here every day. I can't ever thank your mom enough for trusting me with this wedding."

"Why will you miss being here every day?" Rob's voice was low, and he almost whispered it.

"Because I won't have any more opportunities to run into you." Looking into his eyes, I knew those were the words he hoped I would say. There was no way I could hold the truth back from him. I meant the words I had just said. He was the reason I took this job. "It was a disappointing week."

The tension was thick, and I needed to get out of my car before Rob and I went to a place neither of us needed to be right now. Flinging my door open I got out, and took a deep breath of cool country air. Rob had gotten out and walked around in front of me.

"Look, I know you're going to be kind of busy today, but I would like to take you out next week. Supper in town? I will pick you up at six-thirty." He placed a finger under my chin and lifted it so I was looking right at him. "Okay?" All I could do was nod.

"I better go make sure Tyler isn't trying to run away."

"And I should make sure everything is ready. I want today to go smoothly." We both turned to go in opposite directions. "Hey sometime will you explain to me what this shotgun wedding is all about? I've known Kate all my life, and this doesn't seem like her at all."

"Oh, it's a story." Rob arched his brow and chuckled. "I will fill you in on our date."

I turned and walked away first. There was suddenly a whistle behind me.

"You still look fantastic walking away, Jess." I added a little extra sway and heard 'damn.' If he could have seen my face, I was grinning ear to ear. This would not be as easy as it seemed, I was sure, but it was nice to imagine we could just pick up where we left off.

The second installment in the Morton Family Saga, The Atonement, is coming December 2021! Stay up-to-date on Bonnie Poirier's new releases, giveaways and more here: https://sendfox.com/bonniepoirier. author

ACKNOWLEDGMENTS

Terence, thank you for being my Tyler. Thank you for not telling me I was crazy when I told you I wrote a book even if you thought it! You are a wonderful provider, husband and dad to our kids. I love you more than you will ever know.

Emerson and Cassidy, you both are two little to know how much you helped this story along. Putting you to bed at night and laying with you gave me the time and quiet to write most of this book.

To my mom and dad who provided the love and home that taught me it was ok to use my imagination, create and write. Mom, you were my first editor for book reports, creative writing and my newspaper articles. My writing wouldn't be where it is without you! Dad, thank you for believing in me no matter what I was doing. You told me to want more out of life than playing it safe. It took a few years but this is me stepping outside my comfort zone!

Douglas, you were the idea man behind most of our hare-brained ideas growing up and I thank you for being encouraging when I came up with my own! You are the best brother!

Britta you were one of the first people I told about my book, and you have been so encouraging as I finish it. It wasn't just Douglas who lucked out when you found each other, our entire family did!

My father in law Monty and husband Terence you both unknowingly provided the education I needed to write the scenes involving cattle. Thank you for your patience with me when I'm out helping. Maybe one day this city girl will be able to handle more than just opening gates and directing traffic but let's not hold our breath!

To all the Poiriers, thank you for welcoming me into your family seven years ago, and for treating me like I have always been around. You are all the most wonderful bonus family I could have married in to.

Abby, you were the first person to ever look at my work. I will never be able to thank you for encouraging me to keep going and finish this book.

Amie, you read what I thought was a completed book and helped me in so many ways build my characters and story. What started out as just manuscript swap has developed into a friendship that I never expected but am so very blessed to have!

My clitique group ladies, I gained wonderful friends and sisters in writing. Our twice weekly calls are highlights of my week. You have been through this book with a fine tooth comb, it wouldn't be the book it is today without your advice and encouragement. I feel like you have always been a part of my life and I don't know what I would do without your friendship.

My beta and ARC readers, you are a valuable part of this journey and I appreciate your time, thought and input.

Thank you to family and friends who supported me when I finally spoke publicly about this endeavor.

ABOUT THE AUTHOR

Bonnie lives in South Central Saskatchewan in the heart of the Canadian prairies. She's married to Terence, who farms, ranches and is a hunting outfitter and guide in the northern part of the province. Terence and Bonnie have two children. Emerson is five and loves helping with the farm and cattle. Cassidy, who is two, is mom's shadow, talking a mile a minute and loves helping in the garden.

Bonnie has been a Licensed Practical Nurse for the last nineteen years. She's worked in a busy city hospital, managed a long term care facility and is now working casually as a floor nurse to spend time at home raising the kids and helping on the farm.

When she's not writing, helping Terence and keeping the kids busy she enjoys vegetable gardening, tending to her flowers, reading and photography.